NIGHT CROSSING

to

ATHENS

A NOVEL

Irene Magers

Shady Tree Press, New York

iMg BOOKS
Published by SHADY TREE PRESS
136 East 64th Street, 7th Floor
New York, NY 10065
U.S.A.

PUBLISHER'S NOTE
This is a work of fiction. Names, characters, places, and incidents stem from the author's imagination, except where historical or political names and places enter into the story.

ISBN-13: 978-0-9841211-2-0
ISBN-10:   0-9841211-2-9

OTHER BOOKS BY IRENE MAGERS
Coach From Warsaw
Last Train From Berlin
Down And Out in Manhattan

Cover design by Sonja Lohmeyer and Dennis Kreibich

www.ShadyTreePress.com
Printed in the United States of America

NIGHT CROSSING

to
ATHENS

A NOVEL

Book II in a Trilogy

For my three bright stars
Tom, Kati, and Laurence

Chapter One

Berlin 1924...

"I wish you wouldn't go into town today," Dorrit said and got up from the table, tightening the belt on her green morning coat and walking over to the rosewood sideboard for another helping of scrambled eggs. Replacing the cover on the chafing dish, she reached for the coffee pot. "Want a refill?" She turned to her husband seated at the opposite end of the large table covered in a blue-flowered breakfast cloth and set with fine Meissen china. A center crystal vase held stalks of forsythia, the yellow buds forced into an early bloom.

"Yes, please." Glancing over the top of the newspaper, Johann smiled ruefully because he had no intention of granting her wish about not going into Berlin today.

The coffee pot felt light and lifting the lid, Dorrit frowned. "Oh, it's empty." She replaced the carafe on its warmer and returned to her seat to ring a small bell.

Frau Schmidt came into the dining room with freshly brewed pot and a basket of warm rolls. As she poured the coffee, she nodded toward an empty place at the table where a glass of milk stood half full and a portion of eggs remained largely untouched. "Shall I clear Fritz's dishes?"

"Yes, he's finished." Dorrit took a roll from the basket, split it and let butter melt on each half before adding a dollop of raspberry jam.

"Talk of the devil..." Johann grinned toward the arched doorway leading into the center hall where Fritz could now be heard thundering down the staircase and sliding across the parquet, dragging his leather school bag behind him. This commotion was followed by a shout of *Wiedersehen!* as the front door opened -

1

sending a shaft of cold March air into the house - before closing with a resounding thud. "It confounds me why that boy is always in such a hurry." Johann shook his head and went back to the newspaper. "And why slam the door?"

"Max was the same at the age of sixteen." Dorrit smiled indulgently and bit into the warm roll.

Nurturing a fair amount of familiarity with a household she'd served for three decades, Frau Schmidt never missed an opportunity to opine and, in the years following the Great War, lament about food shortages. "Max always cleaned his plate before running off to school," she mumbled. "There was never anything wasted with that boy." She left the room, her expression clearly implying the firstborn was her favorite and that she missed him now that he was attending Heidelberg University.

Once they were again alone, Dorrit repeated her concern about Johann venturing into the center of Berlin. "I do wish you'd reconsider," she said. "Yesterday the radio warned of riots."

"None took place, darling."

"I know, but what about today?" Dorrit glanced at Berlin Zeitung next to her plate, scanning its front page for articles to support her fear. An item in the upper right hand corner caught her eye. "Listen to this!" She unfolded the paper and began to read aloud. "Incendiary leaflets supporting the railway strike were distributed last night on Leipziger Platz the same time posters calling for the blood of the union leaders sprung up along Wilhelm Strasse. Both sides have called for demonstrations. Riot troops have been put on high alert." Dorrit stared down the length of the table. "*Riot* troops, Johann! You know perfectly well that demonstrations spell trouble. When crowds converge in large numbers tempers boil, anarchy takes over, and bloodshed follows. After years of hardships the threshold is at an all time low. You know that better than most. You treat the injured."

Nodding, Johann stirred his coffee. "It's too late to cancel the forum with Dr. Carrel. He's here from Paris and if he, a foreigner, is not deterred by threats of riots it'd be a sorry situation if I were."

Something in Dorrit's anxious mind prompted the thought that this intrepid French surgeon and Johann could conduct their medical experiments here in suburban Grunewald, a safe distance from the center of Berlin. "Maybe it's not too late to change the venue?" she suggested. "Why don't you invite Dr. Carrel out here to your clinic?"

"I don't have the university's fresh supply of corpses."

"Please, I'm eating!" Dorrit made a face and pushed some auburn strands behind her ears. After rounding the corner of forty, she'd cut her hair and now wore it in a short, modern bob that stubbornly retained the curls from her youth.

"In addition to a lack of cadavers," Johann said with a half smile, igniting that silvery glint in his gray eyes that invariably disarmed her, "my clinic lacks an observation gallery." He put his napkin on the table, pushed back his chair and got up. "Besides, a great number of physicians have signed up for today's forum. How do I get word to them? How can I suddenly require them to come out here en masse?" He reached for his suit jacket hanging on the back of a chair standing against the beige satiny walls under an exquisite painting of fruits and flowers. Thrusting his arms into the sleeves, he walked over to Dorrit, bent down and kissed the top of her head. "If it'll make you feel better, darling, I'll take the bus this morning."

"I suppose it'd ease my mind a little," she said, snatching at the relief she felt with his offer to make use of public transportation. It was well known that if caught in the vicinity of a riot, chauffeur-driven automobiles risked being pelted with rocks; civil violence the press blamed on communist factions within Germany. She rose from her seat and followed Johann into the hall where Schmidt stood ready to drive the baron into town.

"I won't need you this morning," Johann told him. "My wife believes driving is unsafe."

"Very well," Schmidt sniffed, slanting a look at the baroness, wondering if she had insulted his ability at the wheel.

3

Chapter Two

Leaving the house, walking through the wrought-iron gates, Johann turned right and continued along Lindenstrasse, where each of the stately homes faced Grunewald Park, the green woodland that lent the neighborhood its name. After a few blocks he reached Halensee Strasse where his clinic occupied a prominent corner. Before catching a city-bound bus, he stopped in briefly to consult with his friend and colleague, Dr. Benjamin Tarnoff, who ran the facility in his absence.

An hour later, riding a bus nearing central Berlin, Johann saw that a great number of demonstrators were gathering on the sidewalks along Potsdamer Strasse. As the crowd swelled, people spilled into the street, forcing motorized traffic to proceed slowly. The bus eventually stopped altogether near Leipziger Platz rather than risk colliding with the ever-increasing number of pedestrians joining the surge. Agitators with bullhorns were climbing atop lampposts on the square, trying to out-shout each other. Union leaders promised jobs with no layoffs, while strike organizers promoted picket lines and called for the overthrow of President Ebert. There had been a string of presidents and chancellors since Germany sent Kaiser Wilhelm into exile in 1918, none had lasted long; still, it would require a brave soul to call for the Kaiser's return. After all, he had waged a war where the peace following the conflict was almost as bitter.

Deciding a roundabout way to Humboldt University was preferable to sitting idle in traffic with a faint-hearted driver who might feel kinship with the rioters and be reluctant to move, Johann concluded he would be better off skirting this trouble spot on foot. A couple of blocks east of here he could catch a trolley toward Unter den Linden and probably arrive at the medical school before

4

this jam cleared.

Stepping off the bus, no sooner had he set foot on the curb, buttoning his overcoat against the cold wind, when a shot whizzed by his ear and tore into the brick building behind him. Ducking into a nearby doorway, believing the bullet might have grazed the side of his head, he removed his hat to test for blood. There wasn't any. He gave a slow whistle with his narrow escape. The random shot had obviously come from the rioters brandishing guns brought home from the war, never turned in, and now used indiscriminately in the streets. Civilians regularly fell victim to sporadic gunplay, and it was an unsettling thought to realize that he'd come within a hair of being a statistic.

From the relative safety of the doorway, Johann took stock of a situation that was deteriorating right before his eyes. The sound of more shots could be heard, but it was impossible to tell who was responsible. People sitting on the bus ducked down and, feeling singularly exposed, Johann turned to test the door he was leaning against, hoping to get inside the building. It was locked and no apartment dweller was foolish enough to open the vestibule while anarchy ruled the streets. *Where are the riot troops the papers promised?* he wondered and hoped Dorrit wouldn't turn on the radio at home and learn about this. He glanced up and down the sidewalk for signs of some police presence. There was none, and of course it would require more than foot patrols to handle this escalating mayhem.

A few doors down, he saw a woman huddled with two children and a half-grown dog in a precarious spot similar to his. The woman stuck her head out from the doorway like a turtle from its shell; her face a picture of panic as more rioters filled the street, many wielding homemade weapons, which in their crude form looked more menacing than guns. Johann motioned for her to stay in the shelter, figuring that as long as the little group remained there, they'd be safe until things blew over. He, however, couldn't wait. He must try to get through these rioters now marching like an undisciplined army toward Leipziger Platz.

Perhaps he could join them, melt into the crowd, and work his way to the opposite side where he could peel away at the first intersection and then head east. After a few moments of deliberation, he decided it was that or nothing. Rolling up his collar, he jammed his hat down on his head and fell into step with the revolt.

He had elbowed himself halfway through the churning multitudes and had the opposite curb in sight, when columns of uniformed troops materialized on Leipziger Platz, barricading the square and arresting those with bullhorns. This so angered the mob that it let out a unifying roar before suddenly storming forward.

An attack on armed troops was not something Johann had planned to be part of. But, trapped within the angry swarm, he was swept along in a maelstrom of a terrifying strength. Realizing the troops would surely open fire, he did his level best to break free, dodging bodies and the weapons they carried, all the while gritting his teeth with the irony of the situation and his blistering hand-to-hand combat. To have survived two years at that wretched field hospital on the Russian front, only to be maimed by his countrymen on the streets of Berlin, was a galling thought but gave him that extra rush of adrenaline needed to reach the opposite curb.

Stumbling up onto the sidewalk, Johann leaned against a lamppost to catch his breath. He spotted several injured individuals lying on doorsteps, companions hovering over them, comrades-in-arms who had pulled them to safety. Above the din, the sound of repeated rifle fire could be heard. The troops were dispersing the rioters. Johann prayed they were aiming over their heads and that those carrying guns did not return fire. But, dismissing a situation he could do nothing about, he got down to the business of attending the injured, something he *could* do.

"I am a doctor," he said, approaching each victim in turn and finding mostly bruises, welts and fractured ribs, made quick work of his examinations until he came upon a man who was unconscious with blood seeping from his mouth. A scruffy boy was kneeling next to him.

"Move aside," Johann ordered the distraught lad, who looked to be Fritz's age. The boy did as he was told and watched as the Good Samaritan knelt down and loosened his father's collar.

"Papa f...fell..." the boy stammered, compelled to explain himself while his father's vital signs were being checked. "He couldn't keep up when everybody started running. They trampled him...like...like a discarded shoe...or...or something."

"That's mob mentality for you," Johann said and determined that the victim's blood stemmed from a badly cut lip. "Your father will be all right. He'll need some sutures and he might have a concussion."

As Johann was saying this, the man regained consciousness and began retching, cradling his head between callused hands. Once the dry spasms ceased, he sank back down on the sidewalk, wiped a dirty sleeve across his mouth, and looked at the well-dressed individual bending over him.

"The nausea will pass," Johann told him. "You've had a blow to your head. You need to get to a hospital. They'll repair your lip and keep you overnight for observation." Too dazed to speak, the man nodded, indicating he understood.

Johann got up, his knees stiff from the cold sidewalk. Pivoting his head, he noted that the revolt had lost some steam, the rioters' fervor dampened by the troops' firepower. He turned back to the boy and his father. "There's nothing more I can do for you here," he said. "Ambulances should come along shortly." He reached into his pocket for a clean handkerchief and gave it to the injured man. "Use this on your lip." Again he dipped into his pocket, this time extracting a card, making several notations on it before handing it to the man. "Show this to the admitting physician and there won't be any charge for your treatment." Looking at the boy, he added, "Make sure your father gets on the first ambulance that arrives."

"I...I will..."

Johann walked away with a heavy heart. The fronts had silenced six years ago but the war hadn't ended. It had simply moved home.

Chapter Three

Johann caught a streetcar and as it approached Wirchow Hospital, made a snap decision, got off and went to the emergency entrance to make sure ambulances had been dispatched. Years ago, he and Kurt Eckart had interned here. Kurt was still with the hospital as Chief of Surgery.

Entering through the familiar doors, Johann was struck by *déjà vu;* the place hadn't changed. The same assortment of patients were waiting for treatment, a pristinely uniformed nurse walking among them, jotting down names and complaints, prioritizing the cases for the doctors, one of whom was bent over a gurney, examining a woman with burns on her legs. Johann approached the blond, bespectacled resident at the admittance station.

"Have you been notified of the riot?" he asked.

The young doctor looked up from a ledger, shook his head, and then suddenly got out of his chair as if to stand at attention. Not on account of the riot - such news was commonplace - but because he recognized the esteemed surgeon standing before him. "Herr Baron Doctor von Renz!" he exclaimed, grinning cheek to jowl and offering his hand. "It's a privilege to meet you. I'm Dr. Witt."

Johann shook his hand and came to the point of his visit. "There's been some street trouble. Several people in and around Leipziger Platz need medical attention. Have you been notified?"

"No." Dr. Witt snapped his brows together. "Any life-threatening injuries? Deaths?"

"None that I saw."

"Good." Dr. Witt brushed aside the riot. Being face-to-face with this renowned individual took precedence over minor injuries on Leipziger Platz. "I've attended many of your demonstrations at

Humboldt," he continued eagerly. "I read today's *affiche*. Is it true that you and Dr. Alexis Carrel will attempt to repair blood vessels?"

"Yes."

"I wish I could attend. But I'm on duty and can't get away. Do you really believe blood vessel surgery is possible?"

"Someday it will be routine." Johann shifted his feet impatiently.

"Seems to me it'd be like trying to sew together pieces of wet spaghetti."

Johann grinned at the comparison and stole a look at the clock on the wall above the young man's head. The rust around the edges had encroached on the white enamel since his days here, otherwise the timepiece looked the same and he figured it was still dependable.

"I'm in a bit of a hurry," he said. "You'll have to excuse me. Perhaps we can talk some other time." He dug out his card and handed it across the desk. "Give me a call."

Dr. Witt fingered the card with reverence. "Thank you! I will."

"I'm surprised no calls have come in," Johann said, as he turned to leave. "Perhaps facilities closer to the riot were called."

"Yes." Dr. Witt seemed to remember something. "You know, our telephones have been down most of the morning. We had a fire in one of the transformers last night. But since you've now reported the trouble, I'll go ahead and dispatch an ambulance to Leipziger Platz. Just to be on the safe side."

"Good." Johann left.

Walking across the sidewalk toward the trolley stop, he was pulling on his gloves when a taxi stopped at the curb to discharge a passenger. What luck! In view of gasoline shortages since the war, an unoccupied taxi was a rare sight. Johann got in.

"Humboldt University," he told the driver and sank gratefully into the soft leather upholstery.

Chapter Four

"The mail's here, Ma'am." Schmidt walked briskly into the mahogany paneled library, carrying an assortment of envelopes on a silver tray. Bending forward at the waist, he held it out to the baroness seated in a tufted red leather sofa by a soaring glass-fronted bookcase that took up an entire wall of the room. The sofa, flanked by matching chairs, faced the fireplace and the mullioned windows on both sides of the carved oak mantelpiece. "Will you be needing anything else?" Schmidt glanced toward the hearth, happy to see that the logs he'd lit earlier were still burning adequately. "Perhaps a cup of tea?"

"Thank you, no." Inserting a marker, Dorrit placed the book she'd been reading on a side table before gathering up the letters.

Tucking the empty tray under his arm, the butler withdrew. Dorrit got up, brushed out the pleats in her navy blue gabardine skirt and walked over to the Queen Anne desk by the window, sat down and began to leaf through the envelopes, turning one of them over in her hand. It was from Heidelberg University and addressed to Herr Baron Doctor Johann Maximilian von Renz; nonetheless, she tore at the seal. Opening it was a clear invasion of privacy, but it was done to spare Johann. Mail from the Dean at the College of Archaeology invariably communicated details of Max's escapades and, depending on the scope of the complaints, took a toll, which was why Dorrit intercepted these missives whenever possible. If an account of Max's offenses was particularly bad she found ways to soften the blow. Johann's former patience with the vagaries of youth was a thing of the past. The Great War had changed him. He laughed less readily, worked like a man possessed and slept little as if life was too precious to be spent sleeping. The enormous fatalities at that field hospital in Kapsukas would haunt him till the end of his days.

Dorrit's breath escaped in a deep sigh; she was again remembering Hans. Whenever the Great War was resurrected in thought or in speech, Hans Konauer figured prominently. The passing of time had not dimmed the memory of the young soldier arriving in Bernau in a pine coffin too narrow for his shoulders, making it look as if his last act had been to shrug at his fate. His death had caused Dorrit such pain that Gerlinde's and Karl-Heinz's crushing heartbreak might as well have been her own. As it were, her friends' anguish endured like a streak of bad luck when the elder Konauer slumped to the ground in a fatal heart seizure as his beloved grandson was laid to rest. Weeks later, when Ursula followed her husband into the grave, Gerlinde - stressed to the breaking point by three consecutive trips to the cemetery - raised her voice to a pitch never before wrung from her gentle lips and ordered her twin daughters not to leave the house if there was the slightest hint of trouble anywhere in the countryside. Berlin was completely off limits, the result being that Dorrit and Johann only saw the Konauers when summering in Bernau.

Massaging her temples, Dorrit looked up at the old pendulum clock on the mantelpiece. Its cracked wooden case looked out of place in this opulent library, but it had been her father's favorite, traveling with them across Eastern Europe, sheltering their paltry savings in its pendulum well. So, while the rest of Herman Zache's clock collection was stored in the attic, Dorrit displayed this one prominently; it was a keepsake from her childhood. She heard it chime and play a little melody, signaling it was three o'clock. It would be hours before Johann returned home. After his session with the French surgeon, he would no doubt go to his clinic and see patients. Since he was one of only a handful of physicians attempting the risky procedures associated with facial reconstruction, he was besieged by veterans who came from all corners of the country in the hope that their burned and shattered faces might be repaired. Of course, with the passing of time the flow of these veterans had tapered off, now leaving the clinic to accident victims or injuries associated with street riots.

Riots! With fear of what she might hear, Dorrit had purposefully not listened to the radio today and again resisted the temptation to touch the dial, instead turning her attention back to the letter from Heidelberg. As she skimmed the familiar complaints associated with her oldest son, she wondered why - with so much wrong in

11

Germany - the college felt compelled to summarize Max's misadventures. Clutching the parchment in her hand, she considered tossing it into the fire; Johann need not learn of this latest complaint. Max was not on academic probation, on the contrary, his marks were excellent, so these latest capers could be ignored like others before them, except those that had required a bank draft to disentangle him from gambling debts or from a non-virtuous female who'd discovered his family's name and wealth. If Max could not be persuaded to share the former, women invariably became determined to relieve him of the latter.

Dorrit made up her mind, crumpled the letter from Heidelberg and, taking careful aim, threw it into the fire where it was instantly devoured in a small puff. The offending mail disposed of, she turned her attention on more pleasant correspondence, such as an effusive letter from Anna von Steigert reporting on Enno's new post in Greece, describing in dramatic whorls and arcs the details of their splendid ambassador's residence in Athens. "You must come visit," Anna's fine penmanship begged in closing. "The weather is absolutely fabulous." Dorrit smiled and put the letter aside for Johann to read, but doubted he'd make time for a pleasure trip. Dipping her pen into the inkwell, she composed a reply to Anna. That done, she wrote out an acceptance for an invitation to Lillian Eckart's birthday party. Lillian was turning forty-five in April, a milestone she guarded with obsessive secrecy; so Kurt had obligingly shaved the number, asking friends to come celebrate his wife's fortieth. Of course no one was fooled except Lillian who put her head in the sand with the slightest displeasing statistic.

The clock on the mantelpiece was pealing the hour of five when the heavy brass hinges on the front door groaned, signaling Johann was home. Schmidt could be heard, walking across the hall to relieve him of his coat and hat. Dorrit jumped from her chair, her bones complaining with the sudden movement; but, staunchly rejecting any notion of middle age, she adjusted the lace collar on her blouse, gave the pleats in her skirt another shake, and proved her vitality by running lightly into the foyer and into Johann's embrace. As he bent down to kiss her, he decided not to burden her with talk of this morning's riot.

"Where's Fritz?" he asked instead, walking through the French doors and finding the library empty.

"At Helmut Niemann's. He telephoned earlier to say he was going there directly after school. He and Helmut are practicing an American piano piece...*Maple Leaf Rag;* I believe it's called. I've heard him play it here at home. It's a catchy tune. Full of spirit."

"Like most things American," Johann smiled, lifting a crystal decanter and pouring two glasses of sherry from the cart behind his desk, a massive affair, which stood by the window opposite the Queen Anne. He handed a glass to Dorrit. "Will he be home for dinner?"

"Yes. I insisted on that."

"Good." Johann walked over to the fireplace, put his drink down on the mantle, picked up a poker and stirred some life into the fire. Flexing his fingers in front of its warmth, he raked a hand through his dark brown hair peppered with gray at the temples. He nodded toward the pile of mail on Dorrit's desk. "Any news from the front?"

"No," she lied, her eyes scanning the embers for any telltale signs of the burned mail. *The front* was a reference to Heidelberg. Johann used the term whenever he inquired about Max and the personal complications that dogged his oldest son.

Chapter Five

Three years later, June 1927...
While in the process of wrapping up an archaeological dig
sponsored by Heidelberg University on Aiyina, a remote Greek
island, Max received a letter from his mother that contained
unsettling news.

"Your father suffered a nasty cut while experimenting on a
cadaver," Dorrit wrote, her usual neat penmanship shaky, indicating
the state of her anxiety. "The wound is slow to heal and I'm afraid it
is infected. Yesterday he ran a fever." She went on to say that while
she didn't want to alarm Max, she was growing concerned and
suggested that he come home for a visit. "As you know, we're about
to go out to Bernau for the summer. We're leaving Berlin a bit
earlier than usual. I expect the fresh air and languid pace in the
country will work wonders; still, your presence will be an additional
catharsis. But for heaven's sake, don't let on. If your father suspects
that you left your work on his account, he'll be furious."

Max made immediate plans to return to Germany rather than travel
with his colleagues to their new assignment on the Greek mainland.
He arrived in Bernau on a picture perfect afternoon in mid June;
never guessing this would be the blackest summer of his life.

The taxi that brought him from the train station made an awful
racket as it circled the courtyard fountain before coming to a
grinding halt on the gravel. Max got out, paid the fare, and cringed
as the driver worked the tired clutch, maneuvering the car back
through the gates and down the long tree-lined drive, dragging a
loose muffler. The noise should have roused a crowd, but not a soul
appeared; it was as though the barony was deserted. Max picked up
his bag, glanced up at the imposing facade of his ancestral home and

14

climbed the broad stone steps to the massive front door, pushed it open and stepped inside.

The cavernous hall, which ran from the front of the house to the back showed no signs of life, no manifestations of Rolf shuffling across the white marble floor in a blind and deaf bid to welcome home the firstborn. Max wondered if the ancient butler had passed on to his reward. He also wondered if his father had taken a turn for the worse, causing everyone to remain in Berlin. A cable or letter to that effect would have missed him once he began his journey home.

"Anybody here?" he called out, dropping his leather bag on the floor with a resounding thud.

Someone stirred on the landing where the wide staircase divided and continued in opposite directions to the second floor. A maid peeked over the mahogany banister and snapped to confused attention.

"Oh!" She curtsied and pushed some blond hair under her black cap. She had worked here only a few months and had never seen the eldest son but recognized him from the photographs the baroness kept on her dresser. He was even better looking in person, she noted, and realized the gossip in the servants' wing pertaining to his looks had not been exaggerated. Details about his work in the out-of-doors bore true as well. His face was bronzed by the sun while his sandy hair was bleached almost white, a devastating combination. As he walked to the foot of the stairs and looked up at her, she couldn't help notice his green eyes, if only because they were a matched pair, for nothing else on his person matched. Unlike his brother, who was always fastidiously dressed, this one appeared oblivious to fashion and wore his clothes with haphazard indifference. His khakis were worn and dirty and she suspected his gray pullover had been blue at one time. Moreover, he was unshaven. Still, despite his dishabille, he was uncommonly handsome.

"Is my mother outside?" he asked, nodding toward the far end of the hall where the double doors stood open to the terrace, the breeze carrying in a sweet scent from the rose garden.

"No. The Baroness is visiting Frau Konauer," the girl said in a low voice as if it were necessary to maintain a level of quiet in the house. "She left less than twenty minutes ago. Heinrich drove her. I don't believe anyone expected you until tomorrow."

"Yes, I'm a day early. Is my father down at the stables?"

"No. Herr Baron is resting upstairs."

"Resting?" Max felt an uneasy twinge. He had never known his father to take to his bed in the middle of the day.

"*Ach!* I thought I heard voices," Heinrich said, surprised, as he walked through the front door, taking off his cap and driving goggles and immediately picking up the heap of dusty leather on the floor. "Welcome home, Herr Maximilian! I'll bring your luggage up to your rooms at once."

Recognizing the valet who had been groomed to take over from Rolf, Max realized the old butler had died. "Did Rolf pass away?" he asked.

"Yes. Last month."

Max hadn't known a day in Bernau without Rolf. "I'm sorry to hear it," he now said, wondering why he hadn't been informed. Of course he frequently traveled faster than mail and any number of letters could have gone astray, chasing him down around the Mediterranean rim.

With the mentioning of his predecessor's demise, Heinrich looked appropriately solemn before Herr Maximilian's unfortunate attire came to his attention. "Do you require a change of clothing?" he now asked. "Perhaps a bath before I wake Herr Baron and announce your arrival."

"Run a bath, but don't wake my father." Max concluded that if Johann was sleeping, woe be it for him to disturb him. "How is he?"

"Herr Baron is having a good day, all things considered. He decided to rest only after the baroness left for her visit with Frau Konauer. He prefers that she doesn't know about any midday naps." Heinrich flashed a conspirator's smile that stopped short of incorporating a wink.

Max crossed the floor to the library. The room was empty. "Is my brother out riding?" he asked, remaining in the doorway.

"Yes. You weren't expected until tomorrow."

"So I've been told." Max grinned at the maid still hanging over the banister. She found her feather duster and went back to her chores. "Any cold beer in the cellar?" He turned to Heinrich.

"Of course." The butler, quick to recognize priorities, dropped the luggage and rushed off, anxious to prove himself worthy of his recent promotion.

Max strolled into the library. Its light furnishings - white damask chairs and sofa - set it apart from the one in Berlin. An exquisite pastel Aubusson covered the floor and silk drapery the color of sea foam framed the large bay windows. While waiting for Heinrich to return, he eyed a stack of unopened mail on his father's desk. Walking over and rummaging through it, he was looking for an envelope with an Aiyina postmark, his pulse quickening as he searched.

Moments later, having gone through the pile twice, he came up empty-handed. Of course it was unrealistic to expect anything this soon; besides, mail from Aiyina might spell disaster; he ought not be so eager. He turned away from the desk and looked out the windows, pondering his recent dilemma. Narrowing his eyes, he raked his fingers through his hair in visible agitation and continued to stare at the garden as if something out there held the answer to his considerable problem on Aiyina. As his eyes roamed the beautiful green lawns dotted with groves of majestic elm, he wished himself back on that rocky and arid island, a remote crust of land, a dot on the map, nothing but a blemish on the blue Mediterranean, which nonetheless pulled him with both longing and dread; a paradox of emotions completely foreign to him and therefore all the more aggravating.

Chapter Six

When Max came downstairs to join the family in the library before dinner, he was a changed individual. A white linen jacket hugged his broad shoulders, and he was wearing newly pressed slacks with a blue-striped shirt open at the neck where a yellow ascot was tied in a rakish knot. Of course, credit for this ensemble went directly to Heinrich and his former stint as valet.

"Max!" Dorrit cried with delight and jumped up from her chair the minute he strolled through the doorway. "I'm sorry I wasn't home when you arrived." She ran to embrace her son. "I was visiting Gerlinde. We all thought you'd be arriving tomorrow."

"I know," Max grinned engagingly and lifted her clear off the floor in a crushing embrace, an easy assignment for someone at his height with the strength of a trained athlete. Releasing her, he nodded in Fritz's direction before walking over to a high-backed wingchair where Johann was watching the happy reunion without attempting to get up. Max landed a fond blow on his shoulder. A man of untiring energy, his father looked peculiarly pale and drawn. He had obviously reaped little benefit from his rest this afternoon.

"You're looking good, Papa," Max lied.

"So are you, son. It's wonderful to see you." Tapping his pipe against an ashtray, dislodging some powdery remains, Johann smiled with great pleasure. "And a day early. A wonderful surprise. I guess we misread your telegram."

"No. I was on a milk run two days north from Athens when I got lucky in Zagreb and secured the last couchette on an overnight express to Berlin. It pulled in today at noon."

"I see. Did Schmidt meet the train and drive you out?"

"No, I figured it was quicker to hop on the *Ring-Bahn*. Say, are we riding in the morning?"

"Seven sharp if you can shake yourself out of bed."

"Count on it." Max turned his attention to Fritz whose head was buried in a newspaper. He marked a column before putting it down to acknowledge his older sibling.

"Welcome home!" he said, standing up and embracing Max with a brotherly back thumping.

"God Almighty!" Max broke loose and lifted his eyebrows, pretending to measure the space between the ceiling and his brother's dark head. "Is it my imagination, Frederick Alexander, or did you grow a foot since my last visit?" His eyes flicked over Fritz's conservative attire - navy jacket with gray slacks - making him appear older than his nineteen years. "I'll soon be obliged to look up to you."

Fritz, who didn't think Max would pay him a compliment if he could help it, merely said, "How was Greece?"

"Fantastic!"

Dorrit straightened in her seat, pushing a pink cushion behind her back for support. "Does that mean you found some important artifacts on Aiyina?"

"No. The site's been scratched. My colleagues are now in Koropi on the mainland, working with that slave-trader Professor Krugg. I have to join them there in about two weeks."

"Two weeks?" Dorrit looked crestfallen; she had her heart set on at least a month. Max hadn't been home since last Christmas. "Will you be back later in the summer then?"

"Yes. I can take a break in August after a quick trip back to Aiyina." The latter part of that comment slipped out inadvertently. Max immediately regretted it.

"Aiyina?" Johann said, surprised. "Didn't you just say the site has been scratched?"

"Well, yes. But...uh, something else... Never mind. It's not important." Max cleared his throat and clamped his mouth shut. This was not the time for a confessional. He'd just arrived and his father looked as if bad news might kill him.

A puzzled look passed between Dorrit and Johann, but they didn't press Max. He was twenty-four. They respected his privacy. If something needed to be clarified, he would do so in his own time.

Suffering no such reticence, Fritz spoke up. "If there are no artifacts on Aiyina why go back?"

The query netted him an evasive shrug and the sight of his brother's back as Max turned and walked over to one of the

19

bookcases. He opened a false front revealing a well-stocked liquor cabinet and proceeded to take requests. While pouring drinks, he fired questions at Johann about the goings-on in the stables, safe pickings for conversation and an effective way of changing the subject. He inquired about the new Hanoverian gelding his father had mentioned in a letter some time ago. He also asked about his favorite hunter, as well as the general soundness of an aging stallion. Max shared his father's passion for horses and whenever he was in Bernau they spent many hours riding.

Chapter Seven

He met Johann down at the stables at seven sharp the following morning. Their horses were saddled, and they were soon riding the familiar trails across the estate.

It had rained during the night and the bridle paths remained wet, which required a slower than normal pace; too slow to suit Max who, furthermore, registered surprised each time Johann suggested they take detours around hedges on the property rather than jump them. Max couldn't recall a single occasion in the past when his father had avoided the thrill of a good jump.

He shifted in the saddle and took a long hard look at him. Johann was in his mid fifties and by anyone's measure still a strikingly handsome man. There were lines across his forehead, but his square jaw was firm, his shoulders straight, and although his dark hair was graying, it remained thick. His vitality, on the other hand, was at an all time low with a grim twist hovering about his lips as if an inner pain bothered him. Max figured the infection Dorrit had mentioned in her letter was to blame, and remembered her wish that he pretend ignorance. He glanced at the bandage wrapped around his father's index finger that along with a slight swelling of the hand precluded him from wearing riding gloves. The horror of blood poisoning crossed Max's mind. He decided to pry without revealing what he already knew.

"What happened to your hand?" he asked casually after a while of riding along in silence.

"Pardon?"

Max pointed to the bandage. "Did you cut yourself?"

"Yes." Johann nodded. "Cuts are common in my profession, Max. I've had them before. This one is a bit more stubborn than usual. It's nothing to worry about."

"I suppose you're treating it with some medical ointment?"

"Yes." The deafening sound of a period at the end of the word made it obvious that Johann didn't wish to pursue the matter.

Max pulled down the brim of his hat to shield his eyes against the morning glare. There was no shade on this stretch except for the diffuse shadows some brambling berry bushes threw across the path. The foliage was glossy and drooping with moisture from last night's rain now being released as vapor, signaled a humid day was in store. Max decided he would shortly make a subtle suggestion that they return to the stables, subtle because one had to be careful when dealing with a proud man. If he proposed they turn around prematurely, Johann would no doubt insist they press on, if only to prove that he could.

Skirting the wheat fields, they halted their horses at the crest of a gentle hill where a forest marked the eastern perimeter of the von Renz property. Guiding their horses into the shade of the trees, the sudden presence of man and beast roused a flock of ravens roosting among the conifers. For an instant the motionless air came to life with beating wings as the birds flew in clumsy circles overhead.

Johann removed his hat, wiped his sleeve across his brow before jamming the hat back down on his head, soundlessly cursing his dwindling strength. His back against the cool forest, his eyes caressed the wheat fields undulating like a gentle green sea as far as the eye could see. Directly west, built on a rise and nestled among elms and sloping lawns, his family home stood in baronial splendor; its red brickwork faded pink with age and tinged green in places by climbing ivy. To the east, the slate roof of the old Konauer estate rose above a copse of trees. One of the twins lived there now with her husband and children; Gerlinde and Karl-Heinz preferring the home they'd built years ago after the twins were born. It lay in a glen behind the old manor house and was not visible from here.

"Some sight," Max said, studying the cultivated landscape where a river was left to meander through the countryside without any interference from man except where a bank of white sand was periodically deposited at a gentle bend. Max smiled with childhood memories of the river beach, memories that were particularly seductive on this hot summer morning.

Johann leaned down to pat his stallion's long slender neck, a russet color when they started out this morning; its coat was now black and shiny with sweat, making him a carbon copy of his sire Asmodeus. "You and Fritz are the sixth generation to hold this land," he said, sweeping his arm in a half circle. "Take good care of it."

"Is Fritz showing any interest in farming?"

"No." Johann chuckled softly. "I realized long ago that neither one of you yearn for the land. Be that as it may. I'm proof that love of agronomics is not a prerequisite for keeping the soil productive as long as you employ a competent manager like Klausen. He's getting on in years, but keep him on as long as he wishes to stay and be sure he trains a new manager before he retires. The place is only as good as the people you hire. Remember that."

"I will. But there's no harm in reminding me from time to time."

Time? Wondering how much he had left, Johann smiled nonetheless and although conversation taxed him, continued. "You're the oldest, Max, so whatever it's worth, the title comes with your share of the estate. Of course titles don't mean much in our world today. It was different when Germany was a monarchy. Still, it will give you entrance into pleasant society."

Max shrugged. He had no interest in the prospect of carrying the family banner in society, but said nothing, for to speak his mind would only sound ungrateful. "On the subject of something pleasant," he grinned, his teeth gleaming white against his tanned face.

"Such as?"

"A cold beer."

"Before breakfast?"

"Why not?"

"All right." Johann laughed, reached over and touched his son's knee affectionately before turning his horse and proceeding down the path ahead of him.

Chapter Eight

It was a week later that the Konauers' hosted their summer solstice party; a yearly tradition that drew guests from near and far, one and all arriving in the finest peasant attire money could buy.

At noon on Saturday, when Dorrit and Johann set out for the festivities, the Mercedes was already idling in the courtyard with Heinrich at the wheel. Max and Fritz would follow in the Daimler-Benz because both automobiles were needed later to ferry back a number of overnight guests; these large weekend gatherings required that Dorrit help Gerlinde accommodate the overflow.

Settling into the back seat, Dorrit spread out the folds in her colorful dirndl skirt so the material wouldn't wrinkle during the ride. The skirt was topped by a green peplum vest laced over a white cotton blouse with puffed sleeves and, to further achieve a peasant look, she had fastened some fresh daisies in her hair. Johann scoffed at the idea of a costume for himself and was dressed in his usual riding garb: tan jodhpurs, brown plaid shirt, a suede vest, and high boots.

Rolling down the car's window, Dorrit took a deep breath of the heady air, marveling at the perfect weather and recalling how incessant downpours had forced last year's extravaganza indoors. Today no rain was expected; it was clear with a balmy warmth more akin to August, the temperature taking a toll on the roses climbing the sunny brick walls of the house. She noticed clusters of the red blooms hung upside down, yielding their weight to the midday heat, a look of defeat yet their fragrance was all the more potent because of it.

Heinrich put the car in gear, drove through the gates and down the tree-lined drive where the uppermost branches of the poplars formed an arch dappling the lane in spots of shade and sun glare. Yellow buttercups dotting the grass at the edge of the driveway bobbed their glossy heads in the wake of the car. Dorrit sank into the soft gray leather seats, turned and looked at Johann leaning into the opposite corner of the car.

"I hope Max and Fritz won't delay setting out," she said. "This is one of the rare occasions when Max is home for the Konauers' party. It'd be a shame if he missed the hunt, which he'll probably enjoy the most."

"I believe he's more concerned about missing the mail," Johann said.

"The mail?"

"Yes. Haven't you seen him pacing the hall each day, waiting for the delivery?"

"No." Dorrit shook her head. "Is he expecting something important?"

"I guess so. According to Heinrich, he grabs the mail directly from the carrier before Heinrich can sort it and put it on my desk."

"Hmm, maybe he's expecting a letter from a young lady," Dorrit said with a speculative glint in her eye.

"If so, he is finally interested in someone who can read and write."

Dorrit laughed with the truth in Johann's statement. In the past, Max had befriended a number of uneducated women and, happy in the thought that he might finally be romancing someone of quality, she conjured up the image of a well-bred girl.

Heinrich shortly turned into the familiar lane where the ancestral Konauer home came into view on the left. Leni, the first-born twin, lived there with her husband, Emil Lange, and their three boys. Klara had married a year after her sister and lived in Eberswalde, where her husband worked in his father's business, a large tool manufacturing concern he hoped to control one day. He was ambitious; something Leni's husband was not. Emil displayed an aversion for any kind of labor, forcing Karl-Heinz to endure him like a pinched nerve.

Passing the old manor house, Heinrich continued down the gracefully curved drive that led to what was known as the "new house," although it was more than a quarter of a century old. Of yellow masonry, it had oversized windows with wooden slats decorating the upper story, while red Spanish tiles comprised the roof; a mélange of aesthetic blunders that Gerlinde had insisted on at the time of construction, much to the dismay of both builder and architect.

On this festive day in late June, the entire Konauer clan including two sets of in-laws, one from Eberswalde the other from hell, because Karl-Heinz blamed Emil's parents squarely for his laggard ways, stood harmoniously under the large portico, greeting the arriving guests. In prior years, the party had been for family and close friends only, but since Gerlinde's democratic heart couldn't bear to leave anyone out, the guest list continually grew, the event eventually becoming something of a county fair.

Chapter Nine

Heinrich pulled up behind other cars in the driveway, spilling out revelers, their greetings to one another interspersed with the happy high-pitched shrieks of children. Setting the brake securely, he jumped out and opened the car doors. As Dorrit alighted she saw Johann falter exiting on the opposite side before he steadied himself against the hood. It tore at her heart but she knew better than to comment. Anyway, once they were under the portico, he appeared to have regained himself, proving it by picking up one of Leni's little boys and giving him a flying tumble in the air.

Dorrit embraced Gerlinde who, despite her frail build, looked very convincing dressed as a burly peasant woman, complete with wooden clogs and a babushka covering her pale hair. Glancing down, Dorrit pointed to her clogs, disproportionably enormous on her small feet, making it look like she was standing in feeding troughs. "You'll break your neck, dancing in those," she cautioned.

"You're right." A twinkle in Gerlinde's blue eyes lit up her plain face, momentarily disguising the lines marking her years and the one heartache she would never recover from. "I'll change shoes before the dancing starts."

Dorrit turned to Karl-Heinz heaping abuse on Johann for his lack of a costume. Karl-Heinz enjoyed a masquerade and was wearing something that looked wonderfully troll-like with a wide black leather belt and a pointed felt hat. He had even grown a bit of a grizzled beard. "Your husband is an unimaginative bore!" he scoffed as he kissed Dorrit, his whiskers tickling her. "To show up here dressed like, well...like himself, for Christ's sake! I ought to ban him for non-participation in the festival. Next year I just might. Don't think that I won't."

Dorrit laughed. Karl-Heinz said the same thing every year.

Once inside the house, Johann stopped in the hall to chat with a horse breeder from Potsdam. The man's wife was so completely lacking in conversation that Dorrit was glad when the crowd swelled and people began moving toward the open doors to the terrace, putting distance between her and the trite woman.

Bathed in the midday sun, humming with conversation, the terrace was a sight to behold: a sea of colorful costumes as bright as the assortment of flowering potted plants in its four corners. Trestle tables standing against the house were being set with tempting edibles, servants holding the sumptuous dishes aloft, depositing them on blue checkered cloths. As she walked past the buffet, Dorrit's nose twitched with the aroma of sausages stewed in sauerkraut and platters of smoked ham glazed in tangy currant sauce. There were bowls of vegetables drowning in parsley cream, and plates of tiny sugar-braised potatoes heaped into pyramids. Catering to a variety of thirsts, kegs of beer, wine, and assorted fruit juices were placed among blocks of ice in a far corner, but not so far away that guests found the trip inconvenient. Johann's gaze swept the mostly male crowd gathered there, but spotted neither Kurt Eckart nor Philip von Brandt among the thirsty. Beyond the confines of the patio, a dozen youngsters of varying ages raced across the grass, chasing each other, the wind, and a hapless hound. Several girls sat quietly on the wide steps leading down to the lawn, watching the chase and weaving freshly picked violets into each other's hair, their hands moving like monkeys grooming one another.

"Hi!" a familiar voice called out above the din. "Over here!" Lillian Eckart was standing on tipped toes and waving to Dorrit and Johann from where she and Isabel von Brandt had secured seats under a yellow umbrella. Lillian was wearing a pink concoction that could not be identified, except for the fact that it was expensive. Isabel wore the same blue muslin shepherd dress she'd worn last summer, this year adding a straw bonnet.

Some years ago, after a lengthy courtship, Philip von Brandt had finally married Isabel Thimm, a refined widow from Dusseldorf with two teenaged daughters. Moving his new family into his old home in Berlin's posh Charlottenburg, Isabel immediately transformed the house into one of the most glamorous, causing relief to ripple through the community. Not only was the restoration project welcomed, but gone was the fear that one of the coarse and painted ladies Herr Doctor von Brandt had heretofore found

28

irresistible, would snatch him in a weak moment and impose herself on the neighborhood.

Dorrit and Johann crossed the terrace to the blessed shade of the umbrella, Johann approaching with a mocking remark. "You look more princess than peasant at this humble affair," he teased Lillian. Isabel laughed out loud. It was safe for her to do so because her costume was not adorned with shiny palettes and festoons of French lace.

"I'll have you know that this is a milkmaid's outfit," Lillian pouted but made no excuses for her finery as she pivoted, patting her blond hair and allowing the flounces in her costume to billow about her. "It's an exact replica of an outfit Marie Antoinette wore at Petit Trianon."

"Doing what?" Johann wanted to know.

Lillian slapped his arm. "Really! Don't be so dense. Everyone knows the French queen was fond of milking cows."

"Wearing *that?*" Johann laughed. "She obviously lost her head long before the guillotine."

Lillian chose to ignore the remark, instead reporting that Kurt was down at the stables. "He and Philip left a few minutes ago to select their horses for the hunt," she said.

"You can still catch them," Isabel added, pointing across the lawns in the direction they'd taken. "But I recommend the shortcut through the house or all the good mounts will be spoken for before you get there."

"Isabel!" Lillian frowned. "Don't be so helpful. Johann won the crown last year. Remember? This time Kurt has promised me the pearls." Turning to Dorrit, she said, "Kurt ought to win for once."

"No reason why not," Dorrit agreed without reminding her that Johann held the record of several consecutive wins; a feat that required skill because the ring of orchids entwined with Majorca pearls was hidden in the woods by a professional game warden.

"You'll get some pearls," Johann assured Lillian. "All Kurt has to do is stop in at Friedlander's."

Lillian sputtered at the mentioning of Berlin's famous jeweler, and Johann took the opportunity to excuse himself, nodding to the ladies and pressing a kiss on Dorrit's forehead. "See you later, darling."

"Is he usually this exasperating?" Lillian wondered out loud after he was gone, but quickly forgave him. She had known Johann since childhood and had always been a little bit in love with him.

Strolling across the flagstones, Johann was detained by friends but, making his excuses, moved on, only lingering a moment when

Max and Fritz arrived. They, too, were hatless and dressed in typical riding gear, which had no doubt earned them a good ribbing from Karl-Heinz.

Disappearing into the house, Johann had no intention of going to the stables; he was merely looking for a quiet place to rest; something Dorrit suspected the minute he left. As she now sat down with her friends under the umbrella, taking a glass of lemonade from a tray a maid was passing around, she was glad that Gertrude and Ben Tarnoff would shortly be here and would, furthermore, stay at the barony tonight. By this time tomorrow, Ben would have examined Johann and given him a strong prescription. Medical intervention was needed because topical ointments, country air and rest alone were not providing results. Max's homecoming last week had cheered Johann, but the low-grade fever persisted and the situation was not helped by the fact that he refused to admit anything was wrong. Ben would set him straight. He would listen to Ben. Dorrit was pinning her hopes on it and, knowing that the Tarnoffs were in synagogue this morning, she now only hoped that an emergency at the clinic wouldn't delay them further. She had her own emergency. She'd burst if she didn't discuss Johann's deteriorating condition with a woman who was older, wiser, and had once been a nurse. Gert had a wonderful calming aura about her. Dorrit could unburden her fears; in truth, she often thought of Gertrude as the mother she'd never had.

Chapter Ten

A sudden shout from the children playing on the lawns stirred Dorrit from her inner musings and she realized Lillian was talking to her. Dazed and confused, she looked at her friend as if waking up from a deep sleep and finding herself in a strange place, which might as well have been the case because she hadn't heard a word. Moreover, she looked at the plate of food in front of her without the faintest idea about who had placed it there.

"Really, Dorrit!" Lillian was not fooled by her sudden alert and wide-eyed expression. "What's the matter with you? What on earth are you daydreaming about?"

"*Me?* Daydreaming?"

"Well, you certainly weren't listening." Lillian picked up a fork and toyed with some glazed ham and vegetables. "So tell me, what do you think? Shawl or apron?" Dorrit realized the conversation had again centered on Lillian's gaudy costume.

"Using the shawl as an apron would make more sense," Isabel spoke up, defending her position.

Dorrit nodded, wishing they could talk about more important matters, namely Johann's illness. But she didn't dare bring it up. Lillian had a loose tongue. In no time flat the entire party would be buzzing with speculation about his health or lack thereof. He would be furious.

"All right, what's wrong?" Lillian demanded, studying her inattentive friend and arching her lightly penciled eyebrows. "Where's your gifted tongue? Have you swallowed a toad?"

"No." Dorrit cleared her throat to prove there was no frog in it. "I…I guess I'll have to agree with Isabel. An apron would make your dress more authentic." Reaching out and running her fingers

31

over the exquisite lace on Lillian's multi-tiered skirt, she added, "Pink becomes you. But I can't imagine that anyone, including Marie Antoinette, would dream of wearing silk and satin around cows."

"The queen's livestock behaved commensurate with their royal caretaker," Isabel said, fighting to keep a straight face. She found the conversation mindless and knew Dorrit did as well - why else was she so absentminded? Of course they both loved Lillian too dearly to let on, and were nicely distracted a moment later when Anna von Steigert walked up to their table. Home from Greece, she and Enno were spending a few weeks at their Wannsee villa, a yearly vacation that coincided nicely with the Konauers' summer gala.

"We arrived just as the horn sounded for the hunt," Anna explained, embracing everyone and accepting compliments on her Greek peasant dress, complete with leather sandals. The opulent gold jewelry she wore detracted from the costume's authenticity, but no one commented on the obvious. Anna would be crushed, and perhaps Greek peasants were more affluent than one was led to believe. "Enno wasted no time and joined the men. I can only imagine what sort of an old nag they left behind for a latecomer."

Chapter Eleven

Lunch plates were being cleared away when a breathless Elsie rushed up to Lillian. "Mama!" she cried. "Can I see your purse a minute?"

"Sweetheart! Where are your manners?" Lillian smiled indulgently at her only child.

"Oh? Sorry..." Elsie made a token curtsy to her mother's friends at the table before she quickly got back to business. "Now, may I?"

"Yes, darling." Lillian handed her daughter a small beaded bag. "Did you have some lunch?"

"Uh-huh. Lots." Elsie rummaged through the purse, pocketing a lipstick and some rouge. She handed the bag back to her mother who didn't seem to notice how light it'd become. Poised to bolt, Elsie turned toward the house.

"Wait!" Lillian grabbed her arm before she could run off. "Aren't you joining the lawn games?" She pointed toward a group of girls and boys gathering on the grass with colorful mallets and wooden balls.

Elsie made a sullen face. "Only old people and little kids play croquet," she said. "Besides, it's much too hot out here." Planting a dutiful kiss on her mother's powdered cheek, Elsie remembered to smile at each of the ladies before making her escape, dodging between the people and tables on the terrace. As she ran, her blond hair bounced with youthful energy, as did the hem of her gypsy skirt, displaying four tulle petticoats and two shapely ankles.

"Don't any of you dare breathe a word outside this room!" she warned moments later once she and six other pubescent girls had sequestered themselves in an upstairs room in the rambling Konauer house and prepared to admit to burning crushes on certain boys at

33

the party, all of whom were safely away on the hunt and out of earshot. "I think Fritz is divine!" she whispered, kicking off the confessional. "Even if he can't dance."

"What makes you think he can't dance?" A girl offended on his behalf was demanding proof.

"Because I've never seen him dance, *silly!* And I see a lot of him. His parents and mine are best friends. Believe me, Fritz can't dance."

"Maybe he just doesn't want to," the same girl suggested, deciding the boy in question was far too cute to have any faults.

"Yeah!" another girl chimed in. "Or maybe he just doesn't want to dance with you, Elsie."

"Hah!" she snorted. "You only say that because you're jealous and because you know he likes me."

"Me? Jealous? Not in a million years!" the girl countered. "He's not my type."

"Yeah! Right!" Elsie challenged. "Let's see you decline if he asks you to dance tonight."

"I most certainly will." The girl elevated her small stubborn chin.

"Not in a million years!" the rest chorused, nudging her. She turned beet red.

Once harmony was restored, and after several other boys had been swooned over, another girl was prompted into admitting that she'd prefer to dance with Fritz's brother. "He's squeamishly handsome," she giggled.

"Max?" everyone protested, shocked with her declaration.

"Yeah, why not?"

"Because..." a girl in a red-riding-hood costume shrieked as if she'd just seen the wolf, "he's too old for heaven's sake!"

"And he's always off somewhere," another girl said. "In some desert or some such place where he digs up old bodies and moldy stuff. My parents say that even though he's rich, he'll make a poor husband."

"Poor?" Everyone turned on her, questioning her logic.

"Uh...well, you know. Not only is he never around, but he has a certain reputation."

"What do you mean?"

"I don't know. My parents didn't say."

Sounds of disappointment rippled through the group.

Eventually everyone ran out of material, grew restless, and returned downstairs to primp in front of a large hall mirror. Jostling each other, they smoothed their hair and chewed their lips to bring out some color. Elsie applied a trace of the lipstick and rouge she'd lifted from her mother's purse and, secure in the belief that the cosmetics made her look much prettier than the rest of the girls, was soon leading her inferiors toward the library in search of candy dishes with soft-centered peppermints.

Once inside the door, she suddenly pulled up short, her entourage bunching up behind her. Shades drawn, the room lay in semidarkness, but she immediately spotted Baron von Renz stretched out on a hunter green leather sofa. His hands were laced casually behind his head and he appeared to be asleep, one booted foot on the floor, the other sprawled across the armrest.

The bemused girls tiptoed backwards. Once clear of the door, they turned and, hanging onto each other's shoulders, exploded in fits of giggles as they crossed the hall and ran outside in embarrassed decorum at having spied upon the formidable baron in the privacy of his sleep.

Chapter Twelve

The sun was sinking behind a bank of haze in the west and with this last gesture painted the sky purple. Riders were returning from the hunt, arriving singly or in small groups that were met in the courtyard by grooms waiting to take the horses to the stables. As the men dismounted, they commiserated about difficult trails and clues that had failed them. Good-humoredly, they laughed at their misadventure while counting heads and speculating on who was still out there and might return the victor. Talking animatedly, they strolled around the side of the house to the terrace, where a hundred colorful paper lanterns now illuminated the scene. Tables, chairs, and kegs had been moved out onto the lawns, clearing the space in preparation for the dancing. The men immediately headed for the kegs and casks and placed bets on riders still in the woods. As thirsts were quenched, bets were doubled and redoubled.

Finally, riding his horse across the lawns toward the terrace, Max appeared with the orchids looped over the pommel of his saddle. Groans of dismay could be heard because large sums of money had been lost with this first glimpse of the victor. No one except the horse breeder from Potsdam, who in his ignorance had bet on the horse, not the rider, thought Max had a chance. After all, he was so rarely at this event that he wasn't expected to have the necessary familiarity with the treasure hunt to triumph.

Guiding his horse to the edge of the tables and chairs, he jumped down, grabbed the ring of pearl-entwined flowers and gave the animal a brisk pat on its rear flanks, sending it on a stampede toward the stables, clods of grass flying behind it. Taking the steps to the terrace in a single leap, his roguish gaze surveyed the crowd. He had no wife or fiancé. His choice was wide open. His eyes came to rest on Gerlinde standing toward the back, head bent in whispered conversation with one of her grandsons begging to be picked up to view the proceedings; a plea she prudently resisted because his weight, much as she loved every ounce of him, would surely snap her back.

"For our hostess!" Max announced, holding the prize aloft as the crowd parted for him.

Gerlinde looked up in bewilderment, tears springing to her eyes as Max placed the crown atop her babushka before lifting her grandson up so he could be the first to kiss the festival queen. Putting the boy down, he sent him off with a pat such as the horse had gotten. The musicians scrambled to their station, picked up their instruments and broke into a waltz as Max escorted Gerlinde to the center of the floor for the opening dance. With this unexpected attention, Gerlinde forgot to remove her clogs, which hampered any approximation of a graceful waltz. If she hadn't been so loved by all, some might have been tempted to laugh at the comical figure she presented.

The next dance was a lively polka. Husbands found their wives and young lads shyly approached the unattached girls, while children joined hands and skipped around in circles. The terrace was soon vibrating with boots hitting the flagstones while the swinging of skirts fluttered in the light of the lanterns, colorful and iridescent like butterfly wings in the sun. From the distance, from under a tall birch tree on the lawn, where Fritz had found his niche among fellow students more interested in debating than dancing, the scene took on folkloric qualities.

"He's at it again," Kurt remarked, dancing with Dorrit after Lillian ran into the house, dabbing at her skirts soiled by a clumsy guest sloshing around with a full wine glass.

"Who is at it again?"

"Fritz. Look!" Kurt swiveled on his heels so Dorrit could see the group on the lawn, arguing furiously. "If he's debating issues of a political nature, I commend him."

Dorrit laughed. "As long as he champions views not too foreign with yours."

"Well, of course."

"To tell you the truth, Kurt, I wish he'd break off the debate and dance." She glanced toward Elsie who had found a spot under the same tree and was looking at Fritz with dewy speculation. She was a pretty little thing but shamelessly spoiled. Dorrit wondered if the damage was irreversible; still, all things being equal, she'd welcome her into the family someday. Fritz could do worse. "There are a number of pretty girls here tonight," she said. "Your Elsie, for instance."

Kurt glowed at the mention of his pride and joy. "In due time," he said as if he had read Dorrit's mind, "a match between our respective offspring would be enthusiastically embraced by Lillian and myself." As he was saying this, he smiled toward his daughter, who just then happened to glance in the direction of the dance floor. Catching her eye, Kurt blew her a kiss.

She stuck out her tongue in the classic childish display of having been embarrassed by a parent.

Chapter Thirteen

The music woke Johann. He sat up, rotated his shoulders, smoothed down his hair, and switched on a lamp on the table next to him. Perched on the edge of the sofa, he tried to determine if he was ready to join the festivities.

The rest has revived me, he told himself, searched for some corroborating evidence but found none and figured the simple exercise of getting on his feet would cost him. He swore under his breath and was selling himself a bill of goods about mind over matter when he heard familiar voices in the hall. Karl-Heinz was greeting the Tarnoffs. Johann heard them express apologies for arriving so late.

"My goodness, Johann, is that you?" Gertrude, having caught sight of him through the doorway, walked into the library. "Hiding out?" she asked cheerfully. "It's a nice spot you've chosen. Cool and quiet."

Johann struggled to his feet. "How was your trip out?" he said, noting Gert was dressed in a Tyrollean costume and suspecting that Ben would be in Lederhosen and green-feathered cap. "You're awfully late."

"Traffic was abominable," Ben said, coming up behind Gertrude.

"No crisis at the clinic then?" Johann grinned at the sight of Ben's bony knees, and gave him credit for being a good sport, subjecting himself to short pants at the age of sixty-five.

"Nothing worth mentioning."

"Good," Karl-Heinz cut in. "There's to be no shop talk tonight. Come on, let's join the party." He took Gertrude's arm and led her from the library. As he passed through the doors, he glanced over his shoulder to confirm that Ben and Johann were following. When he saw Johann take a couple of faulty steps, he threw a questioning look toward Ben, who simply waved him on.

Of course Ben knew that Johann was not well. Some time ago in Berlin, once it became clear that his cut was not healing, they immediately rushed to consult with other professionals. A number of remedies were attempted to no avail; there was no known cure for blood poisoning and not wanting to distress his family, Johann decided to keep it quiet. Ben obliged him only because he remained guardedly optimistic. A strong individual with a mild infection could recover, which he hoped would be the happy outcome in Johann's case.

As they stepped out on the terrace, Johann spotted Dorrit dancing with Philip von Brandt. He stopped in the doorway to watch.

"Aren't you coming?" Ben said, motioning toward Karl-Heinz and Gertrude making their way around the perimeter of the dance floor toward the refreshment bar on the lawn.

"No. You go ahead. I'm going to pry my wife away from Philip."

"All right. But don't exhaust yourself," Ben warned and left to catch up with the others.

His eyes on Dorrit, Johann remained standing in the open doorway a while longer to dispel a stubborn lightheadedness. Her short copper curls glistened in the lamplight. The daisies she'd pinned in her hair earlier had wilted and hung like floppy earrings against her cheeks. The neck of her blouse was open and he caught sight of the emerald heart she always wore. He'd given it to her years ago the night of his clumsy proposal and, amid her vast collection of jewelry, she treasured that piece above any other; a sentimentality that meant a great deal to him. Mobilizing some strength, and once the music changed to a slower dance, he elbowed his way through the crowd and tapped Philip on the shoulder.

"Go trample someone else's feet," he shouted above the music, sending Philip in search of another partner.

"Did you miss me, darling?" Johann said as his arm went around Dorrit's waist, his feet falling into step with hers, glad the slow tempo wouldn't tax him. "I got too comfortable in the library and lost track of time."

"Of course I missed you," she laughed, her green eyes sparkling like the flash of the gem around her throat. "But you missed the excitement."

"Excitement?"

"Yes! Max found the crown. He gave it to Gerlinde, making her festival queen. It's the first time anyone has ever done that."

Johann smiled. "With all his rough edges, Max is a thoughtful fellow. I suppose our Fritz has withdrawn into an intellectual retreat and can be found nowhere near the dance floor? Did he go on the hunt?"

"Yes, but he returned early. His horse was favoring a leg and he didn't want the animal to go lame."

"And now he's favoring his own legs and not dancing." Johann grinned.

"I'm afraid so. But don't worry, Max is covering enough ground for both of them." Dorrit tossed her head toward Max and the young woman in his arms. "She's the fourth one I've seen him with. No girl will be a wallflower tonight."

"Like I said, he's a thoughtful fellow."

The music changed to a sarabande and before their feet made the necessary adjustments, Johann bent down and brushed his lips against Dorrit's cheek. The instant his mouth touched her skin, she felt his fever and jerked her head up to stare at him.

"Do you want to go home?" she asked, realizing any benefit from his rest in the library had been short-lived.

Although the suggestion had much to recommend it, Johann shook his head. A lavish supper followed by colorful gypsy dancers with tambourines and burning torches lighting a huge bonfire by the river was yet to come; pageantry Dorrit enjoyed and something he didn't want to deprive her of. Besides, an early departure would draw unwanted speculation.

But how long could he keep the truth from his family? How long could Dorrit be fooled? How long could he stave off pitying looks and artificial smiles from friends? He was familiar with people's brittle gaiety when visiting hospitalized individuals not expected to survive. He wanted none of that. So long as he was not confined to his bed, he wanted to keep the real nature of his illness to himself.

Chapter Fourteen

It was a number of days later when the last of their houseguests had departed, that Dorrit and Johann sat down for dinner alone with their sons.

The evening remained warm, the kitchen staff compensating by serving a cold supper and leaving the French doors open to the garden to encourage a breeze. However, except for a winged insect nothing stirred the air in the banquet-sized room where, in spite of the heat, tapers in the candelabras on the dining table and on the sideboards were lit, casting light across the rare tapestries that had hung on the walls for over two hundred years, not aging, while the beveled glass in a mirror of similar vintage - hanging over the alabaster fireplace - was as mottled as a rain-splashed sidewalk.

A wonderful dry Montrachet was served with the meal. Johann abstained, instead drinking an inordinate amount of water while repeatedly dabbing his napkin against the sheen of moisture on his forehead; something he hoped would be attributed to the heat. Likewise, he hoped his distinct lack of appetite would go unnoticed. There had been some tense moments just before the Tarnoffs went back to Berlin because Dorrit had not been placated by Ben's assurances and had insisted that he leave a prescription. Obliging her, he left a bottle of placebos.

His condition deteriorating, Johann felt himself wedged into an ever-shrinking space between despair and denial. Inasmuch as his pride wouldn't allow despair, denial emerged the winner as he continually refused to accept the truth. And tonight, engrossed in his own sorry deliberations, he missed some of the conversation around the table until he heard Dorrit pose a pointed question to Max.

"So tell us, why are you going back to Aiyina?" she was asking.

Surprised with her directness, Johann listened carefully; he remembered Max being cagey the day he arrived home.

"Aiyina?" Ambushed, Max looked up from his plate and took a sip of wine while gathering his thoughts.

"Yes." Dorrit leveled her gaze at him; this time not letting him off the hook. Her curiosity was at a breaking point because she suspected that his eagerness to intercept the mail and his need to return to that island were somehow connected.

"Hmm, yes…" Max spread some pureed gooseberries on a piece of cold chicken with measured deliberation while formulating a reply that would both satisfy and be evasive. "Aiyina is a small island in the middle of the channel between Peloponnesus and the Greek mainland," he said. "Approximately thirty nautical kilometers from Athens."

"Max, please!" Dorrit laughed, stopping him. "I can read a map. I'm simply curious as to why you're going back there when Professor Krugg needs you in Koropi."

Max managed a shrug. "I have to attend to a bit of unfinished business."

"Having to do with archaeology?" Johann asked.

"Of course, Papa." Max avoided Johann's eyes. He hated to lie, but justified it with the fact that his father was too ill to hear the truth.

"I see," Dorrit said. "So you *did* discover something there?"

"Uh-huh, and it needs to be explored further." This was as close to a truthful answer as any Max could come up with on such short notice.

"I was surprised that you and your colleagues stayed in a hotel on Aiyina," Dorrit said. "Don't you usually make do with a campsite?"

"Our assignment was brief. It wasn't worth shipping the gear needed to set up camp. Besides, the hotel was sufficiently cheap not to strain Heidelberg's budget. It was a pleasant change of pace."

"You disappoint me," Fritz mumbled, dishing up some potato salad and clucking his tongue in a way that irritated Max. "I always thought de facto scientists shun creature comforts when working in the field."

Refusing to be baited, Max leveled his eyes on his brother. "My stay at the Hotel Miranda was well worth the loss of your esteem."

"I assume the von Steigerts have stayed there at one time or another," Dorrit said. "They've traveled extensively around the Greek islands. Did you have a chance to talk with them at the Konauers' party?"

43

"No, not really and I doubt the Miranda would appeal to them. It's hardly a five-star resort. There are no porters to carry luggage. No room service and only one bath per floor."

"My goodness!" Dorrit laughed. "Were there any guests?"

"Sure, there are always tourists looking for a bargain with genuine local ambience. And of course the proprietor was not about to disappoint them with plumbing and fresh paint. Hot water was rationed, the walls were peeling like a bad sunburn, and I swear nothing but bougainvillea held the roof in place. Oddly, the food was extraordinary and the view was spectacular. The hotel was built on a high bluff overlooking the Mediterranean."

"Food and views?" Fritz figured there was more to the story than Max was telling. "*That* warrants another visit?"

Ignoring him, Max turned his attention to the maid walking around the table with a fresh platter of sliced chicken. As he took a second helping, he made an offhand comment about driving into Berlin tomorrow morning, explaining that he needed to do some research at the university library.

"Can I take the Benz?" he asked his father.

"Of course."

Max looked across the table at Fritz. "Want to come along?"

"Why not?"

Thus the topic of Aiyina was closed. In truth, there was nothing Max could add unless he was willing to mention Cassandra, which he was not. It would serve no purpose and only cause a major uproar in the family at a time when turmoil was least needed. It was obvious that Johann was under the weather. Of course he was probably sufficiently robust to declare his eldest son a damned fool before scrambling to hire a team of tough attorneys to keep him from the long arm of the law.

Chapter Fifteen

Cassandra was employed at the Miranda Hotel, but Max had not spotted her until one morning toward the end of his stay after he'd spent a sleepless night tossing and turning on the thin horsehair mattress in the room he shared with a fellow student from Heidelberg.

As the first gray hint of dawn crept across the room's small window, Max knew the sun's glare would not be far behind and since he hadn't been able to sleep in the dark, he sure as hell couldn't sleep in broad daylight. He threw off the bedcovers, got up and decided yesterday's clothes were none the worse for having spent the night on the floor. Making quick work of getting dressed, he left the room, glancing at Ernst Horstmann in the opposite bed. All manner of strange rasping sounds escaped from his throat, but didn't wake him; Ernst was an exasperatingly sound sleeper.

First among the hotel's guests to come downstairs, Max walked into the empty dining room, anticipating an immediate infusion of coffee to combat the dismal feeling that results from lack of sleep. He plunked himself down in the far corner at a table with an unobstructed view of the Mediterranean. Opening the window, he inhaled the pleasant smell of kelp and saltwater and glanced down a hundred meters below to where shrieking sea gulls hovered over the surf pounding against the rocky shore. Reaching across the table for one of the week-old Athens newspapers that littered the place, Max opened it with a rustling sound in the hope that someone in the kitchen might take notice. When that didn't work, he righted his cup noisily in its saucer, another distress signal.

The clinking china got results. A waitress walked in with a steaming pot of the house brew, a strong Turkish blend, which Max knew to be an eye-opener; so was the waitress, he discovered. In fact, the sight of such an alluring female restored him same as a good night's sleep. Smiling broadly he called upon his command of Greek, said *Yassou!* and added a pleasant remark about the weather.

Without responding, she simply poured his coffee before rudely turning away. Employees at the Miranda were not known for small talk but this individual's discourtesy was of a new order. Even so, Max's smile remained in place.

"Ahem!" he said to her retreating back. "Any specials this morning?"

"No," she said over her shoulder, her tone so unenthusiastic that a more discriminating guest might have considered taking his business elsewhere. But elsewhere meant the *taverna* in town, a long walk on an empty stomach. One of the Miranda's many charms was its seclusion and distance from civilization, if indeed the small fishing village hugging the harbor qualified as such.

Narrowing his eyes, Max's gaze followed her, if only to confirm that other guests suffered the same icy treatment. He watched her walk over to a table being claimed by a middle-aged Belgian couple he recognized as the bird watchers he and his colleagues had had a run-in with yesterday on the other side of the island. Patient as saints, the couple had been perched on a rock for hours. However, they were none too understanding when the Germans began exploring the terrain nearby, an activity the Belgians claimed would frighten away a rare aquatic bird they had traveled the length of Europe to spot.

"Can't you go dig somewhere else?" they'd suggested, waving their binoculars as if shooing away kids with pails and shovels. Max had given them a dire look and, if not for Ernst's levelheaded intervention, would have said something he would have to apologize for. Sipping his coffee, he now dismissed the Belgian birders and again focused his attention on the Athens newspaper to hone his Greek.

It was only a matter of minutes before the pretty waitress brought breakfast to his table: fried eggs and bread dipped in honey. As she poured orange juice, Max studied her every move and wondered how on earth he had missed seeing her before this. Although she was sullen, the symmetry of her perfect proportions begged to be noticed, and her face epitomized the classic beauty around which the ancient Greek legends were spun. Her hair was black and braided, the two plaits fastened behind her neck with a rubber band. As she leaned closer to refill his coffee, he noted that her dark eyes were dull with something he recognized. He was familiar with the ravages of a hangover and decided she'd be worth befriending once she recovered. Unfortunately, he didn't have much time. He was leaving Aiyina the day after tomorrow; still, he'd been known to move fast when a situation warranted. He resolved to approach her as soon as he returned from the dig this afternoon, timing which might coincide nicely with the end of her shift and her headache.

As guests began to fill the dining room, a proportional number of waitresses walked among them, serving breakfast and pouring coffee. Max lost track of the pretty one when she went into the kitchen and failed to reappear.

"Good morning!" Ernst Horstmann joined him at the table with the irritating buoyancy of someone who had slept well.

"Where's the rest of the gang?" Max said, referring to their four colleagues and knowing full well that all were late sleepers - another sore point with him.

"I kicked their doors before I came down. They'll be here shortly." Ernst measured sugar and cream into the dry well of his cup in anticipation of some coffee. "What got you up so early?"

Max shrugged, only the elderly complained of insomnia. He eyed his friend's red hair - generally an untamed disaster - this morning being the exception because it was soaking wet and combed straight back from the forehead. "You're dripping," he muttered, pushing an extra napkin across the table.

"Thanks." Ernst wiped his eyeglasses before tending to the water trickling down his neck. He was as tall as Max but lanky, which gave him the appearance of being all arms and legs. He hailed from Hamburg and had been Max's roommate since their freshman days at Heidelberg. Both were now working toward their doctorates and regularly hooked up on these foreign assignments. Laboring in close and punitive quarters had tested and proved their friendship many times over, and a shared hunch had brought them to Aiyina in the hope of finding Phoenician artifacts.

The ancient Phoenicians - the world's first traveling salesmen - had sailed the Mediterranean at the dawn of time. Evidence of the goods they'd traded was discovered on several neighboring islands, encouraging Max and Ernst to apply to the Greek government for permission to explore Aiyina and petition Heidelberg for the necessary funds. Nothing was heard from the Greek government, which they took as consent. A pittance was received from Heidelberg, which they managed to stretch. However, they couldn't expand the number of days Professor Krugg had allotted them.

"Our time is just about up," Max said, wiping honey residue from his fingers. "I stayed awake half the night, wondering why we even bothered coming here. We need at least a month for any kind of preliminary exploration. I still say a full-scale dig on the west side of the island would pay off. There's a natural harbor and fresh water. Things the ancient mariners required."

"I don't know. I'm beginning to think this island is too small for them to have bothered with."

"For trade, yes. But it's a perfect refuge. Plenty of game and fresh water before crossing the treacherous sea to Athens. I'm sure they established shelters here."

"We haven't found any proof."

Max shrugged. "We didn't have enough time."

"If you feel so strongly about it, take it up with Professor Krugg once we're back on the mainland."

"I might do that. I still can't imagine why Heidelberg gave him such a large grant for the Koropi dig."

"They got caught up in all the hoopla when those local Greeks digging wells found relics sufficiently ancient to be worth both time and money. If I remember correctly, you were pleased when Krugg handpicked us for that assignment." Max rolled his eyes; Ernst had an irritating habit of coming to the defense of his superiors. Seeing the expression, Ernst added, "A bit of gratitude would become you. Like it or not, we're heading for Koropi."

"Sorry to spring this on you, but I need to go home first. Remember that letter I got yesterday?"

"From Berlin?"

"Yes. My father has some sort of an infection. My mother asked me to join them in Bernau as soon as possible rather than wait till the August break."

"Krugg won't be pleased."

"Christ Almighty, Ernst! My father is ill. I don't give a damn what Krugg thinks."

"All right!" Ernst held up his hands. "You head home. I'll cover for you."

Chapter Sixteen

At the end of the day on his way to the common bath down the hall, Max raced past four barefooted Norwegians built like triathletes and wearing towels around their waists.

"The shower on the floor below has cold water today," he said in German. When they looked confused, he put his finger to his lips, tried English and added, "Don't tell or there'll be a stampede."

"*Ja...?*" The Scandinavian jocks looked at each other.

"*Ja! Ja!*" Max beat his chest, rubbed his upper arms and pointed to the floor below.

"Ah-hah." The men caught on. "*Tak! Tak!*" They nodded, turned and padded down the hall toward the stairs.

Having secured privacy and plenty of hot water, Max went into the bath and bolted the door. He peeled off his clothes, turned on the shower and impatiently began to rid himself of the day's dust and grime; impatiently because when he returned from the dig minutes ago he had spotted the pretty waitress from this morning behind the bar in the lounge adjacent to the dining room; a perfect place to make contact.

Stepping from the shower, he dried himself, shook out his clothes and put them back on, figuring the hot steam had refreshed them. He ran a comb through his wet hair and left the room, thrusting his arms into the sleeves of a worn jacket. Stopping at the top of the stairs, he adjusted the open collar of his faded chambray shirt and slapped at some stubborn dirt clinging to the knees of his khakis.

It was not yet the dinner hour. The restaurant was empty except for two women setting tables. The lounge was also empty except for the waitress behind the bar, polishing glasses - a chore she'd probably gladly abandon to have dinner with a guest. Surely, she had put in enough hours today to take the night off. Approaching her, Max envisioned a leisurely stroll to town followed by a pleasant meal at the *taverna* near the harbor, add a good bottle of wine and the possibilities were endless.

Fashioning a friendly smile, he put some money on the varnished counter and ordered a cold beer, knowing full well it'd be room temperature, but it never hurt to ask. This waitress looked like she might perform miracles.

She put the polishing rag aside and without as much as a murmur filled a glass from the wooden keg under the counter. Setting it down in front of the customer, she counted out his change before turning around and again attending to her chores.

His smile fading, Max took a sip; where he came from barmaids polished glasses only when there were no customers. Something was wrong here. Her disposition was no better than this morning; in his experience hangovers didn't last this long. Was she married? Did her husband beat her? Did a cranky child keep her up nights? As she reached up to place some stemware on a shelf, he looked at her hands. No wedding ring. Good. He decided to persevere, ruefully reminding himself that catching a female's eye usually didn't require this much effort. Legally blind women noticed him. Of course, if there'd been another waitress around with half the looks of this one, he'd quickly enough redirect his charms. Generally speaking, he was easy to please, insisting on only three things: a respectable measure of physical appeal that included good teeth, no last names, and plenty of prior experience.

"New on the job?" he asked, addressing her back. Since he hadn't spotted her until this morning, it occurred to him that first day jitters might account for her lack of conviviality.

Without turning, she shook her head.

Max clenched his jaw. This was not going well. "What's your name?" he tried. He was usually more inventive, his lines were known to hook the most fickle fish, but the language barrier was a handicap. It wasn't easy to come up with clever expressions in Greek. He had studied it at Heidelberg, enjoyed a fair command, but was by no means fluent. He was far more comfortable with English or French - taught by governesses from the day he took his first steps. He was about to give up on this surly lady when much to his surprise she turned around.

"My name's Cassandra," she said so softly Max wasn't sure he'd heard correctly.

"Cassandra?" he tested. She nodded. Cloaking his triumph in a controlled smile, he dug more money from his wallet and ordered another beer. Now that he had her attention it was important to keep the momentum going. "My name's Max," he said, watching as she refilled his glass; her movements more graceful than other women he'd known in the servant coterie.

Putting the beer down in front of him, she again counted out his change, this time remembering to put the coins in a deep dish like her friend Marie had shown her. Marie claimed that while customers might automatically sweep their change off the counter, they'd be less inclined to scoop it out of a dish; therefore, employing that little bit of artifice, she stood to make a small fortune. Greed had recently found fertile soil in Cassandra's bosom and her hopes of riches grew with every passing minute because this customer was ignoring his change and hadn't even looked to see if he was being cheated. Her calculating heart went into high gear; it'd behoove her to keep him at the bar, ordering. He appeared to want conversation and for the purpose of enriching herself, she'd talk herself hoarse and watch him get drunk in the process.

"Where are you from?" she asked, wishing he was drinking something more expensive than beer.

"Heidelberg University." When she looked puzzled, he simplified his answer and said, "Germany." In his experience barmaids were not scholars.

"Ah..." She gave him her prettiest smile. "We get a lot of German tourists. We even had an American film star once." As she spoke, she studied her customer; although he was poorly dressed, he was every bit as handsome as that film star. She now recalled Marie talking about a group of Germans who spent their days digging in the hills, which annoyed Dimitri Vrachnos, owner of the Miranda and a great deal of island property. Marie claimed she had overheard Dimitri tell his cousin Pavlov to keep an eye on them. An involuntary shiver ran down Cassandra's spine. Pavlov Recachinas made her blood curdle. He was a brute without a conscience. Marie called him the devil incarnate, and it took some effort for Cassandra to toss aside her fear and loathing and again concentrate on her customer.

"What are you looking for on our island?" she asked, assuming this was one of the diggers.

"Phoenician artifacts."

"You mean bits of pottery? Old jugs?"

"Yes, but we'd settle for some gold bars and a handful of jewels," he said flippantly.

"Like the stuff they found in Tutankhamen's tomb?"

"You've heard of Tutankhamen?" Max was surprised.

"It was in all the papers. They're still writing about it. Was he really buried in solid gold?"

"From head to toe."

Cassandra sighed. "The Englishman who found the tomb must be very rich."

"Howard Carter?" Max shook his head. "He hasn't made a penny. The Egyptian government laid claim to the entire find."

"That unfair!" Cassandra cried. "I mean...all that work! No payment? No reward?"

"That's right. But it hasn't deterred him. He's still bringing artifacts to the surface. I suspect he and his team will be at it for a few more years."

"I don't suppose there's any gold here on Aiyina?" Cassandra said, a speculative gleam in her eyes.

"If there is, we haven't found it."

"What have you found?"

"Earthworms writhing indignantly at being exposed to daylight."

Cassandra laughed. Max noted that she had beautiful teeth and remembered that she hadn't offered her last name or asked for his.

Two out of three. Good.

The talk of gold reminded Cassandra of her own quest for riches, and to make sure this individual didn't scoop up his change, she discreetly nudged the dish of coins out of his line of vision. He might be poor, but so was she, and profoundly desperate as well.

"How much longer are you staying on Aiyina?" she asked, wishing he'd finish his beer and order another.

"We leave the day after tomorrow. Our time and our money have run out."

Cassandra felt ashamed at her avarice and glanced at the coins.

Max studied her lovely face, marveling at her smooth, creamy skin. His eyes dipped to the embroidery around the revealing neckline of her white blouse held together by some flimsy strings. Worn with the narrow black skirt, the entire outfit had a come hither look. Displaying herself so provocatively, she clearly had plenty of experience.

Three out of three. Bingo!

He was lifting the beer to his lips when she turned back to the glasses and began polishing as if her life hung in the balance. A look over his shoulder told Max that the hotel proprietor had stimulated this resurgence of industry. Evidently the man needed only to stroll through the dining room to remind his employees of their duties. The women setting tables moved a little quicker, while another assumed a battle position (hands on hips) and used her tongue as a sharp instrument to ensure that an aging male employee was placing the wine bottles correctly in the cabinet next to the bar.

"Labels facing up!" she hollered at him. "We can't be turning them over to see what's what." When she issued a stern look toward Cassandra, Max ordered another beer to prove she was generating business. While she filled his glass, he finally came to the point of this entire exercise.

"How about having dinner with me tonight?" he said, digging out some money. "At the *taverna* in town. It might be a nice change of scenery for you."

"I am working." This time she left his change on the counter.

"I'll wait till you get off."

"Then you'll go hungry. I'm not free until the kitchen closes. By then the *taverna* has stopped serving food as well."

"When do you eat?" he pressed her, concerned that one so lovely worked such long hours.

"Whenever I wish. I work in the kitchen. Our cook, Marie, is training me as an assistant. I'm just helping out in the restaurant today because one of the regular girls got sick."

Max now knew why he hadn't spotted her before this morning. He leaned on the bar counter and sighed melodramatically. "You're condemning me to suffer another meal with my tiresome colleagues," he said, pulling down the corners of his mouth. "Would you grant a doomed man his last wish?"

"What might that be?" Cassandra grinned with his theatrics.

"Have a drink with me here at the bar after you finish work."

"I...I guess that'd be all right."

"What time does the kitchen close?"

"Around ten o'clock."

Guests were filing into the dining room; several headed for the bar.

"See you at ten." Max winked and walked away.

As she had hoped, he left all the coins in the dish and even ignored the change on the counter. Before getting busy serving the new customers, Cassandra quickly pocketed her windfall.

Chapter Seventeen

Max sat down in the dining room with his colleagues for a splendid meal of egg and lemon soup, followed by large sautéed prawns and grape leaves stuffed with rice. The bar was visible from his seat and he was glad to see that Cassandra had put on that sullen face again. He liked to think that he, alone, was able to make her smile.

"Want something from the bar?" Ernst asked, noting Max's preoccupation.

"Huh?"

"Do you want some wine?"

"Absolutely." Max signaled the wine steward and ordered for the table.

"It'll have to come out of your own pocket," Ernst felt compelled to remind him.

"Shut up!" Walter, the most junior member of the team, kicked Ernst under the table. Heidelberg covered their room and board and unless Ernst intervened, Max who could easily afford it provided extras such as something decent to drink.

"You got plans for that pretty waitress over there?" Richard, familiar with Max's roving ways, threw his head in the direction of the lounge.

"Maybe…"

Walter turned toward the bar. *Oh boy!* "Could you be more specific?" he said, staring at the female in question and making his own plans.

"Hands off."

"What?"

"You said to be specific."

Walter worked his jaw.

"Relax!" Franz cut in before Walter's famous temper could surface. Only the orals stood between Franz and his PhD so his opinion generally carried some weight. "Believe me, neither one of you will get a word out of her." Everyone looked at Franz in surprise. He spread his hands, saying, "I tried."

"You did?" Richard sounded skeptical. He'd been Franz's roommate since their sophomore year and knew him like a book. He also knew that Franz was betrothed to a girl in Heidelberg, the engagement sealed with a ring Richard had lent him the money for.

"Yes, I approached her earlier today when I came back to fetch the lunch Kasos forgot to bring us. She was picking those vile things that grow on the trees in the courtyard." Suddenly frowning, Franz looked down at his plate, wondering if an olive had found its way into his meal.

"You...you propositioned her in broad daylight?" Max sputtered.

"Propositioned her? Of course not! I'm not as brazen as you. I was simply curious about the Miranda. I asked her if it had been the residence of some wealthy Greek at one time. It has remnants of a former dignity, not a commercial enterprise like a hotel. My Greek's fairly good, but I might as well have been talking to trees."

Martin looked pointedly at Walter. "Hear that? Don't waste your time."

Max sent Martin a kind look.

The steward arrived at the table with two bottles of Saint-Emilion. Max gave him the nod to pour and told him to remove the pitcher of Retsina, a local wine that came with meal and tasted like cleaning solvent. It'd kill before one felt pain. Not even Walter drank it.

By and by, as people finished their meals, the restaurant began to empty. Some guests headed back to the bar, others went outside to light up cigars in the courtyard. Franz and Richard joined this latter group, continuing a chess match they'd begun before supper, a game made all the more challenging now by the lack of light. Miranda's proprietor wanted his guests to enjoy the twilight and was loath to waste electricity until absolutely necessary.

Eternally optimistic, Walter and Martin walked to town in search of some nightlife. The sinewy Norwegians climbed down the cliffs to prime their hamstrings along the rocky, moonlit beach. The Belgian couple left the dining room and disappeared down the hall, presumably to get to bed early so they could rise with the birds. Ernst left Max at the bar and went upstairs to enjoy the solitude of the room they shared.

Propping himself up on his bed, he put pen to paper and wrote a long letter to Ellen in Hamburg. He'd been sweet on her for years and regularly reminded her that he was alive and well. He corresponded diligently in the hope that she wouldn't rush to the altar with her father's hawk-nosed accountant, an established individual with a steady income, attributes her parents held in high esteem all the while hoping that a certain impoverished archaeologist would lose his way in the desert and never be heard from again.

Chapter Eighteen

It was ten-thirty before Cassandra left the kitchen and walked over to where Max was waiting, beginning to fear he was being ditched. Most hotel guests had now retired to their rooms; only a few diehards remained. At a table next to him some Italians were conversing in English with a Swedish couple and although it was difficult to botch the English language, they managed to do an admirable job of it. The minute Cassandra appeared, Max jumped up and pulled out a chair.

"Now, what can I get a hardworking lady to drink?" he smiled.

"Metallikos," she said and sat down. She was wearing the same outfit she'd worn all day and Max noticed the blouse hung a little lower on her shoulders, making for an even more tantalizing décolleté. She had removed the rubber band that held her braids together, freeing the plaits. This less severe look made her appear younger. This morning Max had believed her to be twenty or thereabouts. Now he wasn't so sure. Only one thing was certain: it was difficult to get a woman into bed on mineral water.

Feeling slightly less optimistic about the evening ahead, he walked over to the bar, which Dimitri Vrachnos was now tending, though he seemed more fixed on bingeing with a local chap leaning heavily on the counter; both appeared well on their way to an appointment with the floor. As Max was paying for the drinks, Vrachnos experienced some trouble distinguishing between a lepta and a drachma, something his drinking buddy found so hilarious he elbowed him, causing the drinks to spill. Pushing the wet glasses toward Max, Vrachnos gave him a venomous look as if it was entirely his fault. Seeing the man up close, Max noted that despite the Mediterranean sun and a head of black hair, he lacked color and his skin hung flabbily on his face as if no bones supported it. Only his eyes remained sharp, embedded in their sockets like two chunks of granite on either side of a large fleshy nose, its tip sagging over a full mustache obscuring his upper lip. His shoulders hunched, gargoyle came to mind, and definitely nasty when hitting the sauce. Max walked away with the glasses and a prickly feeling at the back of his neck as if a dagger was about to find a home between his shoulder blades. He sat down opposite Cassandra, felt better instantly, and raised his brandy to her mineral water.

"To the most beautiful girl on the island," he smiled, hoping charming words would soften her up, same as if she were drinking brandy.

"Where do you go from here?" she asked, sipping her drink.

"To Koropi and hopefully a more successful dig. Actually…" Max corrected himself, "my colleagues are going to Koropi. I'll be joining them in a couple of weeks."

"Where are you going?"

"Home."

"Where's your home?"

Max bit his tongue, made a pretense of sniffing the brandy, and tried to think of some obscure German town.

Help came from an unexpected source. "Hey, Cassie!" Struggling with his zipper, Dimitri Vrachnos waddled away from the lounge in a powerful hurry. "Watch the place a minute!"

Cassandra got up and went behind the bar counter. Alone at the table, Max realized the interruption had been a godsend.

Cassandra stayed at the bar until the proprietor returned. She walked back to Max, carrying another glass of brandy. "This one is on the house," she smiled.

"Thanks," he mumbled, annoyed with her charity, before remembering that it had come out of Vrachnos' hide. He glanced toward the bar; the man made his skin crawl. "Your proprietor ads a bit of perverse ambience around here," he said. "I have the distinct feeling he'd like to drink my blood."

Cassandra giggled nervously as if such a worry was not too far-fetched. "If he looks angry," she said, "it's because I'm socializing when I should be in bed."

On that score old dagger-eyes and I agree, Max thought. Out loud he said, "He worries about his employees' bedtime?"

Cassandra nodded.

"That's surprising. He doesn't strike me as the altruistic sort."

"He concerns himself with me because he's my uncle."

"Your *uncle?*"

"Well, yes. Kind of..."

Kind of? That said a mouthful. Max digested the connotation in silence, not quite sure what to make of it.

"Not by blood," Cassandra qualified.

Max realized it was entirely possible that she was the man's mistress. He also realized he'd better clear up a few details before going any further. Dimitri Vrachnos looked like he'd eat anyone who crossed him. Cassandra was pretty, but not pretty enough to die for. "You live with him?"

"No, I live in one of the cottages behind the hotel. I share it with Marie. She's the cook here."

"My compliments to her," Max said. "The meals have been exceptional." He raised his glass and took a small measured sip; the brandy - unlike the food at the Miranda - was of an inferior quality.

"I'll tell her." Cassandra smiled engagingly, and it was the height of absurdity that Max felt compelled to pose another question about something that was none of his business. He was anxious to seduce this girl, not probe her life story. It was sufficient to know that she was not living with her boss.

"Do you have any family besides him?" Max nodded toward the ogre.

Cassandra shook her head.

"Been on your own long?"

"About three months. My mother died in March. She had cancer. The doctor called it pancreatic cancer. Dimitri paid for her treatment."

"What about your father?"

"He died a long time ago. I was six years old when he drowned."

Max's eyebrows shot up; he'd always had a morbid interest in accidental deaths. "Your father drowned?"

"Yes. During a fishing trip," Cassandra said tonelessly. "With Dimitri."

"Fishing?" Max jerked his thumb toward the bar. It was hard to imagine that brute had sea legs. "With *him?*"

Cassandra nodded and took another sip of mineral water.

"Did they fish for sport or for a living?" Max asked.

"For Dimitri it was sport. For my father it was a living. He was an expert seaman but he didn't have a boat of his own. Dimitri did but didn't know much about sailing. It was a good partnership until the day of the storm."

"They went out in a storm?"

"No, it was calm that morning or my father wouldn't have gone out. He had great respect for the sea. When evening came and they didn't return, my mother was not alarmed. Fishing vessels were occasionally disabled at sea. The stranded men would simply wait for assistance. In this case it didn't work out that way. When a search party went out the following morning, the boat was found with its hull half submerged and only Dimitri clinging to it. There was no sign of my father, which was strange because he was a strong swimmer. Dimitri explained that a sudden squall had hit the boat broadside, capsizing it and throwing them both overboard. Before he went into the water, he managed to catch hold of a line and pull himself up on the hull. He called out to my father but got no answer. When he saw sharks circling nearby, he knew what had happened."

"Good God!" Max shuddered.

Her eyes downcast, Cassandra took a deep breath before continuing. "With my father gone, my mother had no means of support. Dimitri offered us a home with him. He said we were to consider him family from that day forward."

"Gallant fellow," Max mumbled and asked Cassandra how she and her mother had fared under his auspices.

"All right, I guess. We had no choice. My mother had a brother, but he had too many children and couldn't take on additional responsibilities. And for some reason his wife couldn't stand the sight of us. Anyway, they shortly moved to Athens where she had relatives. We never saw them again."

"What about your father's relatives?"

"He didn't have any. He was an orphan. He'd come to Aiyina as a stowaway on a trawler. After the accident, I used to imagine that when the Agrippa capsized he was knocked unconscious and had drifted into the shipping lanes where he was picked up by a tanker. In due time he'd make his way back to Aiyina. When he didn't, I convinced myself that his exposure in the cold water had cost him his memory. It was more bearable than to think that sharks..."

"I know what you mean," Max finished for her.

Cassandra produced a smile; it wouldn't do to dampen the mood of a hotel guest. "We were fortunate that Dimitri came to our rescue," she said in a lighter voice. "My mother got her own room at the hotel and I was moved into Marie's cottage. Dimitri even paid so I could go to school in the village. No small thing. Girls on the island are not educated. I've been lucky with my job as well. It's full time. The hotel business is seasonal. Part time work is the best most can hope for."

Max figured that Dimitri Vrachnos had obviously made her mother his mistress. But why had he educated Cassandra then launched her as a kitchen assistant? That didn't make sense. And she was grateful? There was obviously much he didn't understand about these island people. He certainly didn't understand Cassandra. She was not at all what he had expected. She seemed vulnerable now and, except for the provocative way she dressed, was no temptress. He was no longer anxious to seduce her. Pretty or not, she was not his type. Getting her into bed would require too much of an effort, something he should have known this morning by her surly face.

"Would you like to go for a walk?" he asked as a way of concluding the evening and disentangling himself. A walk wouldn't appeal to someone who'd been on her feet all day.

Cassandra appeared to consider the idea. She glanced around. Dimitri Vrachnos was slumped over the bar counter, asleep. His drinking companion had disappeared. The lounge had emptied of customers.

"It was only a suggestion," Max said. "I'm sure you're too tired."

"No," Cassandra said and rose with such determination that she tipped her chair over. "I'd love to go for a walk."

Chapter Nineteen

Strolling along the road toward the village, Max was suddenly glad he had suggested a walk. It was pleasant to be outside. Along this stretch, the road followed the edge of the cliffs where far below rolling waves collided with the rocky shore, spraying the cool night breeze with a tangy sea mist. A dog was barking in the distance, a belligerent rejoinder to the softly creaking blades on the windmills dotting the rugged landscape. Dwarfed by the arid terrain, canted cypresses leaned inland, silhouetted in the moonlight and casting eerie shadows across the dirt road, ghostly shapes from which imagination springs and tales are born.

Max soon discovered that Cassandra was something of an expert on Greek mythology. She had been talkative in the hotel's lounge and here under the endless black sky she became a veritable muse. By the time they came down from the hills and reached the narrow cobble-stoned streets of the village, she had put a whole new twist on the old legends, bringing Persephone, Aeolus, and Pallas to life as no Heidelberg pedagogue had ever done. With each passing minute, Max grew more intrigued.

Although no food was served at this hour, the *taverna* near the harbor was active. Several men sat at the tables outside, smoking long pipes and drinking ouzo. Passing by, Max looked through the open doors and spotted Walter and Martin at the bar with some younger citizens of Aiyina. All were chatting animatedly, the locals laughing at the Germans butchering their ancient language. Walter saw Max and waved him in. Max shook his head and continued walking.

"You don't want to be with your friends?" Cassandra said.

"Not tonight."

"Oh, look!" She pointed toward the wharf. "Look! The lights of Athens!"

"You can see Athens from here?"

"Yes, depending on the weather." She grabbed his hand and rushed him across the square. "Tonight it's perfect. The water's flat as a plate." At the edge of the harbor she stopped and let go of Max's hand. "To get a really good look we have to go out on the pier away from the lights of the village. Come! Hurry! The moon is almost at a point where it'll cast a reflection on the water and dim the view." She broke into a sprint. In her excitement it never occurred to her that Max might not be dazzled.

They made their way out on the wharf past fishing vessels rocking gently in their moorings. Maneuvering around an obstacle course of crates, piles of netting, and glass buoys, Cassandra worried the moon would soon be too bright while Max gave thanks for the light it provided.

"There! What did I tell you?" she cried, once they reached the tip of the pier where she looked eagerly into the distance. "Have you ever seen anything more beautiful?"

Peering into the vast expanse of the night, Max tried to focus on the horizon. Sure enough, once his eyes adjusted, a wavy line of glimmering light was visible where the black sky met the sea. Not one to spoil a lady's delight, he agreed that he'd never before seen anything quite so sensational.

"I've often wondered why the Miranda was not built facing Athens," Cassandra said. "Then the lights would be visible from the hotel."

"It was probably built before electricity was invented," Max offered as an explanation. "So it never occurred to anyone."

"Of course!" Cassandra hit her palm against her forehead. "Electricity! Why didn't I think of that?"

"Do you get to the mainland occasionally?" he asked her. "To Athens?"

"I was there once. When my father was alive."

Max gazed down at her. "You mean to tell me that you've only been off this island *once?*"

"Yes. But I'm going again soon."

"You're planning a trip?"

Cassandra nodded. "You may think it odd, but I've got something in common with my namesake, the youngest daughter of Priam. She got her gift of prophesies from Apollo. I don't know where I got mine from but, like her, I can predict the future."

63

"Really?" Max grinned. "Well, if there's a trip to Athens in your future, what's in mine?"

Cassandra pinched her lips together and shut her eyes. "You'll be world famous," she said after a moment. "As famous as that archaeologist, the one in Egypt, the one who discovered Tutankhamen's tomb." She opened her eyes. "What was his name?"

"Howard Carter."

"Yes. One day you'll work with him because you are not afraid of the pharaoh's revenge."

"You've heard of the curse?"

"It's been written up in the papers. Several times."

Again Max was impressed with her *au courant*.

"Of course, telling your future was easy," Cassandra admitted. "You're already in the profession and I know you're not afraid from the way you ran along the pier minutes ago."

"The way I ran?"

"Without fear of tripping and breaking your neck."

Max laughed. "I wish there was a way to transmit your favorable prophecy to the eminent Mr. Carter. I'd give my right arm to work with him. But I don't think he'd give a student - shy of a doctorate - the time of day."

"The time of day?" Cassandra looked confused.

"An idiom. A figure of speech. Forget it."

"Oh." Cassandra turned back toward the lights of Athens, her face aglow. Max was studying her lovely profile when he suddenly noticed a chill pass over her. Her shoulders slumped, her expression darkened, and she appeared as morose as this morning. He wondered at the transformation and looked out over the water to see what had frightened her. But except for the running lights of an approaching boat, the view remained unchanged.

"Are you game to go back along the beach?" he asked when the hum of the boat's motor grew louder and the water began to slap against the pier. "It'll probably take longer." He checked his watch. It was almost midnight. "Do you suppose Uncle Dimitri is worrying about your whereabouts?"

Cassandra shook her head. The gesture seemed to throw off her bleak mien. It vanished as abruptly as it had come. "He's had too much to drink," she said. "When he binges, the hotel can burn down around his ears and he'd never notice. He's been known to pass out at the bar and sleep there till morning."

"A class act," Max muttered.

"What?"

"Another idiom. So what do you say? Shall we take the scenic route?"

"The tide is coming in. We might get wet."

"You'll be our insurance. Neptune wouldn't dream of swamping a pretty local like yourself."

Cassandra smiled and turned away from the lights of Athens. She felt strangely happy in this foreigner's company, and if he wanted to go back along the beach so did she.

No sooner had they left the pier and climbed down the rocks to a narrow strip of sand, when a wave came out of nowhere and caught Max while he was bending down, removing his shoes. Cursing, he shook himself like a shaggy dog. Having avoided the wave, Cassandra ran ahead, doubled over with laughter. Scowling at her irreverence, he fished his shoes from the surf before sprinting after her.

"That does it!" he said, clamping an arm around her waist. "Just goes to show that I was right. From now on you'll stay glued to my side so old Neptune won't fool with me again."

Glued to my side. The words carried ripples of pleasant sensations up and down her spine and as she walked along the beach, Cassandra was conscious of Max's warm arm on her waist. Of course no sooner was she reveling in this wonderful new phenomenon when a dose of reality pushed it aside. She might conjure up rainbow forecasts and delude herself with impossible dreams, but in the end nothing would come of it. Her future was carved in stone. No amount of prognostication she fancied herself capable of could alter it. She had worked for three months and saved a fortune, at least what she believed to be a fortune, until she learned that it wouldn't buy passage to Athens. She figured she'd have to save for an additional six months and by then it would be too late. Like the legend of Tantalus, anything she wished for would always be just beyond her reach. And it was no use to beg or borrow from friends; they were as poor as she and beholden to evil, sworn to a power stronger than friendship; even Marie would thwart her. In the end, her pleadings would count for no more than the wind rattling leaves. But she mustn't think about that now. Tonight was special and the evening was full of magic, which she sensed each time she looked at this foreigner. She liked the way his green eyes narrowed when he laughed, and the way the breeze ruffled his blond hair. She decided he looked exactly like Apollo.

She recalled the early part of this evening and now regretted having encouraged him to spend money at the bar and greedily pocketing all his change. Using the deep dish was wicked and conniving. Her cheeks grew hot. Maybe she could think of a way to return the money before he left Aiyina. It was a good thing that she hadn't accepted his dinner invitation. Judging from the elbow patches on his corduroy jacket and the frayed collar on his shirt, he probably couldn't afford it.

Chapter Twenty

The midnight strollers had gone quite a distance along the beach when they came to some steep rock formations extending out into the water, leaving no sand to walk on. It was high tide; there was no way around the cliffs unless they waded into the sea, which was risky business. The surf was rough. Scratching his head, Max appraised the situation.

"I don't think we have a choice," he said after a moment. "We'll have to climb these cliffs. It shouldn't be too difficult. There are plenty of footholds. If the other side is sheer, we'll jump."

"Jump?" Cassandra didn't relish jumping off high places, especially in the dark. Of course once they climbed to the top, they could go inland to the road that ran parallel with the shoreline, but not along this stretch. Unfortunately, Pavlov's sheep farm lay between them and the road, and if they walked through his herds, the sheep would bay and the dogs would bark, rousing Pavlov, a man Cassandra did not wish to rile; definitely not at this hour. "Maybe we should go back to the pier," she suggested.

"We're already half way to the Miranda," Max said, putting his shoes on. "Let's first try scaling these cliffs." He started to climb, leaving Cassandra little choice but to slip on her shoes, hitch her narrow skirt above her knees, and follow.

They reached the summit without mishap but once there, it became clear they had to jump. The other side was a smooth vertical wall.

"This doesn't look good," Max conceded. "If we go inland, I suppose we'll come to the road?"

"Yes, but we can't cross here. This land belongs to Dimitri's cousin. We'd be trespassing. He wouldn't allow it."

"It's dark. He won't see us."

"He'll hear us. His dogs will sound the alarm. He keeps a gun."

"All right, you talked me out of it. Here goes..." Max looked over the precipice and jumped. Much to Cassandra's amazement he landed without injury. Picking himself up, he brushed sand from his clothes and held out his arms. "Your turn!"

She looked into the dark void.

"There's a sandy spot right here. It'll be a soft landing."

Cassandra remained on her dizzying perch. "Where?"

Max pointed to what looked like a postage stamp, most of which he was standing on. "Come on! I'll catch you."

Cassandra spit over her left shoulder to ward off evil, closed her eyes, and flew off the edge of the cliff. An instant later, her feet sank harmlessly into the wet sand. As promised, Max caught her, and as he now gazed at the dark-eyed beauty in his arms, he felt a sudden and profound attraction, a direct opposition to his earlier assessment that she was not his type. Her face gleamed in the moonlight, her black hair shimmered; she seemed ethereal...unreal.

Cassandra heard a strange roaring in her ears and thought it was the surf until she became conscious of an odd hammering inside her rib cage - soft and pleasant - not born of fear from her jump. For endless moments she remained motionless, content to stay like this forever. She felt safe, happy, special, and the fact that a virtual stranger made her feel this way didn't matter. She just wanted it to last a little longer; she needed to feel the warmth of another human being, if only for a minute, because in her future there would be no feelings at all.

When Max's hands slid up her arms and cupped her chin, she embraced her euphoria. He studied her face, and she held her breath in anticipation as he bent his head down, touching his lips to her forehead, tenderly tracing a path across the bridge of her nose, before reaching her mouth with a sudden and fiery intensity.

Cassandra felt hot waves engulfing her.

Theirs was a combustible combination.

Releasing her to draw breath, Max leaned her against the smooth surface of the cliff, bracing his hands on either side of her, trying to requisition some sanity while deciding whether he ought to proceed in this rude environment. Of course it was also rude to chase Ernst from the room and into the night without proper warning.

"This is not an ideal place, Cassandra," he murmured, taking her face between his hands, again kissing her.

The timbre of his suddenly husky voice drew her away from the support of the rock wall and back into his arms. "I like it here," she whispered.

Max took that as an invitation and dismissed the idea of a bed and a roof over their heads. He shrugged out of his jacket and threw it on the sand. As he pulled her down on the scant comfort it provided, he began to struggle with the ribbons on her blouse; struggle, because his fingers were for some cockeyed reason trembling. Even so, essential garments eventually fell away in a dreamlike sequence, offering him paradise.

After an eternity of racing heartbeats - and much too late - he realized he had stolen her innocence.

The shock of it sobered him same as a spray of cold seawater. Moving away, supporting himself on his elbow, he looked at her as if seeing her for the first time. This was something he had not expected; moreover, it was accompanied by a queasy feeling. How had such a gorgeous creature remained untouched for so long? And why had she given herself to him, a foreigner about to leave the island? There was a great deal Max suddenly wanted to know.

"Cassandra…" he said, giving her a narrow-eyed look, "what's your name?"

"My name?" In a belated bid for modesty, she pulled her discarded clothes about her. "That's a foolish question."

"Yes," he allowed with a grin. "I guess I'm asking about your surname. What's your family name?"

"Chandros. My middle name is Helen."

"Cassandra Helen Chandros." Max tested the sound of it. "It's very pretty."

"And it's not common," she said proudly. "No one on Aiyina has the same name."

"It's not common on the mainland either," he assured her. "I've spent time in various parts of Greece and I've never heard it before. Of course there's a shipping company by that name. The Chandros Line." He leaned down and kissed the tip of her nose. "To be named after a ship is quite noteworthy."

"Only if it's sleek and elegant. I've seen some tankers pass Aiyina I wouldn't name a mongrel after."

Max threw his head back and laughed.

"Tell me something," he said with renewed curiosity, for she was truly an enigma. Clever and beautiful, she slaved in a hotel kitchen, hoping to be a cook, not a high water mark on a résumé. Earlier she'd mentioned going to Athens. Was she thinking about getting a job on the mainland and bettering herself? "Tell me, how old are you?"

"Fifteen."

"*What?*"

"Fifteen," she repeated.

Christ Almighty! Max drew away as if he'd been scalded. He fell flat against the sand where some large pebbles dug into his back, but he didn't feel a thing. *Fifteen?* His mind was reeling. *God have mercy! I've seduced a child!* Lambasting himself, he wondered when in the course of the evening his brain had left him? He, who routinely cleared up any and all important details, had had plenty of time and opportunity to learn her age. By nature he was a suspicious bastard and proud of it. What the hell had happened?

"I'll soon be sixteen," she volunteered, seeing his agitation.

"Yes, well, I suppose that's of some consolation," he said, a wry twist on his lips.

"Why are you angry?"

"Huh?"

"Why are you angry with me?"

"*You?* I'm not angry with you! Far from it. I'm angry with myself. Had I known that you were only..." Max clamped his jaw shut because if she didn't know the problem her tender age presented, perhaps it was better not to enlighten her. Why complicate things with talk of statutory rape. Now there was an ugly term! Imagine, earlier this evening he had believed her to be Dimitri Vrachnos' mistress.

Maximilian von Renz, you're losing it!

A dire thought struck him. Suppose her benevolent "uncle" got wind of this little tryst. Suppose Cassandra got it all mixed up with love and romance and other silly notions women delight in chatting about. Sooner or later word might reach her guardian. Dimitri Vrachnos kept his pulse on everything that happened on the island. Why else had he sent those big-boned goons out to the dig to lurk around whenever Max and his team put shovels into new ground? Digging for artifacts was no crime - they had credentials - but violating a minor *was* a crime and the law was painfully specific. Max suspected Vrachnos would not be a pleasant fellow to deal with. The man had a dark side the size of the moon's.

Good night! Maximilian von Renz...*rapist!* Wait till it hit the papers back home. Like lead in a bucket, it'd sink a fine old German name. The ramifications, including jail, the gallows - and on a lesser scale - expulsion from Heidelberg, roared through Max's mind. He wondered if he could swear Cassandra to secrecy. No, that would be cowardly. Besides, he had never known a female who could keep her mouth shut.

He pulled his jacket protectively around her slim form. On the one hand he was overcome with self-loathing and on the other he was overwhelmed with reverence for this lovely girl. He pushed the hair away from her face and held her close without speaking. His mind was in turmoil. He needed to think. She'd been a willing partner but was not old enough to give consent. Did she realize that some future husband would denounce her? Great premium was placed on virtuous women in these parts and there was a particularly unattractive Greek term for a bride who comes to the marriage bed deflowered.

Chapter Twenty-one

Considering the lateness of the hour when he'd stumbled into bed, Max felt strangely alert the following morning. Of course it didn't take genius to figure out that his good humor stemmed from the prospect of seeing Cassandra again. Thinking about her when he awoke was so all consuming that Ernst's wheezing in the next cot didn't bother him. Ernst suffered from a number of allergies that brought on asthma-like symptoms, plus he had a skin condition that required he lather his face with petroleum jelly. Max attributed most of the afflictions to a doting grandmother who had raised him since infancy after his parents died. Of course, an old woman's coddling was not responsible for Ernst's sensitive skin, which took a beating from the sun and peeled mercilessly.

Getting out of bed, Max walked over to the window for a glimpse of the new morning. The rocky hills and sparse vegetation - heavy with dew - glistened in the light of the rising sun. There was no view of the sea from the hotel's economy rooms, but the stark landscape was just as enchanting and, mesmerized, he watched some sheep rounding a crest in the distance, breakfasting on tufts of grass growing between the rocks. He threw open the window and leaned out to try to see the cottage where he had left Cassandra last night. It wasn't visible from here. Hearing some squeaking below, he spotted Kasos, the kitchen boy, wheeling a cart of fresh comestibles toward the kitchen.

Regretting this was his last day on Aiyina, Max decided he would return as soon as possible and would also break his own rules and tell Cassandra how to get in touch with him; God forbid there were unwanted results from last night. Max knew he had been careless. What he didn't know was what to expect from one so young if she found herself with adult problems. She would probably panic and turn to her "uncle" who looked sufficiently corrupt to handle all sorts of problems with aplomb. To circumvent that ogre, Max must give her his address and stress that he wanted to be the first to learn of any calamity.

He turned away from the window. The alarm clock on the small table between the two beds had another twenty minutes on it and whereas he would normally have taken advantage of the added sleep, he now gathered up his shaving gear and left the room for the bath down the hall.

While lathering his face, it occurred to him that perhaps he was a little bit in love with Cassandra. Reaching for the razor, he started to shave only to suddenly stop and stare intently into the mirror as if looking for the fool who'd come up with that idea. He shook his head. *No!* He was definitely not in love with Cassandra. Charmed? Yes, but he'd been charmed before, and was much too fond of females in general to love any one of them in particular. He continued shaving, nicked himself, cursed, finished the job and discarded the dull blade. He washed his face, went back to the room and rummaged through his clothes, trying to find some that were clean enough to wear another day.

Ernst awoke, threw off the blanket, and put his long skinny legs on the floor. After a moment of sitting on the edge of the bed, he stood up and went through a number of stretching exercises.

"See you downstairs." Max finished dressing and left the room.

"Be there in a minute," Ernst said in a strained voice, doubled over as he was, trying to touch his toes.

Cassandra did not appear in the dining room during breakfast and she was not in the kitchen, something Max learned when he went to look through the small glass pane in the door. Deciding that she was sleeping late, he warmed toward the proprietor. Apparently, Dimitri Vrachnos wasn't cracking the whip this morning. Perhaps he was still comatose after last night.

Max spent the day with his colleagues, restoring the exploration sites to their natural state. It was early evening before the job was done, the equipment cleaned and packed for tomorrow's early departure.

After dinner, when he still hadn't spotted Cassandra, Max became concerned and walked brazenly into the hotel's kitchen; a futile exercise, as it were, because Marie - waving a large soup ladle - immediately evicted him with a string of curses. But before backing away, he got a good look around; there was no sign of Cassandra.

Bewildered, he headed for the courtyard, stopping to ask several hotel employees where she might be. Everyone shrugged as if her whereabouts was none of their business and should be none of his either. It was almost as if Cassandra was deliberately avoiding him and had enlisted the help of her coworkers.

It occurred to him that she might be ill. Perhaps she'd caught a chill last night? With that thought, he left the hotel and walked around the side of the building to the small white stucco cottages that housed the staff. The cottages were identical, but he remembered the one Cassandra shared with Marie because it had a fresh coat of blue paint on the door. Approaching, he saw no lights but knocked anyway. After several moments, when repeated tapping got no response, he tested the handle. The door was unlocked. Feeling like a thief, he opened it and went in, calling out her name and switching on a ceiling light as he proceeded to walk through the narrow space between two rooms. Marie's name was etched on her door, which was left wide open, advertising a domain strewn with neglect. A pillow lay on the floor and clothes were piled on her bed. A number of mismatched shoes littered the floor while brushes and combs and various hair ornaments cluttered the windowsill. A framed picture of Madonna and Child hung askew on the wall above the bed, benignly looking down upon the holy mess.

By contrast Cassandra's room was tidy. A doily covered the scarred top of a small dresser. Her garments hung on a wall hook and, seeing the two simple outfits and concluding they were all she owned, Max experienced a strange flutter in his chest and was sorely tempted to leave her some money. However, after last night that would be the ultimate insult. Looking at the clothes, he realized there was no sign of the embroidered blouse and the black skirt she had worn yesterday, nor were her wet shoes anywhere. A pair of slippers stood by the foot of the bed. The entire scene was almost too perfect. Something was wrong with it. Max began to wonder if Cassandra had slept here last night. But why wouldn't she have? He left her right by the door and saw her enter.

He felt an uneasy chill, probably due to the fact that he was trespassing. He prepared to leave. As he took one last look around, he spotted a framed photograph on the windowsill. Walking over and picking it up, he brought it into the light of the hall. It was a wedding picture. He guessed it was Cassandra's parents. There was a certain quality about the man that Max couldn't put his finger on, but he didn't look like your average fisherman. Max studied the woman. She was lovely. It was not surprising that Vrachnos had taken her in after her husband died.

Laughter erupting somewhere outside on the hotel grounds reminded Max that he shouldn't be here. He replaced the small photograph, turned off the lights, and left the cottage, carefully closing the door behind him. As he walked away he was still at a loss. Where the devil was she? Was she visiting friends in the village? But even if she had taken the day off to spend in town, surely she would have returned by now. They had made plans to meet this evening. Of course, Max realized it was also entirely possible that she was being coy, playing games, making an ardent suitor stew.

A relic of a bus arrived from the village the following morning to take departing hotel guests, including the Heidelberg team, down to the harbor in time for the noon ferry to Athens. The ferries ran only every couple of days and since the bus pulled up to the Miranda late, there was a frenzy of activity as luggage and equipment was loaded onto the roof rack of the ancient van.

Max left a letter for Cassandra with the desk clerk and, still hoping she would materialize to say goodbye, delayed the bus, using one ruse after another. However, when it was about to leave without him, he finally hopped onboard, taking a seat among his colleagues and homebound tourists. The bus lurched forward. He looked out the window and saw the kitchen boy hauling a wagon with empty bottles along the road. The bus sputtered and died. While the driver attempted to revive the motor with some lofty oaths, Max stood up and pried open a window rusted shut from years of exposure to the salty air.

"*Yassou!*" he yelled to get the boy's attention, for although he had delivered lunch to the excavation sites several times, Max had momentarily forgotten his name.

The lad stopped and squinted against the sun to see who was calling him. Recognizing Max, he waved as the engine caught and the bus began to roll.

"Kasos!" Max shouted, finally remembering the boy's name. "Have you seen Cassandra?"

Kasos shook his head.

"When you do, tell her I left a note..." Max's efforts were lost to the rumbling bus and the growing distance between himself and the boy standing by the roadside.

Defeated, he sat down.

His colleagues eyed him with dry amusement.

Chapter Twenty-two

Johann checked his watch. It was almost noon and time he headed back. Guiding his horse out from the woods, he turned west and rode along the edge of a meadow, staying under the shade of the trees for as long as possible.

A shot pierced the serenity of the forest behind him, sending a flock of starlings on a clumsy flight path across the meadow. Another shot rang out, and had Johann possessed an ounce of spare strength, he would have ridden back into the woods and flushed out the poacher. But he could no more confront a lawbreaker than flap his arms and fly. For although he'd felt relatively well this morning, his low fever coupled with the midday heat had now drained him. He would need a long rest this afternoon if he were to hold his own at dinner tonight, a meal he didn't want to miss because both his sons were in Bernau. Max, home from Greece, would shortly be off again.

Horse and rider were soon trotting along a bridle path on the lee side of a tall hedge bordering the village road where cars roared past on the new asphalt laid down between Berlin and Bernau, a smooth surface encouraging speed and allowing each driver his personal pursuit of a wreck. The pavement was supposed to accommodate increased traffic, but Johann suspected it had simply been a work project for the chronically unemployed. Joblessness remained prohibitively high and he had no quarrel with make-work projects. In fact, he had ordered Klausen to hire any man who came looking for work, the result being that the estate had never looked better. Not a blade of grass was bent, no fruit was left on the ground in the orchard, the gravel in the courtyard was raked daily, and the stables smelled like a summer morning. The only down side was an army of pullets that now had the run of the place. In view of the lingering economic uncertainty, Klausen had some time ago begun raising all manner of eatable fowl. With hyperinflation evaporating the buying power of money before it could be spent, wage earners preferred to take their pay in chickens and eggs.

The Allies' punitive reparation demands after the war had crippled German industries, causing deep and long-term ills persisting to this day. One of these ills was a proliferation of political parties. Anyone with a grievance could form a coalition in parliament, resulting in twenty-eight factions now holding seats in the Reichstag, making the government virtually ineffective.

Johann reflected on the latest opportunist, Adolf Hitler, a raconteur who'd clearly lost touch with reality that day in 1923 when his political party of less than five thousand members granted him dictatorial powers. On such insignificant support, he declared himself Germany's new Fuehrer and attempted a coup. He served a prison sentence for his wild attempt to seize power, but was now a free man and once again popping up among the disenchanted with lavish promises of full employment. This pleased the jobless while his talk of the superiority of the German people spoke to others.

Shifting in the saddle, Johann dismissed the troubles in Berlin, touched a heel to his mount, and quickened the pace. Minutes later, hooves crunching in the freshly raked gravel, the horse cantered through the high iron gates. Bearing left toward the stables, Johann saw that only the Mercedes was parked at the side of the house, reminding him that Max and Fritz had taken the Benz into Berlin this morning to do some work at the library. Both would probably invite friends out for the weekend. Dorrit would like that. She enjoyed having the house full of young people.

Dismounting at the stable compound, Johann tossed the reins to a groom and started to walk up the path toward the house. Once in the courtyard, he experienced a sudden disabling dizziness and leaned against the rim of the fountain, his shadow falling across the reflecting pool, sending goldfish darting under the lily pads. He dipped his handkerchief in the cool water and wiped his face and neck before climbing the stone steps to the front door; a simple exercise that left him winded. Stumbling into the cavernous hall, he threw his hat on a table and slumped down on an upholstered bench, miserable in the knowledge that he might not be able to get up again without assistance.

Cursing his illness, he looked around. The hall was empty. *Where were the damned servants when one needed them?* Johann felt a great urgency for water; a sudden and desperate thirst threatened to close his throat. Trapped by a paralyzing feebleness, he rested his elbows on his knees and held his head between his hands; it was too heavy for his shoulders. He heard Dorrit coming down the stairs. She must have been waiting for him and had started down as soon as she heard the front door.

"Johann!" she cried in alarm at finding him doubled over on the bench. "Dear God! What happened?"

With all the strength he could muster, he staggered to his feet. "I stayed out too long," he said with a crocked grin as Dorrit hurried across the hall toward him. "I ought to know better in this heat."

She flew into his arms, her head tilting back to look up at him. He looked ghastly. His gray eyes glinted, not with the familiar mischief, but with a sudden and raging fever. Her heart cringed. His shirt was damp with perspiration and felt cold against her palms except at the open collar where his exposed skin burned under her fingertips.

Without warning he lurched forward. Dorrit didn't have the strength to hold him up. They both fell in a heap on the floor.

Johann had lost consciousness.

Lying on the cold marble, Dorrit's heart pounded so violently her lungs were rendered useless. Gasping for air, she scrambled to her knees, put Johann's head in her lap and with enough wherewithals to remember that her sons were in Berlin, called for Heinrich. When he didn't immediately answer, she shrieked his name again and again, abdicating all decorum to a flood of panic, her voice that of an animal dying in a trap.

"Heinrich! In God's name where are you?"

Several maids came scurrying into the hall, their mouths dropping open in flustered bewilderment with the scene on the floor. Quickly gathering their collective wits, they joined the clamor for assistance.

Heinrich heard the commotion and came running up from the cellar where he'd taken refuge from the day's heat while selecting wines for tonight's meal. Red-faced, he puffed into the hall, scattering the maids as he went, color draining from his ruddy face the minute he saw the unconscious baron and the overwrought baroness. Snapping to foggy attention like a soldier on watch caught napping, he uttered, "I'll get Klausen."

Barging out the front door, he returned quickly with the estate manager. Together the two men carefully lifted their employer and carried him upstairs to his bedroom. Her heart in her throat, Dorrit followed, grasping the banister with both hands like a blind person.

The minute Johann was safely in bed, she went back downstairs to the library to telephone Ben Tarnoff. He promised to leave Berlin without delay. Dorrit felt better at once. With Ben on the way everything would be all right.

After hanging up the telephone, Ben called Kurt Eckart at Wirchow to relate the grim news. "I'll come with you," Kurt said without a moment's hesitation. "We'll take my car. I'll swing by and pick you up. You can fill me in on the drive out."

Within an hour the two doctors were in Bernau and pulled up to the barony, Kurt's car racing and overheated. The men rushed into the house and up to Johann's bedroom, each carrying a large black bag.

Peeling the bandages away from his hand, they examined the red swelling and checked his vital signs. After drawing blood and running separate tests, they came to the same conclusion: the blood infection had entered its final stage. Fluid was building up in Johann's lungs. He would begin to deteriorate rapidly and probably sink into a coma. His strong constitution had sustained him thus far, but his body's defenses were depleted. He was dying and there was nothing they could do about it.

After huddling and agonizing over their dismal diagnosis, they left the bedchamber to go downstairs to face Dorrit waiting in the library. Walking in, they closed the double doors behind them to secure privacy from the curious maids milling about in the hall. As much as both doctors dreaded this assignment and wished it could be avoided, there was no escaping it. The truth could no longer be kept from Dorrit; there was no soothing her with half-truths and false hope. They walked over to where she was seated in a wing-backed chair, sat down on the sofa facing her, and carefully spelled out the details of blood poisoning, saving the bleak outcome for last, hoping that by then she would have drawn her own conclusion and be prepared when the hammer fell, which it did with Ben's closing words.

"There's nothing we can do, Dorrit," he said in a tight voice. "Nothing except try to make Johann comfortable. There is no serum to combat septicemia. He is dying."

Until that moment, Dorrit had yet to flinch. Her eyes wide open, her gaze never once strayed from her friends' somber faces. However, with Ben's final words, her mind went blank. She stared straight ahead, no longer hearing anything or seeing anybody, her heart shriveling from a pain such as she could not have imagined.

When she remained in what appeared to be a stupor, Kurt spoke up sharply, his voice sounding strange in her ears as if it came from far away. "Dorrit, did you hear what Ben said?"

She nodded feebly, her hands clawing the arms of the chair for support. Ben reached into his pocket for the ammonium carbonate and Kurt inched forward to a perched position on the sofa, ready to catch her. But they didn't need to be concerned. On the edge of her misery she became determined not to trouble her friends with a collapse. She pulled air into her lungs and although there was a sick feeling in her stomach, struggled to her feet. Both men got up as well, their eyes following her as she walked over to the windows, gritting her teeth against a searing hurt slicing through her body. She could no longer face Ben and Kurt without succumbing to hysteria and insist they recant their prognosis, admit they were wrong; after all, doctors were human and made mistakes. She would demand that Johann be hospitalized in Berlin. Surely someone at Wirchow had a cure. Kurt was chief of surgery there. Surely he could do something!

But for all her denial and wishful thinking, she knew no mistake had been made. Kurt, with the power of Wirchow at his disposal, could do nothing. Ben, with all his skill as a surgeon, could do nothing. She knew Johann would die because her heart was being ripped apart and only a true calamity could devour her so mercilessly. Crushing the green satin drapery in her hands in an attempt to stop their trembling, her bitter gaze turned to the outside world where the beautiful flowering shrubs mocked her torment.

"How...how long has Johann known that he w...was...terminal?" she finally whispered and turned around.

"Since the very beginning." Ben put the smelling salts back in his pocket. Dorrit would not need them.

"You mean...you mean since that day of the accident in the laboratory?"

Ben nodded. "The cadaver was diseased and transmitted the infection."

"But that was a month ago."

"I know. During the first week or so, Johann thought he could fight off the contagion. As we know, there's no cure for blood poisoning. A few patients survive. Most don't. I allowed myself a bit of optimism on his behalf. I felt his strong constitution was in his favor and might pull him through. I was wrong."

"Why didn't he tell me? I knew he wasn't feeling well. But he always belittled my concerns. Ben, you examined him last week after the Konauers' party. Why didn't *you* tell me?" She turned up the full force of her agony. "Or you, Kurt? Why did you all conspire to keep me in the dark?"

Kurt was busy clearing his throat, so Ben spoke up. "I gave Johann my word not to say anything."

"I was not aware of his illness," Kurt added defensively. "I hadn't seen Johann in a while. When I saw him at the Konauers' I knew he was ill. I confronted him but he brushed me off."

"He brushed everyone off," Ben said. "He wanted whatever time was left to be as normal as possible. He didn't want anxious eyes watching him. He didn't want sympathy."

Dorrit's head fell on her chest. She wept openly. Ben came over and put his arm around her. Kurt handed her a handkerchief. No one spoke. Between sobs she heard the baroque clock on the black marble mantelpiece chime plaintively; a befitting sound reminding her that time was passing; Johann's life was ebbing away. She must go to him. He must not be alone upstairs.

Using Kurt's handkerchief, she mopped her face dry, stiffened her spine and turned her eyes - black from the strain of pulling her shattered soul about her - on her friends. With hard-won dignity she thanked them for leaving their responsibilities in Berlin and rushing out to Bernau. She embraced each in turn, all the while staging a private battle for composure. Johann must not know that she'd been weeping. She must help him have peace of mind. He mustn't see her wretchedness, her desperate anguish at facing life without him. If Johann wished that the time remaining be as normal as possible, so be it.

That much she could accomplish.

Chapter Twenty-three

Days passed, warm summer days that swept like caliginous shadows over the entire von Renz household. Although their father could no longer communicate, Max and Fritz spent hours in the sickroom, and Karl-Heinz visited regularly. Gerlinde accompanied him to the barony, but before reaching the second floor she would invariably begin to weep and rush back downstairs in a flood of tears. Her affection for Johann ran deep. She couldn't bear to see him in decline.

Dorrit was alone with Johann the evening he died. It was past nine o'clock, not yet dark, one of the white nights of summer. The windows were open and the smell of moist grass wafted inside, mingling with the fragrance of the many flowers in the room left by visitors. Tiny gnats buzzed about and Dorrit swatted at the ones that might bother Johann. She had sent the nurses to their quarters and was sitting by his bed, encouraging him to drink some broth. He couldn't swallow and waved it away. But he appeared more lucid than earlier in the day and at one point attempted to speak. When he couldn't, he immediately looked impatient with himself.

Dorrit took his hand in hers, caressing his long slender fingers, remembering how her father had once said that Johann's hands were not only those of a fine surgeon but those of a pianist. Of course Johann had never played the piano; Fritz was the musician in the family.

Again Johann attempted to speak.

"Don't try to talk, darling," Dorrit said, putting his hand to her cheek. "Save your strength. Save it for tomorrow."

A ghost of a smile touched Johann's white lips with her optimism about tomorrow.

"There...won't be a...tomorrow..." he whispered.

"Don't talk nonsense," she scolded sweetly and, knowing how he hated having the nurses around, added, "I might be forced to send for assistance."

A chuckle escaped his chest with her idle threat.

"I've never thanked you..." he murmured a moment later.

"What on earth for?"

"For...a wonderful life...for our...sons..."

"Don't be silly," Dorrit managed to say lightly even as an obstruction in her throat grew, forcing water into her eyes. She blinked against the hot, stinging tears. He mustn't see her cry.

Suddenly Johann gave her that wide glamorous smile she remembered from bygone days. She wondered how he found the strength for it.

"You made me so...happy," he said in the next instant, his voice amazingly strong, his hand tightening around hers, even as the smile faded into the corners of his mouth; he couldn't sustain it.

Dorrit was bringing his hand to her lips when his face - drowsy with death - lost its color. She felt a tug on her hand before he relaxed his grip, looked at her for the last time and closed his eyes.

"Johann!" she cried.

There was no answer.

"Johann!" she cried again and again; her restraint crumbling as the dam burst. Her head sank down on his chest and her shoulders shook with the violent tremors of overwhelming grief, her agony suffocating her.

Max and Fritz rushed in and found their brokenhearted mother unwilling to let go of her husband's cold hands.

Newspapers throughout Germany carried the story of the untimely death of the renowned Herr Baron Doctor Johann Maximilian von Renz. On the day of the funeral, the centuries-old Parish Church on the village green in Bernau was overflowing; never before had it been asked to accommodate so many. People arrived in caravans from Berlin. Some traveled the length of Europe. Local villagers, farmers, and merchants came. Dr. Bergen and his wife came from Hamburg, Olivia insisting on sitting in the very last pew and leaving immediately at the close of the ceremony.

A long procession followed behind the casket as it was carried to a gated corner of the church cemetery, where Johann was laid to rest next to his ancestors. The sky was heavy and overcast. The mourners moved slowly and methodically, two and three abreast, along the narrow paths under the weeping willows, past marble

83

monuments and moss covered statues. The funeral cortege was not deterred, nor was it rushed by the threatening summer storm.

Dorrit had endured the church service, did not falter along the path to the gravesite and when Johann's coffin was lowered into the ground her eyes remained dry, desiccated from tears already shed. However, with each clump of black earth falling onto the mahogany lid, her heart withered. She felt faint. Her knees buckled. Standing solemn and erect on either side of her, Max and Fritz caught her and, together, supported her.

The sky darkened. Thunder rolled in the distance. It began to rain, heavy drops mottling the ground. Umbrellas popped open. People gathered silently beneath them.

The pastor's voice droned on.

"From dust to dust..."

Chapter Twenty-four

For one blissful moment each morning when Dorrit awoke, she stretched and listened to the chirping birds outside her bedroom windows, relieved that her nightmare was over. Of course only a fraction of a second passed before reality came crashing down.

Waking up was her nightmare!

Never again to hear Johann's determined steps in the hall was unthinkable. Never to hear his wonderful laughter was unimaginable. Well-meaning friends told her to treasure her memories for they would sustain her. But her friends were wrong. The memories hurt far more than they comforted, and the only reason Dorrit got out of bed each morning was to go to the cemetery. Visiting Johann's grave provided her with the impetus she needed to struggle through another day.

When summer finally drew to a close, she was reluctant to return to Berlin. How could she leave Bernau? How could she leave Johann here alone? It was too quiet in the cemetery; too desolate for someone who had been so full of life.

However, with colder days came the realization that she could no longer procrastinate. Fritz needed to return to his studies at Berlin University, and Max had long since grown restless with his leave of absence from his work. It was high time that he joined his colleagues in Koropi. Dorrit finally acknowledged that she had been selfish and possessive, too absorbed in her grief to remember to be practical. She must not entrap either one of her sons with her sorrow. She must return to the house on Lindenstrasse, if only to restore some semblance of normalcy in everyone's routine.

Once back in Berlin, Max was preparing to travel to Aiyina and then on to Koropi when a cable from Ernst Horstmann changed his

85

itinerary. The world had long known about the unexplained deaths at Tutankhamen's Tomb and when another one occurred, it was the last straw for several archaeologists working there. They packed their bags and abruptly left the site. After hearing about these latest defections, Ernst wrote to Max, saying that he felt sure a couple of doctoral candidates might now get access. He explained he'd wrung a sabbatical from Professor Krugg and was leaving Koropi for Cairo to plead his case with the Egyptian Office of Antiquity, where he would present Max's résumé along with his own.

When a cable arrived from Ernst, telling Max to meet him in Luxor posthaste, he knew they had gotten the green light and, putting all other considerations on hold, now prepared to travel directly to Egypt. He wrote Cassandra, informing her of his new itinerary and delay in returning to Aiyina. As he dropped the letter into a mailbox, he wondered why he bothered. He had sent her several letters during the summer and she had yet to answer a single one.

Fritz and Dorrit went to the train station to see Max off.

"If the pharaoh's curse spares me," he winked at his mother before boarding a southbound express, "I'll be home for Christmas." As he bent down to kiss her good-bye, his flippant attitude lost some ground. Her complexion, formerly so warm and glowing, felt like dry parchment. She had lost a great deal of weight over the past weeks and appeared so frail that he feared a gust of wind might blow her off the platform. Thank God for Fritz. No high-wire act, but he was dependable to a fault and was, in fact, now linking his arm through Dorrit's as though he shared Max's concern about a stiff breeze. Max gave his brother's shoulder a punch loaded with gratitude. Fritz could be trusted to look after their mother.

Chapter Twenty-five

Autumn came and Grunewald Park was ablaze in vivid hues of orange and yellow, the brisk winds playing with the discarded foliage, depositing it across footpaths and grassy knolls in mosaic artistry. Each day before the long shadows of the shortened afternoons chilled the air, Dorrit crossed the street and took a stroll along the familiar paths where she enjoyed watching neighborhood children at play. It didn't seem very long ago when Max and Fritz had romped through these wooded acres and played on these very same swings and seesaws. She noticed the playground equipment was still in good repair; built to last like all things German.

After her walk, she frequently continued along Lindenstrasse to the corner of the Hallensee to gaze at the clinic. Standing on the sidewalk, teary and heartsick, she wished she could go inside and find Johann in his office between patients. But before becoming an object of curiosity to passersby, she wiped her face and went around to the back of the building, hoping to find Gertrude in the garden.

"Hi!" Jiggling with the latch on the garden gate, she alerted Gert to her presence.

"Oh, Dorrit!" Gertrude looked up from her labors, removed her gloves and pushed some wayward hair into the scarf she always wore when working. She rose, groaning theatrically as she brushed soil from the knees of her slacks. "I'm so glad to see you!" Her body was less agile with the piling-on of the years, but otherwise her appearance hadn't changed much in all the time Dorrit had known her. Her figure was still square and her legs remained thin, only her hair had changed, going from brown to mostly gray. "Come let's sit down. There's still a sunny spot on the terrace." She took off her glasses and threw her gloves on top of some gardening tools.

"I'll only stay a minute," Dorrit said, unbuttoning her trench coat as she sat down in a wooden chair after stabilizing its legs on the old brick surface. "I don't want to take you away from your work."

"You're not. I need a rest. The flower beds are almost done and I've picked the fruit." Gertrude pointed to a basket of apples standing under one of her prized trees. "Once they are pureed and canned, I'll bring you some jars."

"Um, that will be lovely. I don't know how you do it Gert, but each year your applesauce gets better and better."

Hearing voices in the garden below, the Tarnoffs' maid leaned over the second floor balcony and, seeing the Baroness von Renz, brought down a tea tray.

Thus a pleasant hour was spent. Dorrit complimented Gert on her hybrid chrysanthemums still blooming and providing spots of color in each corner of the garden. Gertrude asked about Fritz's studies and read Max's latest letter from Egypt, which Dorrit just happened to have in her pocket. The two women chatted about a great number of things but Gertrude was careful not to make any reference to Johann. For the twenty-plus years that she had known Dorrit, she had never been a weeper. However, since this past July she dissolved with very little provocation.

Chapter Twenty-six

November arrived with a blast of frigid air. Schmidt kept the fireplaces throughout the house burning to supplement the temperamental coal furnace in the basement, which meant he was making regular trips curbside to fetch the bundles of wood that were delivered.

"For heaven's sake, have the driver bring in the firewood," Dorrit suggested one afternoon as Schmidt carried a large bundle of kindling into the library. "You ought not lift such heavy loads. If you persist in straining your back, I'll be asking Dr. Tarnoff to make a house call." She looked up from her writing and smiled slyly, knowing full well how Schmidt felt about doctors. He never allowed one within poking range and had not even let Johann examine him years ago when he'd suffered a sprained ankle.

"Dr. Tarnoff will not need to trouble himself," Schmidt said in a deceptively firm voice for a man suffering debilitating arthritis. Straightening his spine, he winced as a pain shot through him but managed to make it appear like a smile, and left the library with a warm spot in his heart for the baroness. Still in mourning, she nonetheless concerned herself with an old butler's aches and pains.

After he was gone, Dorrit put down her pen and pushed aside the letter she was writing to Anna von Steigert in Athens. She would finish it later. Getting up from the Queen Anne desk by the window, she plunked down in a comfortable red leather chair near the warm fire. Stretching out her legs, she kicked off her shoes and wiggled her toes against the hot screen. After a while she got up and padded over to Johann's desk. The Persian carpet under his chair was worn and the blotter needed replacing. She remembered making plans last spring to take care of it right after summering in Bernau. However, as things stood now she couldn't bear the thought of changing anything. The blotter and worn rug would remain. Johann's gold pen and crystal inkwell would also stay exactly where he'd left them, as would a packet of his favorite cheroots in the Limoges container.

A log slipped off the grate, sending a shower of sparks against the screen. Dorrit looked at the clock on the mantelpiece. It was four-thirty and a glance toward the windows told her it was already growing dark. November days were short. Still, she did not turn on any lamps. Feeling peculiarly tired, she sat down at Johann's desk, crossed her arms on the blotter and put her head down. She needed no lights. The glow from the fire would suffice. A gale was whining through the bare trees outside, but the library was warm and sheltered her with an ambrosial past.

Fritz came home a while later, surprised to find his mother sitting in the dark. He walked around the room and switched on the lights. Once the library was fully lit, he saw the state she was in. Her eyes were red and swollen, her pale cheeks glistening with tears.

"Mother," he said solicitously, bending over her. "Have you forgotten about tonight?"

"What...?" Confused, Dorrit looked up, squinted, and saw Fritz.

"The opera," he prodded. "We are going to the opera tonight. Puccini's Tosca. You'll need to get ready."

"Oh? Yes, of course." Dorrit busied herself with a handkerchief. "What time is it?"

"Six," Fritz said. "We have to leave here at seven."

Rising from the chair Dorrit said, "I'm afraid the afternoon slipped away from me, but I'll be dressed in time." As she stepped away from the desk, she experienced a moment of disorientation. "Is tonight formal, Fritz?"

"Opening night traditionally is," he said, arching a dark censorious eyebrow at her lapse.

Noting the expression, Dorrit was gripped by the similarity to his father. It melted her heart to see so much of Johann in Fritz. Perhaps the anamnesis should have pained her, but it didn't. It cheered her. She retrieved her shoes from in front of the fire and walked briskly into the hall. At the foot of the stairs, she stopped and smiled over her shoulder at her tall, dark-haired son who had followed her from the library and now stood, leaning his shoulder against the French doors, watching her with a worried frown.

"Fritz dear, I don't wish to listen to your stomach growling during the performance. Go to the kitchen and have Frau Schmidt fix you something to eat. We'll have a proper dinner after the opera. The Eckarts and their daughter will join us. They'll be in our box tonight."

"Elsie?" he asked.

"Yes, of course. The Eckarts have no other daughters."

Fritz made an exaggerated expression of displeasure.

"Now, really!" Dorrit eyed him severely. "Have an open mind. Elsie is pretty as a picture. And smart. You saw her yourself at the Konauers this summer."

"Yes. I saw that she's still a spoiled brat."

"Bite your tongue! She has just been accepted at Comtesse de Pree in Paris for the spring semester. She is determined to be fluent in French."

"All right!" Fritz held up his hands in mock surrender. "But I warn you, I like Italian opera better than French conversation."

Chapter Twenty-seven

It was swelteringly hot inside the cramped burial chambers but the archaeological treasures were so mind-boggling that Max experienced no discomfort until he climbed back outside and felt the sweat running off his body. His shirt stuck to him like a second skin and, momentarily blinded by the glare of the desert sun, he collided with Ernst and Howard Carter who had stepped out of the tomb ahead of him.

"Your faith moved mountains," Ernst was saying to their host while surveying the man-made hills of sand dotting the area, and happy to flatter the famous Egyptologist with a Biblical reference. Nothing was too good for this acclaimed individual who had welcomed two archaeology students with open arms and was now giving them a personal tour of this extraordinary site in the Valley of the Kings.

"I could never have done it without my good friend Lord Carnavon," Howard Carter admitted.

"The press reported that he fell victim of the pharaoh's curse," Max said. "Any truth in that?"

"No." Howard Carter snorted. "Even if I believed in the curse, which I don't, I find it highly irregular…irresponsible to say the least, for the press to suggest such a thing. First of all, Lord Carnavon was rarely here. He was not an archaeologist. He was simply a collector of antiques and hoped to take some of Tutankhamen's treasures home for display in his library in London."

"After financing your work here, he must have been terribly disappointed when the Egyptian government laid claim to the site and its contents," Ernst said, busily scribbling on his note pad; this was good stuff for an article he could peddle to a Heidelberg magazine.

"Yes, initially," Howard Carter acknowledged. "Of course, once he saw the artifacts, he realized they were far too rare for private ownership and, indeed, belonged in a museum."

A sonorous gong could be heard coming from the direction of an enclave of tents in the distance, housing the international team of scientists, local workers, and uniformed guards supplied by the Egyptian government.

"Come." Howard Carter led the two Germans to the awning sheltering the camp's dining facility. "We'll talk while we eat."

That night as Ernst fell into one of the cots in a tent vacated by three of Carter's men presently in Cairo, accompanying a shipment of artifacts from the tomb, he was smiling from ear to ear. "A month!" he said. "A whole month when all we applied for was a week. Talk about *luck*."

"Timing," Max corrected. "You heard what Howard Carter said during dinner."

"You mean about being shorthanded?"

"Yes. Anyone with a bit of experience and willing to work for room and board would have gotten the same deal had they waltzed in ahead of us." Max turned over and adjusted the net around his cot. The night air was humming with mosquitoes the size of bats and probably fed accordingly.

"I suppose the fact that we speak respectable English helped as well," Ernst said. "That summer I spent in London finally paid off."

"Working in a pub hardly taught you the Queen's English," Max grinned.

"Howard Carter didn't seem to notice."

"Goes to show how desperate he is."

Chapter Twenty-eight

When the month was up and the men in Cairo didn't return as scheduled, Howard Carter asked the two Germans to stay on. They accepted at once, wasting no time questioning what might have delayed the men, until Carter admitted that one had fallen gravely ill, was hospitalized, his two colleagues remaining at his bedside as doctors tried to determine the puzzling nature of his illness.

While such news might have alarmed some with a reminder of the curse, neither Max nor Ernst dwelled on metempirics when work of this magnitude needed their attention; for although Carter and his team had toiled for several years, the job was far from finished. The burial chambers were still stacked with hundreds of fragile objects, which tended to crumble if brought into daylight before being stabilized. While Carter's team was a dedicated lot, some were prone to superstition and the sequence of unexplained deaths now left several unwilling to handle the artifacts until they were brought above ground.

"The world's fascination with this so-called curse is regrettable," Howard Carter said one day as he and Max were working in the depths of a burial chamber and the subject came up while they rested on a couple of packaging crates, waiting for Ernst and the staff photographer to return with fully developed pictures. Carter would move no artifact until he was certain that the film of the original undisturbed piece had been successfully processed. "The deaths are distressing, of course, but can be explained. Our work conditions are harsh. The heat alone is debilitation. The men who succumbed here were old. Not in terms of years. Old in this unforgiving environment."

"The press has stuck to its guns, insisting each death was due to a mysterious revenge of the young pharaoh."

"It sells papers." Howard Carter shrugged. "It's the old adage. If it bleeds, it reads. Like you said initially, the press also reported that Lord Carnavon fell victim to the curse. Nothing could be further from the truth."

"What *did* he die of?"

"Blood poisoning. Confirmed by the best doctors in Egypt."

Blood poisoning! Max drew in his breath sharply. The same disease had claimed his father. But he made no mention of it now, instead asking, "How did he contract it?"

"From a mosquito bite. He was bitten inside this tomb and died four weeks later in a Cairo hospital. When several strange events took place at the precise moment of his death, the press had a field day. I'm sure you remember reading that Cairo fell into complete darkness the night Lord Carnavon died."

Max nodded. "Has anyone ever explained how that blackout happened?"

"No. They can't explain it. No generator malfunctioned. There was no earthly reason for the entire city to go dark. And as if that wasn't odd enough, on Lord Carnavon's estate back in England, his faithful dog - a robust and healthy animal - howled and dropped dead the same moment his master drew his last breath in Cairo. The papers gave little press to a dead dog, overshadowed as it were by another fatality here at the site, which sent reporters swooping down on us like a swarm of locusts. Health inspectors arrived from around the globe."

"Did they find anything?"

"Nothing. No epizootic bug. No disease-carrying organism, which only confirmed in everyone's minds that something of a spectral nature haunted those who worked in the tomb."

"On the subject of death and disease, have you determined what killed Tutankhamen? Surely, his demise at eighteen was premature even in ancient times and especially for a king living in the lap of luxury. Were there any marks on the mummy?"

"None that would have killed him. The tomb established how he lived, not how he died. We'll probably never know. Haremhab, who succeeded him, took great pains to erase his reign from peoples' memory. For reasons of hatred, perhaps envy, he destroyed writings and removed the young king's head from statues around Egypt. The fact that Haremhab went to so much trouble tickled my initial interest. While most archaeologists believed Tutankhamen was a mythical king, I became convinced he'd been an important pharaoh and was buried accordingly. That's why I spent years looking for his tomb."

"It's strange that Haremhab left his burial place alone."

"Perhaps he figured that grave robbers would soon make a mess of it. Maybe he was afraid of offending the Gods. Tampering with a sacred site was serious business in those days."

"Still is…" Max grinned, "for those who subscribe to the curse."

He rose and stretched in the limited space of the chamber where light was supplied by a number of bare bulbs strung on electric wires along the walls. Walking over to a sarcophagus, he let his fingertips glide over the engraved pictures of Tutankhamen. "Since he survived the precarious years of childhood, one might speculate that he met with an accident. Or perhaps Haremhab poisoned him?"

"I doubt he would have dared. For the same reason he left the tomb intact. Tutankhamen might have been a sickly youth. That would be my guess."

"These pictures give no hint of that. Plus the small size of these chambers and the haphazard stashing of his belongings suggest his people didn't expect him to die. They obviously sent him on his journey to Ra with little planning." Max eyed the shrine next to the sarcophagus, its top decorated by a fence of cobras, the sacred symbol of the pharaohs. "Perhaps a snake bite?"

"Pardon?"

"He might have suffered a venomous bite."

"That's possible," Carter agreed, fumbling with some small brushes, splaying the bristles, ridding them of dust. "As good a guess as any. Come to think of it, we did find a peculiar lesion on Tutankhamen's face. The scar was small. There was no way of telling if it contributed to his death. Hmm, I almost forgot about that. As I remember, Lord Carnavon spotted it just as we were removing the burial mask. The very moment he was stung by a rather large mosquito." Suddenly Howard Carter rose from the wooden crate as if he'd sat on a nail. "Now, if that isn't strange!"

"What? The insect bite?" Max said.

"No. The coincidence. The scar on Tutankhamen's face was on his left cheek right above the jawbone. The mosquito that stung Lord Carnavon did so in precisely the same spot."

"I suppose we could speculate that Tutankhamen died of blood poisoning," Max said, "brought on by a mosquito bite."

"In the *same* spot as Lord Carnavon's?" Howard Carter shook his head in disbelief. "That's a striking coincidence." He ran a finger under his collar; the burial chamber felt unusually oppressive suddenly. "God rest their souls…"

The row of electric bulbs hanging along the walls of the tomb suddenly dimmed and went out. Only two remained lit and began flickering an eerie repetitive rhythm: three short blinks followed by three longer flashes. Howard Carter and Max looked at each other. Both recognized the international distress signal. Without a word, and similarly motivated, they quickly headed for the narrow stairs that led thirty feet up into daylight and fresh air. Carter went first. Max followed close on his heels.

Once outside, clear of the ancient burial chambers, and under the full glare of modern day, both men - hands thrust into their white coat pockets - stood around, kicking the sand aimlessly, grinning sheepishly with their brief and momentary credence in the pharaoh's curse.

"We'd better have an electrician check the wires before we go back down," Howard Carter suggested.

Chapter Twenty-nine

Max flung his scuffed leather bag under an empty table at one of the open cafés crowding the sidewalks along the wharfs of Cairo. There was a string of watering holes to choose from, all equally unappetizing, but this particular one had an awning and, though tattered, offered a bit of protection for Ernst's sun-ravaged face.

The two friends had just made the long journey on the Nile from Luxor to Cairo by open barge and had an hour to kill before catching the next river transport to Alexandria. From there they would cross the Mediterranean to Athens and a more hospitable climate.

Sitting down at the table, Max studied his colleague's face; fair and freckled it had taken a beating in the Egyptian desert, the trip on the Nile blistering it further. "No offense, Ernst, but you look like a walking pestilence," he said.

"It's the curse!" Ernst ran a hand through his red hair. "King Tut revenged himself and gave me boils."

"I don't suppose it'll kill you."

"Disappointed?"

"Sure! Imagine the headlines."

"And you'd benefit from association with the latest victim."

"Yes. I'd be hounded by requests for interviews. It'd give my career a shot in the arm."

A tall, thin waiter, wearing a *kaffiyeh* and drying his hands in a stained apron, came over to their table. "What'll it be?" he asked in Arabic, using a corner of the same apron to wipe the table.

"We'll have a couple of beers." With no Arabic in his arsenal, Max responded in English. Egypt was a British colony so he figured the waiter might have a working knowledge of the language.

"And some water, please." Ernst suspected beer alone wouldn't alleviate his thirst.

A few minutes later he and Max remained stoic when they were served two warm beers, a carafe of water as cloudy as the Nile, and a complimentary plate of figs being examined by an enthusiastic swarm of flies. Wisely, both travelers ignored the water and, pushing the ripe fruit aside, didn't begrudge the flies their pleasure. Downing the beer, they shortly left the café to board the launch for Alexandria.

Standing on the aft deck among throngs of passengers and livestock, they watched the docks of Cairo slowly disappear. The café they had patronized remained distinguishable among the rest because of its awning fluttering in a breeze that failed to reach the middle of the wide river delta. It was November but the climate in this part of the world hadn't caught on yet. Leaning over the railing, Max opened a couple of buttons on his shirt and hoped the humid air would begin to swirl once the barge picked up speed. *Speed?* Yes, suddenly, he was in a terrible hurry. He was heading back to Greece where - come hell or high water - he intended to visit Aiyina at the first opportunity. Since leaving the island, Cassandra had loitered in his mortal being like a pleasant ache, and he was still trying to figure out why she'd been a house on fire one night, only to vanish the next. There was also the question of his letters. She hadn't answered any of them. Why not? She wasn't illiterate. She had boasted of being educated; presumably she could write.

"Digging for clay jugs and paving stones looms anticlimactic after the Valley of the Kings," Ernst commented, absently flicking loose paint chips from the railing into the brown river.

"Yes, a distinct reversal of fortune," Max nodded, dismissing the enigma of Cassandra.

"I wonder if Howard Carter was being sincere when he invited us to return."

"I plan to put him to the test as soon as the Koropi dig wraps up and once I've completed my courses at Heidelberg."

"Same here. Pray we finish before Carter is done with the site."

"He'll be there for another couple of years."

"Hope you're right." Ernst found a tube of petroleum jelly in his bag and rubbed it on the blisters around his lips. He was less optimistic about the future than Max. Along with the final Ph.D requirements, he had to rewrite his journals and try to turn them into articles he could sell to magazines. His grandmother had left him a small inheritance, but it was running low. Of course, once he had his doctorate, he could teach, which would give him some security and the courage to ask Ellen's parents for her hand in marriage.

After an uneventful Mediterranean crossing, the two bearded stragglers arrived in Koropi, identified themselves to Professor Krugg and, following a good shave, were recognized and assimilated into the team.

The days passed quickly, not so the nights. In spite of exhausting work and long hours, Max couldn't find a comfortable position on his cot. Sleep eluded him long after it had claimed his colleagues. Of course he knew what ailed him. He needed time off to go to Aiyina. He had to solve the mystery of Cassandra or go crazy. Maybe he already was? It was certainly bizarre to go looking for someone he hardly knew with marriage on his mind. Yet, that was precisely what he wanted. The passing of time had not dimmed his desire for that strange girl. Truth be known, he couldn't get her out of his mind. She fit his lifestyle like no one else. She was no prima donna. She seemed keen on traveling and would go with him wherever he went because he couldn't imagine her complaining about lack of running water or other amenities in the field.

Staring at the moonlight penetrating the worn canvas overhead, Max threw his pillow on the floor. It felt like a brick. He clamped down his eyelids, to no avail. The sounds of slumber erupting from the other bunks began to gnaw on his nerves, and once his cage was rattled, his amiable nature lost ground. He started to nitpick, soon directing his exasperation at an easy target: Professor Krugg. The man was a card-carrying miser. His wallet never saw daylight. Determined no one make a profit, he haggled endlessly with local merchants; hence this crowded and patched tent, rickety cots, and boulders for pillows. Well, cheapskate Krugg might be given an opportunity to improve his image. Tomorrow at first light Max intended to ask for time off; no piddling request, considering the sabbatical he'd recently enjoyed in Egypt.

Chapter Thirty

Two days later he was on his way to Aiyina. Unfortunately, the ferry ran into bad weather, docking at the small picturesque harbor hours behind schedule. Disembarking among locals returning from the mainland, and crates of dry goods, drums of tar and oil, Max left the wharf and boarded the one deplorably shoddy bus servicing the island. He smiled cordially to fellow passengers already seated and nodded to a young couple who had also been on the ferry; he guessed they were honeymooners returning from Athens.

A heavyset woman with a lamb under each arm was last to climb aboard, and the bus soon chugged through the narrow, winding streets of town, stopping and letting people off at various points. When the young couple stepped off, they were met by a handful of smiling relatives waiting by the side of the road. The woman carrying the livestock got off once the bus crested the hills above the town, and Max saw her walking along a narrow path that led to a farmhouse nestled among stunted cypress. He was now the only remaining passenger as the bus headed for its last stop, the Miranda.

The hotel was precisely as he remembered, except the place was unusually quiet. Of course it was November, summer vacationers were long gone and people from northern Europe were not yet sufficiently frozen to migrate south for their annual thaw. The absence of tourists suited Max because it meant Cassandra would have more free time. Entering the hotel, he saw no desk clerk and rang the bell. A woman came running from down the hall, took payment in advance for room and meals and handed him a key dangling on a worn leather strap. "Number eighteen," she said, pointing toward the stairs behind her. "Second floor on your right."

Max thanked her, picked up his bag and headed for the warped staircase covered in the same threadbare runner he remembered. He found the room and went in. It was similar to the one he'd shared with Ernst last June, but it was larger and faced the vast and glimmering Mediterranean. The hotel was obviously empty or a scruffy traveler would never have been given a chamber with such a prime view.

Max threw his bag down, walked over and opened the window to let out a musty redolence as well as a couple of trapped flies buzzing against the glass. He leaned out and took a deep breath of the salty air. Toward the left, he could distinguish the cottage with the blue door where Cassandra lived, and if not for the fact that the staff enjoyed well-earned siestas in the afternoon, he'd go down there right now.

This morning, during the long sea crossing from Athens, he had decided that he would present Cassandra with his proposal the minute he saw her. Krugg had only given him four days off, so he had to come right to the point. No slow dancing. Time was of an essence. He had spent a day getting here and needed another to get back. As he continued gazing at the spectacular view, which could only improve once he feasted his eyes on the loveliest girl in the world, he realized it was not surprising that he'd fallen in love on a Greek island. The arid landscape stirred him. The rocky sun-drenched hillsides were magical, and the cry of the seagulls sounded almost melodic as they glided over the sharp rock formations jutting up from the ocean floor, breaking the turquoise waves rolling toward shore. The Miranda seemed particularly agreeable today. The halls were delightfully quiet. Dinner this evening would be a leisurely affair. He suspected he had the resort all to himself.

The sleepless nights in Koropi had taken a toll and, lulled by the tranquil atmosphere, Max felt drowsy. He pulled off his boots and flung himself down on top of the bed. He had time for a short nap. The mattress was thin but the pillow was filled with real goose down. It was heaven, and it was several hours later when he awoke with a start to the clatter of activity downstairs. Squinting through heavy-lidded eyes, he checked his watch, grunting in annoyance with himself for the time he had wasted sleeping. Moreover, the noise below signaled the hotel was getting ready for a number of tourists after all.

Gripped by an urgency to get a jump on the crowd, Max swung his legs out on the floor and massaged his neck to shake off the residue of sleep. *Crowd?* To hell with the crowd! He'd find Cassandra and have her quit her job. While he finished the work in Koropi, she could get her affairs in order here on Aiyina, say her good-byes, and meet him in Athens for the trip to Berlin where, keeping in mind that the von Renz household was still in mourning, they'd manage a quiet wedding over the Christmas holidays.

Rummaging through his bag, Max fished out a clean blue challis shirt. Putting it on, he rolled up the sleeves, retrieved his boots from where he'd dropped them and stuffed the legs of his gray corduroy slacks into the tops of the supple leather. Checking his reflection in a small wall mirror, mottled with age like everything else in this place, he realized he'd neglected to shave this morning. Never mind. He pushed a comb through his hair, figured Cassandra would have no trouble recognizing him, and left the room.

Chapter Thirty-one

The restaurant was sizzling with energy. Max stood in the wide doorway a moment, taking stock. This frenzied activity would make it difficult to corner Cassandra and, irritated by the thought of even the smallest complication, his eyes scoured the room. Cassandra was not among the women setting tables and she was not tending bar; she was obviously in the kitchen. However, judging from the pace in the dining room, the kitchen would be a regular cyclone; it might not be smart to barge in. He would have to bide his time. He headed for the lounge.

"Has a tour group checked in?" he asked the waitress leaning on the bar counter and chewing on a toothpick.

"Tour group? Nah…" she shook her head and rotated the toothpick to the other side of her mouth.

"Is today a local holiday?"

Again shaking her head, she stared at him in amazement with his ignorance.

"When I arrived this afternoon I could have sworn I was the only hotel guest." Max nodded toward the lavish preparations, winked and said, "Don't tell me you're doing all this for me."

"Eh?" She looked confused and gave him a brazen grin, bringing the unfortunate neglect of her teeth to his attention.

Max tried again. "I haven't seen a soul around. Why are you setting up all these tables?"

"Oh, the tables? That's for a wedding feast. Our owner got hitched."

"Dimitri Vrachnos?"

She nodded.

"I guess he's pulling out all the stops."

"Huh?" Her mouth went slack.

"He's sparing no expense."

"Yeah, and everybody on the island's coming."

"I see." Max decided against ordering a drink; he needed to keep a clear head. Retreating from the bar, he grabbed some almonds from a bowl on the counter and walked out into the courtyard, popping them into his mouth, all the while thinking how different that barmaid and Cassandra were. Their positions at the hotel were essentially the same, their lives similarly influenced by the island environment, yet it was as if an entire world separated them. And it wasn't just Cassandra's beauty that set her apart. It was something else. Her cultured speech. Her refinement. A certain grace. Those were the traits that separated people.

Max strolled across the courtyard also being decorated and since he couldn't sit down without being in the way, he left the premises altogether and followed some well-trodden sheep paths into the hills. A brisk walk would be just the ticket. By the time he returned the preparations would be finished and Cassandra would have time for him.

He had gone quite a distance when the sinking sun reminded him that he'd better head back. Daylight didn't linger in November. Moreover, a thick cloud cover was moving in over the eastern tip of the island. He retraced his steps and reached the road just as the sun began to settle into the sea beyond the Miranda.

A large crowd, obviously the wedding party, was making its way up from the village, the boisterous voices all but drowning out the church bells pealing behind them. Like a boy fascinated by a circus parade, Max stopped to watch their approach. As they came closer, he stepped off the road to let them to pass. Shoulder to shoulder the celebrants were swarming around the bridal carriage, pulled by a once proud animal, reduced by hard work to a swaybacked burro, which for all the revelry around it, held its head dispiritedly low.

Max immediately recognized Dimitri Vrachnos, though the man looked uncharacteristically pleasant dressed in a neat black suit and white shirt with a starched collar. His hair was slicked back behind his ears and his bushy mustache had been trimmed. He wasn't quite the ogre Max remembered; perhaps because he looked washed. The bride sat on the far side of the small conveyance, blocked from view by her husband. Max wondered what sort of woman had found the odious hotel proprietor sufficiently attractive to marry. Of course the Miranda brought in a good living; Vrachnos was by far the richest man on Aiyina, which might compensate for his lack of charm.

Max didn't have long to wait for an answer. The group was alongside him when the groom leaned forward to pull at his socks, allowing the bystander on the road an unobstructed view of the bride.

Cassandra...?

Max felt as if the air was abruptly sucked from his lungs. For a moment he couldn't breathe and, suffocating, couldn't process what he saw. *It's nothing but an optical illusion,* he told himself, *an ocular phenomenon, an aberration brought on by the strange orange light of the sinking sun against the dark clouds closing in.* Because if it were not, why was he suddenly seeing the spectacle in slow motion? In black and white? Why was he hearing no sounds? Why was the wedding party moving, animated and alive, yet silent as the grave? A hundred people were talking and laughing, but the only noise Max heard was a loud roaring in his ears.

He blinked to clear his vision. Nothing changed. Cassandra was still the bride - as enchanting as any he'd ever seen. She was wearing a crown of pink camellias and holding a bouquet of flowers tied with long satin ribbons splaying across her lap. The braids were gone and her lustrous ebony hair was neatly fashioned in an upswept style. A colorful embroidered silk vest set off her white wedding dress and tiny waist. She was as bewitching a picture as Max could imagine; a royal among lesser mortals and like a true sovereign her face was carefully molded. There was no expression in her lovely features.

Max clenched his teeth; a vein throbbed in his neck and his insides ached, same as if he'd been punched. Why, he wondered, why in God's name had she married that hatched-faced lecher? Her uncle, for crying out loud! Not by blood, of course, but whatever Dimitri Vrachnos had been to her in the past, he was now her husband. She had tied herself to him with something stronger than blood: the bonds of matrimony. Max shook his head in disbelief. It didn't make sense. Back in June he'd gotten the impression that she didn't particularly like the man.

He raised his hand to shield his eyes from the last blinding rays of the sun as it sank into the sea. The gesture caught the bride's attention. She glanced toward the lone stranger standing by the side of the road and met his frown with little curiosity until recognition suddenly seared through her. Her hand flew to her mouth, her spine snapped, and she lost her grip on the flowers. They slipped from her lap and fell onto the road. Someone bent to retrieve them, laughed, and handed them back to her.

The procession passed by, leaving Max choking on excruciating disappointment and the acidic dust that the many feet stirred up. But somewhere between the rising dust and descending daylight, a mystery was solved. In June, Cassandra told Max that she was grateful to Dimitri Vrachnos for her education, her job, and the care he'd given her mother. Now there was something additional to be grateful for: marriage, which would obviously be followed by a honeymoon in Athens. A trip she was already planning back then. She'd told him as much that night on the pier.

Max rubbed his neck till it smarted. After months of wanting her, finally coming to claim her, only to discover that she had married someone else was a blow. Things like that happened to other people, not to Maximilian von Renz. His vanity lay like the dirt at his feet and to have been thrown over in favor of an oaf like Vrachnos was, frankly, insulting.

After several minutes of standing immobile by the side of the road, his brain began to rumble again with loathing for the man who had triumphed over him. And it didn't stop there. Unkind thoughts began to swell against Cassandra. Why the rush to marry? At fifteen she was in no danger of becoming an old maid. Max's letters had clearly stated that he would return; only the date had been unclear, being postponed several times as it were. It occurred to him that by not answering, she had played fair; she certainly hadn't encouraged him. He had no one to blame but himself for this foolishness in believing he could come back and pick up where he'd left off. Like a jackass he had pined for a female who'd been busy planning her wedding to someone else. The irony of it, the lunacy, was like a slap in the face. Well, he was now fully awake. He'd been wrong about Cassandra, which was not unusual; men were often wrong about the women they fell for. He had broken no new ground and it was now just a matter of putting this sorry affair behind him. Cassandra had apparently done so. Her display of emotion a moment ago had been cute and appeared genuine because she probably feared he'd come to spoil her party. Former lovers were generally not welcomed at weddings. Suppose he let something slip and her husband learned that she was used merchandise. No wonder she had looked subdued among the revelers. The time was fast approaching when her groom would discover she was not the virgin he expected. No small thing in this society.

That said, Max needed a drink, then it was time to check out. He was not spending the night under the same roof with the bridal couple. It was better to go back to town, rent a room at the *taverna,* take his chances with bedbugs, and return to the mainland on the next ferry, which unfortunately wouldn't dock until the day after tomorrow.

Damn!

This island wasn't big enough for Maximilian von Renz and the honeymooners. They would obviously also be on the same ferry to Athens with him.

Damn!

Perhaps he could charter a boat?

Chapter Thirty-two

Max pushed his way through the noisy crowds in the hotel and elbowed up to the lounge bar, ordering an English whiskey. Tossing it down, he motioned for another. By the time the second shot assaulted his insides, the knot in his stomach loosened; only a tight clenching of his jaw gave proof to any lingering bitterness. He looked around. A hundred revelers were milling about, having a fine time. There was not a foreigner among them. He had been right about the absence of tourists. Everyone here was a local and he suddenly hated them all.

The bridal couple eventually made their way to a long rectangular table in the dining room and took their seats, a signal that everyone else do the same. The lounge cleared and all the tables were quickly filled up, leaving Max alone at the bar.

It took superhuman effort, but he managed not to look at Cassandra even as his jaundiced gaze zeroed in on her husband, a man he'd never in hell expected to envy. He watched as wine was poured from large pitchers and platters of food were passed around. He saw Dimitri Vrachnos grab a lamb shank, clamp his teeth around it, pull at the meat, then gesture with the greasy bone as he talked, stopping only to rinse his gullet with a dousing of retsina, some of which ran down his chin, staining the napkin he'd fastened in his collar. He no longer looked washed.

Seething inwardly at the thought of that man touching Cassandra, Max knew it was time to leave; he'd seen enough. But as he turned away from the bar, he couldn't help looking at the bride. Her expression was still indecipherable. Pushing some food around on her plate, she glanced up briefly when someone offered an off-color remark about her lack of appetite. Vrachnos roared and, wiping his mouth with the back of his hand, leaned over and plastered her face with his wet lips.

Max shook himself loose from the spectacle and began to make his way around the perimeter of the dining room toward the exit into the hall and the stairs up to his room. As a hotel guest, he had every right to remain and partake of a meal he had already paid for, but to stay was nothing short of masochistic. It was high time he found alternative lodgings. A tedious walk to town lay ahead of him. Nothing mechanical moved on the island after dark.

Waylaid by an army of waiters bringing in additional trays of occo buco, Max stopped to let them pass, which afforded him one last glance around. He saw Cassandra looking straight at him, her face becoming rigid like a death mask as she realized he was leaving. The expression caused an icy vibration on Max's spine, never before had he seen such wretchedness. It interfered with his exit, same as the waiters. Suddenly he couldn't walk out. Something was wrong here. This was not the face of a bride worried about her lost innocence and how she might deceive her groom. Something else was afoot. Perhaps it wouldn't hurt to stay a little while longer just to assure himself that she wasn't contemplating *hara-kiri*.

He spotted an empty chair at a table in a far corner of the room and walked over, hoping he wouldn't be obliged to make small talk with the people seated there, or join in the happy toasts to the bride and groom when all he wanted to do was kill the latter. He wondered if Dimitri Vrachnos remembered him, but decided he probably didn't. The hotel catered to Europeans of similar coloring and appearance; there was no reason why he should distinguish one German from another. Max had only been here once before and that was months ago. Moreover, if Vrachnos kept slugging retsina, he'd soon have trouble recognizing his own bride.

Sitting down at the table, Max nodded to his dinner companions and pretended interest in the food, relieved when no one attempted to engage him in conversation. They probably figured he didn't speak their language.

Chapter Thirty-three

It seemed an eternity before the meal was finished and the sated and high-spirited guests got to their feet and slowly meandered through the open doors into the courtyard, where small round tables were placed in a semi-circle to mark the perimeter of a makeshift dance floor. A piano was wheeled out and an accordion and two violas joined the man at the keyboard. The music they produced was wonderful and the soft glow from votives hanging in the olive trees further enhanced the atmosphere. A moon was noticeably absent and not a glimmer of a star penetrated the heavy clouds that had rolled in over the island, but the burning flares in the corners of the enclosure tempered the night air nicely. Bowls of fresh fruit and baklava, along with endless decanters of wine, were placed on a table between two large olive trees.

A charming Greek wedding dance was underway. Max watched the dancers from the dining room doorway and was tapping his foot to the rhythm when someone came up and grabbed his arm. Turning, he found himself looking into the face of the waitress from the bar.

"What did I tell you?" she laughed, the dim light didn't improve her teeth. "Some party, huh? Let's dance!"

Max shook his head, explaining he wasn't familiar with the footwork.

"I'll teach you," she said, demonstrating a few steps before pulling him toward the dance floor. "It's easy. Come on!"

Trapped, he gave it his best shot. The reel required a change of partners and at one point he found himself opposite Marie who gave no indication that she recognized him from his last visit. As they both moved on to their next partners, it occurred to Max that if he

111

remained on the floor, sooner or later he'd be able to take Cassandra for a spin and perhaps learn why she'd been in such a rush to marry and now looked as if death would be her *happy ever after.* Where better to ask questions than on a crowded dance floor, where being with the bride wouldn't arouse suspicion.

Exercising patience - not his strong suit - Max danced with a number of women rapidly losing their sure-footedness; everyone was consuming retsina with suicidal determination. He shuddered. The stuff could strip five coats of paint.

Dimitri Vrachnos eventually left the floor, struggling for breath and motioning for someone else to dance with his bride. He swept a glass off the wine table and drained it before sitting down on a chair near the open doors to the dining room. Two companions joined him and shared some lewd wisdom that caused the three of them to lean back in their seats, slapping their thighs and roaring. With the groom nicely occupied, Max decided to move in on Cassandra.

"Pardon me," he said to the chap dancing with her, noting the fellow was not yet shaving. "I believe it's my turn."

As Max's arm went around her waist and her hand slipped into his, the music took on a profound quality: softly romantic and wildly reckless at the same time. And as if in silent agreement, in spite of the fast tempo, their feet moved to a slower rhythm of their own making. Momentarily numbed by her stunning beauty, Max forgave Cassandra her silence these past months and only wished he could hold her like this forever. But he couldn't. Their dance was bound to be short. His questions had to be asked before someone cut in. How long could he monopolize the bride before drawing attention?

"Hello, pretty one," he said with a wry smile, now leading her through the dancers toward the far side of the floor and out of Vrachnos' direct line of vision. "You've done well for yourself. Congratulations."

Cassandra's chin fell on her chest. The pain of seeing Max was more than she could bear. It hurt far more to see him today than if he had never come back at all. "Why...why did you come?" she asked, her voice raw and miserable. "Why today?"

"Roll of the dice." Max shrugged. "Of course, had you told me that this was to be your wedding day, I would have left nothing to chance and come sooner."

"Told you?" Her head snapped back.

"Yes, I would have liked an opportunity to give Dimitri some competition. You didn't give me a sporting chance. I'll admit my

Greek is not terrific. Still, simple repetition should have made my feelings clear even if I botched the grammar." Max flexed a thin smile. "I kept hoping to hear from you. A postcard would have been nice."

"A postcard?" she echoed, confused.

"I assume the postal service is alive and well on Aiyina."

"Of course."

"Mail still moves on and off the island?"

"Yes. Three times a week. With the ferry."

"So why didn't you answer my letters?"

"What letters?"

It was Max's turn to look confused.

"I never received any," Cassandra said flatly.

Max stared at her. "That's impossible! I can't vouch for the one I dropped in a battered mailbox in Cairo, but I posted several from Germany where moving the mail is a holy experience. Did you at least get the note I left with the hotel clerk?"

She shook her head.

Horrified to realize that his correspondence had been intercepted, Max managed to keep his expression bland in case someone was watching. And, knowing time was short, asked bluntly, "Where were you that last day back in June? I looked everywhere for you."

"I was in the village."

"Doing what?"

"I was being held there."

"What?"

"I was locked up."

"What?" Max said again.

"Two of Dimitri's friends were in my room when I came back from our walk. I didn't think he noticed that left the lounge with you. Apparently he was sober enough to tell someone to follow us. Too lazy, they simply waited till I came back. They told me I had to spend the night with Dimitri's aunt in the village because she was ill and couldn't be alone. I didn't suspect anything until we got there. She was perfectly fine."

"How long did they keep you?"

"Two weeks."

"*Two weeks!*" The words escaped like spit between Max's teeth. "You couldn't get out?"

"No. The room had a window with an ornamental grill bolted to the outside. I couldn't escape but I could see the harbor. I watched the ferry. I saw you leave. After that I didn't care if they never let me out."

"Did the kitchen boy...what's his name, give you a message from me?"

She nodded. "He told me you shouted something from the bus but he couldn't really hear you."

"I thought so. But I'm surprised the desk clerk didn't give you my note."

"The staff makes points by bringing things to Dimitri's attention. Everyone on the island is eager to be in his favor. He makes life pleasant for those who are of use to him."

"And you? You married him because he can make life pleasant for you?"

"Is that what you think?"

"I don't know. What am I supposed to think?"

Before Cassandra could respond, a fellow with a mustache the size of a broom cut in and pressed his partner into Max's arms.

Max smiled and tried his best to appear happy with the switch. However, as soon as the music stopped he excused himself and withdrew into a dark corner to digest Vrachnos' treachery. Locking someone up and tampering with mail were serious offenses where he came from. Evidently these islanders played by their own rules, allowing a scoundrel like Vrachnos to triumph. Standing concealed in the shadows, Max saw several men climb atop a table, clapping their hands and stomping their feet in a matador-like dance. The table finally collapsed under their weight. They sank to the floor, unhurt and laughing with those who had egged them on. The party was growing boisterous. Watching, Max realized the bacchanalian atmosphere might play into his hands. If the celebrants persisted in maiming their God-given sense, the foreigner among them would presumably have more access to the bride.

The foreigner? He picked up a discarded hat from under an upturned chair, a black beret with a small visor, the kind worn by many of the men here tonight. He dusted it off and put it on as camouflage. If he wanted to spend more time with the bride, it'd be prudent to blend in.

Chapter Thirty-four

The minute he had another opportunity to dance with Cassandra Max wasted no time getting back to his question.

"So, why *did* you marry Dimitri?" he asked. "He's no Rudolph Valentino. Was it his money?"

Cassandra shook her head.

"What then?"

"I had to."

"You *had* to?" Max gaped at her because that could only mean one thing and as abhorrence tightened his jaw, he visualized her in bed with that revolting individual. "So he got you in a family way?" Max pressed and wished some local gent would cut in. He was no longer curious about her marriage and was ready to leave. His hand on her waist slackened, widening the distance between them. "Is that it?"

Her eyes darting fearfully around the courtyard, concerned that Dimitri might eventually put two and two together and remember this particular tourist, Cassandra was only half listening until she suddenly realized what Max had said. She paled, her dark eyes flaring with his accusation.

He shrugged. "Don't take it so hard. You're not the first and you won't be the last. It happens all the time. Occasionally it's the only way to get a reluctant suitor to the altar."

"No! You...you don't understand. That's not it. I had to marry Dimitri to honor a contract."

"A marriage contract? I thought that sort of thing went out of fashion years ago."

"It's still common here. I learned about it after my mother died. Our priest Father Stravos told me she had arranged it because she

115

wanted me nicely settled."

"Settled at *fifteen?*"

"No...sixteen." Cassandra's voice sank to a whisper. "Today is my birthday."

Sixteen and married to an ogre more than twice her age! Max weighed the depressing thought and couldn't bring himself to wish her happy birthday, which, under the circumstances, would be nothing short of blasphemous. "There was no way out?" he asked instead.

"I planned to run away. But I didn't have enough money for the fare to the mainland."

"Oh..." Max recalled the night on the pier when she had looked so longingly at the lights of Athens; she had not been thinking about a honeymoon. "Could no one help you?"

"No. I asked Father Stravos but he said I was fortunate that a rich man wanted to marry me. He told me to count my blessings."

"There was no one else?"

Cassandra shook her head. "The people on Aiyina are poor. Nobody has any spare money. Besides, they wouldn't dare defy Dimitri."

"Did you tell him how you felt?"

"Yes. I tried to talk him out of the contract but he claimed my parents owed him money and by honoring the agreement I'd be paying off their debt. I told him I'd work it off. He refused to consider it. He said it'd take too long."

"How much did they owe him?"

"He wouldn't say. He only said that the boat mishap had been my father's fault and was a very expensive loss. So were my mother's medical bills."

"Did he show you any proof?"

"No. But Father Stavros, the doctor, and the boat builder in the village all corroborated his claims."

"Your mother never talked to you about any of this?"

"I didn't see her in the days before she died. Dimitri said she was too sick to recognize anyone. He had moved her in with one of his relatives in the village, where it was easier for the doctor to treat her. When they finally let me visit she could no longer speak."

Max smelled a rat. He'd love to see that marriage contract. Cassandra's mother had obviously signed under duress or was out of her mind with illness. As for Father Stavros, Dimitri probably contributed to the church and the priest wasn't about to bite the hand that fed him. Max began to dig for solutions to Cassandra's problem, his mind testing murderous channels never before explored.

"I always hoped you would come back," she said, interrupting his homicidal thoughts. "For a long time I watched the ferries arriving from Athens, hoping you'd be among the passengers."

"I would have been here months ago. But when I left in June and returned to Germany I found that my father was gravely ill. He died in July. I remained at home to help my mother over the difficult weeks that followed. I must confess, when I could finally leave I decided to meet a colleague in Egypt. Do you remember discussing Tutankhamen when we first met and you predicted I'd work with Howard Carter? Well, your prophecy came true."

"You saw all that gold?"

"Some of it."

Cassandra sighed. "Too bad Tutankhamen died so young. He should have lived to enjoy his wealth."

"He took it with him," Max quipped. "For almost three thousand years." As he was saying this, he happened to glance in Vrachnos' direction, saw one of his cohorts rise from his chair and approach, cutting a determined swath through the dancers. Max whirled Cassandra around, practically shoving her into the man's arms.

"She's all yours," he grinned, slurring his speech with flair and managing to look as if the bride had bored him to death. "I need a drink." Turning on his heel, he headed for the wine table, negotiating the floor with deliberate difficulty. Taking a glass, he put it to his lips and slipped behind an olive tree, discarding the retsina at the base of its trunk. Hidden in the shadows of the branches only a few feet from where Dimitri sat, Max resolved that in view of what he'd just learned he must free Cassandra. But how? She was legally wed in church in front of a hundred witnesses. Still, if he could help it, there'd be no honeymoon.

The sensible thing to do, he concluded, was to go to Athens, come back with a team of attorneys and start annulment proceedings. Unfortunately, the ferry wasn't due until the day after tomorrow, the entire exercise could easily take a week, and since he wasn't about to let Cassandra spend a single night as Dimitri's bride, a round trip to the mainland was out of the question. But other options were wide open. In collision with a rival of Dimitri's ilk, any ceremony associated with a legal dispute was dead in the water. Max was free to resort to...to what? *Dammit!* He was alone against so many, and even if this island had telephone service, it'd be days before help arrived.

Was it too late to approach the groom with an offer to pay off Cassandra's debt? Of course Vrachnos was by no means poor and probably couldn't be tempted with money. At his age, if he expected to have heirs, a young wife was far more valuable, and for that purpose he had blackmailed the loveliest girl on the island. Max wished that Ernst and the rest of the team were here. Suddenly he missed their company as never before. Surely, Franz would come up with a brilliant plan, while hotheads such as Walter and Martin could be trusted to create a world-class disturbance to cover a getaway.

An escape?

Might that be possible? Could he and Cassandra slip away from the festivities, get to the village unnoticed, hide somewhere, wait for the ferry and hop aboard without being spotted? Of course, Vrachnos would have thirty-six hours to comb the island and, if that failed, stand guard at the harbor when the ferry docked.

Max realized that if they expected to make a run for it, they would have to get off the island tonight. If they left the party, how much of a head start could they get? How soon before the bride would be missed? And once they made it to the village, could they borrow a boat and navigate the deep, treacherous water in the dark of night? The clouds were low and heavy. The weather could turn nasty without warning. Even under the best conditions, it was a sobering assignment for a landlubber like Max to tackle the open sea. Chartering a boat might be equally impossible. Any captain worth his salt was no doubt having a fine time right here at the Miranda.

Contemplating several other possibilities - each more impractical than the next - Max kept coming back to the first: run like hell and grab a boat. With each passing minute, the idea gained strength, eventually dominating all sound judgment when he decided it was the only plan available. In keeping with his rash nature, he now left the courtyard. Walking briskly through the deserted dining room and up the stairs, he wondered if he would have a difficult time convincing Cassandra that he wasn't crazy.

Once in his room, he fished through his bag for his passport, stuffing it into the pocket of his slacks that held his wallet. He would have to leave everything else behind; ducking out with luggage was not practical. Turning his back on the room and closing the door, Max felt strangely exhilarated. Abducting another man's bride appealed to his sense of adventure.

Chapter Thirty-five

Max returned to the dining room. The scene in the courtyard looked enchanting without the slightest hint of any corrupt underpinnings. Another circle dance was underway with Cassandra and Dimitri in the center. When the music stopped, a drum roll signaled a speech. The fellow with the broom-like mustache climbed up on a chair and extolled the bride's beauty and the groom's prowess, the latter showing his appreciation by emptying a glass of wine. The guests roared their approval, the music resumed and the party continued.

When Dimitri retreated to his chair along with his bodyguards, Cassandra danced with a tall fellow working his neck like a periscope, his eyes sharp. Max got the message, decided to be extremely careful and remained in the doorway. Considerable time passed before he ventured into the courtyard, doing so only after Cassandra was switched between several partners and after he saw the "periscope" disappear into the hotel with Miss Dental Neglect. Both were laughing, had their arms around each other, and it didn't require much imagination to figure out what they were up to.

While biding his time, Max danced with a number of women before deliberately bumping into Cassandra's partner and making a spontaneous switch. The minute her feet fell into step with his, he outlined his plan.

"We'll never get away with it," she whispered, her eyes darting around, afraid someone might have overheard. "They'll catch us. You have no idea what Dimitri is capable of."

"Another glass of retsina, and he won't be capable of much, least of all a chase." Max tried to sound more confident than he felt; confidence usually won half the battle. "If we steal away carefully, it might be a while before anyone notices your absence."

Cassandra shook her head. "It won't work."

"It's worth a try," Max insisted. "I'm leaving tonight, but I'm not leaving without you. We have a good shot at getting away. A head start is all we need."

"It won't work," she repeated.

"We will be long gone before they realize you're missing. Anyway, Vrachnos will have to claim you over my dead body so I might as well put him through the paces."

"That's not funny," Cassandra said, his flippant attitude scared her. Even so, she was torn between incredible joy with his plan and a terrible fear of its outcome. But if Max was not frightened, why should she be? As it were, her life was no bargain. Perhaps it was preferable to die with Max tonight than live her tomorrows with Dimitri. After a few moments of arguing with herself, she took a deep breath. "Maybe...maybe we could try..." she said, barely moving her lips and letting her heart take charge.

"That's my girl." Max squeezed her hand, sealing their bargain before relinquishing her to another partner. Giving the fellow a looped grin, he said, "Hell of a party!"

Cassandra waltzed away with Pavlov, and although her palms were wet with fear of him, she smiled and made frivolous small talk. But with each step of the dance, any escape plan lost its appeal. Pavlov would think nothing of committing murder. He had done it before. When the music stopped and he left her at the dessert table with a group of women, Cassandra decided she could not let Max risk his life.

"If we are caught," she said a while later and once they managed another spin on the crowded floor, "we'll be stoned." Max was about to laugh, but her expression stopped him. "They'll do it," she said under her breath, her eyes downcast. "Dimitri and his cousin Pavlov once gathered a mob together and killed a couple caught in adultery."

"You saw it?"

"No. Marie did. The woman was Pavlov's wife and Marie told me that since he beat her regularly for no reason, it was no wonder he killed her when she finally gave him cause. They hadn't been married long. She had come here as a bride from Poros. After the murder, Pavlov told her people that she'd suffered a miscarriage and died."

"How was her lover's death explained? Was he from another island as well?"

"No. His family was told that he'd lost his footing and fell down a

120

cliff during an attempt to rescue a sheep. His injuries corresponded with a nasty fall. No one questioned it."

"All right," Max conceded, "Dimitri and this Pavlov fellow play rough. But our case is different. I can't imagine Dimitri would hurt a hair on your pretty head. Killing his cousin's adulterous wife is one thing. His own bride is quite another. And I'm a foreigner. I'm sure he'd figure that some meddlesome souls would come and investigate. Germans are efficient to a fault. They don't leave loose ends. There'd be a full-scale inquiry. Something I'll explain to him if it comes to that."

"He's drunk. The men are all drunk by now. They'll not stop and listen to reason."

"Perhaps," Max said, glossing over the unfortunate truth. "But the fact that they're drunk is also to our advantage. If we get a jump on them, I doubt they can catch us." Max looked around and saw Dimitri's head lolling on his chest. "Listen, we won't be seen together again. I'll leave now and pretend to go upstairs, but instead I'll slip out the back, circle around the rear of the hotel and wait for you along the road to the village. Once you see me leave and once you think sufficient time has passed, tell someone you're going inside to freshen up, then use the back exit."

Nodding, Cassandra agreed to his dangerous game. The outcome didn't really matter. A string of crushing misfortunes had cursed her life. This would be just another one. If only she had someone in the village - not beholden to Dimitri - that would shelter them until the ferry docked. Their prospects were good for slipping onboard. The captain would not tolerate Dimitri's mob, and would be obliged to at least offer Max, a foreigner, safe passage to Athens. But where could they hide until the day after tomorrow? Who would conceal Dimitri's runaway bride and her lover?

No one was the only answer that came back to her.

Chapter Thirty-six

Max was standing on the road leading to town, impatiently shuffling his feet and repeatedly checking his watch. An hour had passed. Why wasn't she leaving the party? Had she lost her nerve?

Suddenly a dark figure darted out from behind the far side of the hotel. He tensed before realizing it was Cassandra coming from a direction he hadn't expected.

"Sorry," she whispered, breathless, as she ran up to him. "I had to get something from my room."

"What?" he asked, taking her hand and now hurrying down the road, surprised anything in her Spartan cottage was important enough to waste time on.

"A picture of my parents." She patted a pocket in the folds of her dress. "I left the frame behind but I couldn't leave the photograph. It'll bring us luck. You'll see."

We'll need it, Max acknowledged silently and said out loud, "Was anyone suspicious when you left?"

"No. For a while I complained about my fancy new shoes and made sure everyone saw me examine my feet. I finally told Marie that I'd gotten a couple of huge blisters and needed to go to the cottage to find some bandages. While there, I changed to some old flat shoes I could run in."

"Smart girl," Max said and increased their pace without breaking into a full run. No point in alerting man or beast to their escape. A barking dog could spell disaster.

They had gone about half a mile when Max decided it was safe to break into a full run. At this distance, pounding feet stirring up dust would not be detected back at the hotel, nor would the howl of a dog. It was time to make like the wind and they now set a pace worthy of Olympian athletes.

Racing down the road, Cassandra's crown of flowers flew off her head, landing in a clump of stunted cypress. Seeing it fly, Max threw his borrowed cap into the trees as well; neither article would be visible in the dark and by morning he planned to be safely in Athens.

The fugitives ran like fire in a parched field.

"Is there a way to bypass the village?" Max asked between rasping breaths, figuring someone might see them.

"We could follow some sheep paths. But the terrain is steep and without a moon it's too dark to see. We're better off on the road. I'm sure no one is out and about at this hour."

Max's ears suddenly pricked with the eerie sound of silence behind them. An ominous lull had fallen over the noisy festivities back at the Miranda. The music had stopped. The quiet made his skin crawl.

They had discovered the bride was missing!

Max cursed a blue streak. He had hoped for more time. He glanced sideways, praying Cassandra would hold up. Beads of perspiration glistened on her forehead, she was panting, but a determined fire blazed in her eyes. He let go of her hand; it was faster to run with both arms swinging. Speed was critical. He'd been blasé when she warned about the perils, but knew she was right. A drunken mob was capable of anything, including a Biblical stoning. While Max was brave, occasionally foolhardy, he was not naïve. From its conception, his plan was full of flaws and the sinister silence now replacing the gaiety back at the Miranda caused cold sweat to run down his back. He prayed Dimitri Vrachnos would spend time searching the premises, every room, every cottage.

Chapter Thirty-seven

The cobblestones on the steep and winding streets of the village made running difficult; it became a choice of slowing down or chance breaking an ankle. But perfectly willing to risk injury, Max and Cassandra continued in blind abandonment down toward the harbor, grateful that the streets were deserted.

They reached the town square blanketed in a damp fog rolling in from the ocean and, although the *taverna* was still open for business, the sidewalk tables were empty, the regular old-timers huddling inside at the bar, preoccupied with a static radio. This enabled the runaways to cross the square without being spotted, a small victory because a far greater obstacle lay ahead of them, that of securing a seaworthy vessel. However, after stealing another man's wife, this seemed a minor hindrance to Max.

An angry buzz in the black hills above town stopped the fugitives in their tracks. Peering up into the foggy darkness, they saw a hazy string of lanterns and flares, like a fiery serpent slithering down the hill.

"Here comes the party," Max said, keeping his voice light to cover a sudden panic. "I guess they weren't having any fun without us."

After a moment of yielding to her fear, Cassandra spit over her left shoulder to ward off evil, turned away from the ugly spectacle in the hills, and ran toward the wharf and the boats moored there. Max followed.

"Which one shall we take?" she said, as they made their way out the pier, stepping around piles of netting and crates, wet and slippery with clinging mist.

"I don't know." Max stopped and scratched his head. "This is a bad time to confess, but I haven't the slightest idea how to handle one of these large fishing vessel. Isn't there anything smaller around here? A rowboat?"

"That would be suicide. They're only used for surf fishing. They can't make it across the open water. Even if we are willing to chance it, we haven't got time now to go back to the beach and launch one through the breakers. One of these motorized boats would quickly catch us."

"All right." Max scanned the armada at his disposal. He might as well be looking at oceangoing tankers. But rather than wait for the mob and suffer the predictable, he'd better pick a boat and apply himself to some on-the-job training. Greatly motivated by the crowd bearing down on the village, he jumped aboard the first skiff only to find its cabin door locked. He ran to the next. Same thing.

Damn, don't these Greeks trust their fellow man?

Four vessels later, now trying to pry open a hatch with his bare hands, Cassandra suddenly pulled at his sleeve. "There's someone on that boat out there!" she cried, pointing toward the tip of the pier where a tiny pinprick of light was visible through the fog. "It might be the Athena. That's where she docks. I know the owner. His wife and my mother were friends." Cassandra now ran ahead in the dark, gambling life and limb as she hurdled herself over marine obstacles. Max followed but - just in case - took time to stop and test the lock on each boat he passed.

It was the Athena! Cassandra's heart beat wildly as she jumped onboard, pounding her fists on the cabin door.

A lifetime passed before someone stirred below deck. When the portal was finally pushed open, her face fell because it was not the person she expected. It was his disagreeable son, whose romantic advances she'd spurned since the age of twelve. Patrik would carry his grudge to the grave.

"Is your father below?" she asked, trying not to project her disappointment.

"No, he's home. Laid up with a sore back." Patrik yawned and with the sudden intake of oxygen remembered to be petulant. "What do you want?"

"Your boat." Cassandra wrung her hands. "Can...can you take the boat out?"

"Sure. Once the clouds lift. I don't know when that'll be." Patrik pursed his lips and gazed skyward. "Damned fog!" Suddenly he looked back at Cassandra. "Hey! Didn't you get married today?"

"Y...yes."

"So what are you doing here?" He studied Cassandra's disheveled hair before his attention snapped to a tall stranger approaching the boat.

"*Yassou,*" Max said, wondering if this individual was in Dimitri's camp. But, friend or foe, this was their last chance at getting out to sea. "We need to charter your boat," he said quickly. "Can you take us across to Athens?"

Patrik stepped all the way out on deck and looked questioningly from Cassandra to the stranger standing on the dock. "What the hell's going on here?" he said.

"There's no time to explain." Max's voice cut through the murky darkness like a whip. "We need your boat." He threw a glance over his shoulder. Dimitri's mob had reached the village, their flares casting a yellow glow through the narrow, tunnel-like street. "I'll make it worth your while." Max dug into his pocket and fished out his wallet.

"Are you running off with Cassie?" This was more a demand for verification than a question.

"Look, just start the engine!" Max unfolded the bills, flexing their persuasive powers. "We'll tell you everything you need to know once we're under way."

Patrik licked the saliva from the corners of his mouth; he was staring at more money than he could hope to earn from a year of sponge fishing.

"This is only half your fee," Max said when the fellow was slow to respond. "You'll get the other half when we reach Athens." For emphasis he patted his passport and the emergency money he always carried between its pages. Tonight it would be spent. This was as close to an emergency as he'd ever come.

"I don't know. If I help you, Vrachnos will have my hide." Patrik glanced at Cassandra. "My life won't be worth a wad of spit. He'll bury me before my body's cold." Cassandra lowered her eyes; his fears were justified. Turning to Max, Patrik raised his shoulders and spread his hands. "I can't help you," he said, truly sorry and again eying the money.

"Look, tell Vrachnos I held a knife to your throat." Max was talking through clenched teeth; it was difficult to reason with a stubborn person while a bloodthirsty mob was nipping at one's heels. "Tell him you were a victim of piracy." In another minute Max might have to resort to violence and it wouldn't be the first time tonight that he'd contemplated murder. At this point, the idea of throwing Patrik overboard and hijacking his boat caused him no qualm of conscience, except for the undeniable fact that he needed his expertise for a safe crossing.

Patrik became aware of the noise in the village and now also saw the flares cutting through the fog. A chill passed through him as he figured he was already in the grave for having Vrachnos' bride on his boat. He made a snap decision and jumped into action.

"All right!" He snatched the bills from Max's hand, shoving them into his pocket. "I get the rest when we reach Athens?"

"Yes." Max, too, sprung into action, untying the lines and freeing the boat from its mooring.

Patrick grabbed the wheel and cranked the throttle. The engine sputtered, coughed, and died. He set a record for fine cussing.

Max grabbed a long wooden pole lolling on the deck and used it to push the boat away from the pier. If the engine refused to cooperate, at least he could put some watery distance between this floating hulk and the mob.

A chorus of angry voices filled the square. The customers in the *taverna* were roused from their comfort at the bar and came out to the sidewalk. When asked, they swore on everything holy that they hadn't seen anyone around these parts tonight.

Patrik worked furiously. He opened the hatch to the motor, blew out the fuel line and tapped a year's worth of corrosion from the top of the battery. Again he cranked the ignition.

Max mustered a grin for Cassandra's sake; her face was white and her hands were wringing tight coils in her hair. Of all the boats in the harbor, he fumed inwardly, they had ended up on a paraplegic. In a few minutes they might have to abandon ship. A one-way swim out to sea was preferable to a stoning.

The engine finally rumbled and it was a decidedly pleasant sound. Patrik revved the old machinery and lightning-quick turned the Athena toward the open water.

"Cut the running lights," Max said, realizing that if Vrachnos' group saw the lights, nothing would prevent them from giving chase in one of the other boats, undoubtedly in better shape than this one.

Patrik hit the switch and the Athena gained some blessed distance in total darkness. The moonless night was a godsend and - coupled with the dense fog - anything a hundred meters from the pier would be difficult to spot.

"Shut off the engine," Max said after a few more minutes, and after the boat had entered a fog bank so thick it felt like rain.

"What?" Patrik turned and gave him a weird look. "What's the matter with you? Are you crazy?"

"Just do it!"

127

Patrik turned off the ignition. "It's your funeral." He shrugged before remembering that it was also his. "I thought you were in a hurry," he tried arguing. "Now we're just sitting here. We might drift back to the pier and..."

"Quiet!" Max hissed.

Patrik pressed his lips together, shook his head at this foreigner's lack of sense and looked toward Cassandra, appealing to hers. However, in the next instant all his attention focused on the noise ashore. He peered into the murky night and dimly saw the large horde of men surging toward the wharf, each carrying a weapon; rifles, clubs, and long sharp blades were reflected in the flares they held aloft. Dimitri's garbled voice could be heard above the din, shouting something. The men immediately spread out and began checking the hatches on the vessels tethered to the pier.

"Where's the Athena?" Pavlov's rough voice wanted to know once the group reached her slip.

"Patrik took her out earlier," someone hollered. "He wanted to be at the sponge reefs before dawn."

"Crazy fool!" a burred voice snapped. "This is no night to anchor at the reefs. You can't see yourself piss in the water."

A chortling erupted, but was quickly stilled by Vrachnos' slurred command for silence. The mob reacted surprisingly fast. A tense hush followed as they edged further out to the very tip of the pier, ears cupped to listen, flares and lanterns held out against the darkness.

Dimitri Vrachnos repeated his order for silence, and had a leaf blown into the water, its splash would have been heard by the three occupants on the boat hidden in the fog bank.

Max wiped at the cold beads of sweat on his upper lip. Cassandra trembled convulsively. He put his arms around her and pulled her up against him. She turned her face into his shoulder. Out of the corner of her eye, she saw Patrik's black silhouette, rooted like a mast to the deck. Max had paid him a fortune and she wondered how he had come to be in possession of so much money. Did he really have more to hand over later? Perhaps he'd been put in charge of funds belonging to his university. After spending it tonight, how would he ever repay it?

"No one's gone out," Pavlov finally determined after a long while of listening. Muttering noisily among themselves, the rest of the men agreed.

"Let's go!" Vrachnos ordered. The men lowered their lanterns and turned their collective backs on the open water.

As they shuffled away from the wharf, Pavlov pointed to a dozen men. "You search the village! Go door to door. Wake everyone up. Enlist every able-bodied man. The rest of us will split into two groups and check the beach in both directions."

"There's a price on the stranger's head!" Dimitri yelled, anger powering his voice. "Find him! I want him dead!"

The flares and lanterns could soon be seen flickering along the beach while others fanned out into the village, rousing its sleeping citizens.

The lights were eventually swallowed by fog and distance.

Patrik looked toward Max before starting the engine. He had gained some respect for his judgment and only cranked the temperamental machinery once he got the signal. After a few false starts, the motor purred like a contended cat. He navigated the shoals and entered the shipping lanes without switching on the running lights. Why chance being spotted? Fog or no fog, he could smell a tanker at a wide enough berth to avoid a collision.

Once on course, he pulled a pipe from his waistband, stuffing it with tobacco he scooped from a folded oilskin pouch crammed behind the barometer. Steadying the wheel with one elbow, he cupped his hands and struck a match; a few determined puffs and the tobacco smoldered nicely, sending warmth to his soul and curls of smoke into the light breeze tossing the boat once it left the shelter of the island. Easy money, he concluded, caressing his bulging pocket. He had never before come across a deal like this and was certainly not going to risk it by letting Dimitri learn of this voyage. If confronted, he knew nothing about the departed lovers because he had spent an anxious night in fog near the reefs on the south side of the island. That would be his story - his only story - he knew his limitations. He could never be convincing if he tried any dramatic stuff about a hijacking. He lived a simple life. Why complicate it? He would have enough trouble figuring out how to spend his newly acquired wealth without drawing attention.

Cassandra and Max remained standing at the stern of the boat, watching Aiyina - a black knoll seamlessly wedged into the murky night - slowly disappear. "You might never be able to return here," Max said, his arm around her. "Any regrets?"

"None," she answered in a voice that left no room for second-guessing.

Max touched his lips to the top of her head. "In that case, you're stuck with a grubby and footloose archaeologist. Would you consider marrying such a fellow?"

Strangling on all sorts of pleasant emotions, Cassandra nodded.

Max lifted her chin, held her face between his hands, and remembered what day this was.

"Happy birthday," he said against her lips.

Chapter Thirty-eight

It was early morning when Patrik put his passengers ashore in Athens, received final payment, refueled, and headed back out to sea.

The sharp smell of boat tar permeated the misty morning air, and the runaways walked away from the large harbor past white cruise ships and oceangoing tankers, their loaded cargo nets dangling precariously overhead. Now flat broke, Max was contemplating thumbing a ride to Koropi where they could lie low while he contacted his attorneys in Berlin. He needed legal advice. Of course, arriving in Koropi with the abducted wife of another man would be the final nail in his coffin. As it were, previous indiscretions had worn his tenure thin. Professor Krugg would drum him out of Heidelberg on a morality charge and deliver Cassandra to a Greek magistrate, who would send her back to her husband at once.

Max dismissed Koropi as a safe refuge.

Randomly crossing streets, he realized that with all that had transpired in the past twelve hours, he had neglected to be practical. During the sea crossing, he should have peeled off a few drachmas from Patrik's last installment. Of course, even if he had some money and could call Berlin, neither his mother nor his attorneys could wire funds to an arbitrary street corner. A bank would have to cooperate. An international transaction could easily take a couple of days and suppose some fastidious official became inquisitive. Cassandra was wearing a wilted wedding dress, not your regular Monday attire, and she looked awfully young in the early morning light. Dirty and unshaven, he could be mistaken for a vagrant. He had his passport to prove otherwise, but once Vrachnos reported the abduction, that document would both identify and indict him. So

131

although the night crossing to Athens had been successful, their troubles were far from over.

Trouble? Max recalled a civics instructor once saying that when in trouble on foreign soil contact the German Consulate. But where might this protectorate be? Athens was huge; they could wander around for days and never see the same street corner twice. *Wait a minute...!* Max stopped in front of a sidewalk café serving mouthwatering omelets. *Consulate? Enno von Steigert?*

Talk about luck. Enno was right here in Athens sure as today was Monday. Max felt a sudden rush of relief. Deliverance was at hand, and although he and Cassandra were obliged to turn their backs on the café with its wonderful aroma of warm bread, he walked away in high spirits. "Once we find the German Embassy," he said, smiling triumphantly, "we'll have breakfast."

Cassandra looked at him, confused and glassy-eyed from lack of sleep. "Breakfast at the embassy?"

"Yes." Max took her hand; there was a new spring in his step. "All we have to do is find it. Which should be easy. Somebody around here has got to know where it is. A traffic officer. Anybody."

"How about over there?" Cassandra pointed to a large building flying the Greek flag.

"A post office? Perfect!" Holding her hand, Max dashed across the street against oncoming traffic, forcing motorists to stand on their brakes.

Inside, the lines were tediously long and rather than wait his turn for a postal clerk, Max decided he had more to gain by going directly to the postmaster who was sure to have a telephone. One phone call and Enno would send a car. Leaving the crowded vestibule, Max strolled down a narrow corridor, ignoring a sign that said: Employees Only!

Stopping outside a door paneled in opaque glass with some fancy gold lettering, Max decided this was a job for Cassandra. "How about if you practice your charm on this fellow so I won't have to practice my Greek," he whispered as he knocked on the door. "Give him your prettiest smile and ask if we can use his telephone. Tell him we need to contact the German Embassy. Explain it's an emergency." Max figured no man could refuse a request that came from her.

"Door's open!" a voice grunted.

Turning the handle, Max stood aside for Cassandra and followed her inside.

Sitting behind a roll top desk cluttered with towering stacks of paper, the only visible part of the postmaster was a shock of graying hair, but clearly visible on the wall behind him were some thriftily framed portraits of past members of the Greek royal family. King George III looked particularly serene and proud in this place of honor, belying the fact that he was currently suffering exile in Rumania. Chewing on an unlit cigar, the postmaster craned his neck and eyed his visitors with a note of wariness as they rounded his desk. He removed the cigar and put it in an ashtray.

"Good morning!" Cassandra began her pitch about needing to use his telephone and admitting that they couldn't pay for the cost of the call.

"Well...uh, being that it's a local connection, I suppose it'd be all right." The man was so baffled with the request that he couldn't offhand think of a reason to refuse it. People usually came storming in here to complain about lost mail and a host of other grievances with the postal service. The polite request from this pretty young thing was a new twist in his routine and he was no match for it. "As long as you don't tie up the line for more than a few minutes."

"Oh, it won't even take that long," she promised.

"All right. The German Embassy, you say?"

"Yes, please."

The man picked up the cigar, again clamping it between his teeth while reaching for a dog-eared directory on a shelf as cluttered as his desk. Fumbling through the pages, he worked the cigar into the corner of his mouth as his fingers slid down several columns until he found the listing.

"Here we are," he said, picked up the telephone, and gave the number to the operator. Once the call was connected, he held out the receiver.

"Thank you." Max stepped forward and took it.

The postmaster leaned back in his swivel chair and continued to work the soggy cigar. As a government official dealing with the public he prided himself in his ability to identify the different species, and could immediately tell that these two individuals had class and rank. They certainly had wonderful manners, and the expensive leather boots on the young fellow were the kind King George himself had worn. But what had brought them to this office, penniless and disheveled? They had probably been celebrating in nightclubs near the harbor and fallen prey to thieves in the wee hours. His eyes fell on the girl's odd dress. It looked like an old-fashioned bridal costume still worn on some of the islands. An idea came to him. Why not offer these two people a ride? It would be nice to accommodate a foreigner who had shown the good sense to marry a Greek girl.

It turned out to be a favor Max was grateful to accept because a nasal twang at the other end of the line informed him that, except in cases of war or revolution, the consulate did not run a livery service for marooned citizens. When Max insisted on being connected directly to the ambassador's residence, the line went dead.

"We're as good as home!" he said half an hour later, getting out of the Fiat as it stopped in front of a white marble building flying the German and Greek flags side by side. After thanking the postmaster for his trouble, Max walked over to the guards at the gate, flashed his passport, and was given entry into a high-ceilinged rotunda, which in spite of its enormous size and gray marble walls was extremely welcoming in that it was German turf.

The receptionist, a woman on the wrong side of forty, regarded their approach, lifting her long thin nose with a measure of the detachment she reserved for fellow countrymen who disgraced themselves when traveling abroad, then without shame had the unmitigated gall to impose on the embassy, slovenly and assuredly broke. The two individuals strolling across the hall toward her fit the mold.

"I'd like to see Ambassador von Steigert," Max said, handing over his passport and scanning the bulletin board behind the receptionist. There was no poster calling for his head. Good. Vrachnos was still searching the island.

"Do you have an appointment?" The woman handed back the passport.

"No. He's a close friend. Please tell him I'm here."

"I'm sorry. Without prior appointment one cannot meet with His Excellency."

Max recognized the nasal twang; this was the trite person he'd spoken to from the post office. "Very well," he said. "Let's make an appointment. I'm free at the moment."

The receptionist looked at him with growing impatience.

"I'll wager ten to one he'll see me," Max challenged her.

"I don't set up appointments. You'll have to consult with the scheduling secretary, Fraulein Knopf."

"All right. Where can I find her?"

"She's not here on Mondays. Perhaps tomorrow..."

"Tomorrow?" Without a shred of tact or good humor left, Max took matters into his own hands and reached across her desk for the telephone. "I'll place the call myself!"

The receptionist mistook his action for a lunge at her throat. Her foot rammed the silent alarm and instantly the intruders were surrounding by guards, while the chief of staff exited his office as if it'd caught fire. Cassandra grabbed hold of Max's arm.

"What's the matter?" she asked. She had not understood the exchange, which had been in German. "What's wrong?"

"Nothing, darling. These men are part of a welcoming committee for special people like us."

"We're special?"

"Yes. I know the ambassador, but this woman refuses to believe it."

"Oh..." Cassandra didn't believe it either, but said nothing, and only wondered how Max could ever have imagined that they would be welcomed here and be offered breakfast. However, fresh from their victory of last night, she wasn't going to question him and simply took his cue, facing down the men without blinking an eye. Elevating her chin, she stared defiantly at the ring of uniforms.

Moments later, having assured himself that these people were no threat to the sanctity of the consulate, the chief of staff called off the guards and turned to the receptionist to inquire about the magnitude of a problem justifying deployment of the alarm system.

Clearing her throat, she writhed like an eel.

"I was attempting to call Herr Ambassador von Steigert," Max spoke up before she could find her voice. "Your receptionist misunderstood my intentions. Perhaps you'd be good enough to announce me."

With an odd twist on his lips, the chief of staff perused the dirty and unshaven person in front of him. "Are you acquainted with His Excellency?"

"Call him. If he says he doesn't know me, we'll leave at once."

The man sighed, inconvenienced, but determined it was worth making a futile call to clear the lobby; there was an unpleasant odor of fish and boat tar about these two individuals. "Let me have your passport."

Max handed it over. The chief of staff picked up the telephone and when he had the ambassador's assistant on the line, opened the document and explained with a touch of apology that - he adjusted his glasses and consulted the passport for accuracy - a Maximilian Johannes von Renz insisted he was acquainted with His Excellency and wished to be announced." Glancing toward Cassandra, he added that the person in question was in the company of a young woman of Greek origin.

"One moment, please." The assistant put the call on hold.

With the receiver to his ear, the chief of staff sat down on the corner of the desk and waited, his eyes roaming the vaulted ceiling, the fingers on his left hand drumming his knee, making it clear that he was a busy man trying to be patient.

The assistant came back on the line.

The chief of staff listened and nodded his head. "I see. Yes...yes, of course. Right away." He hung up and looked at Max with ill-concealed astonishment. "I have been instructed to escort you to the ambassador's residence. Please, follow me."

Chapter Thirty-nine

"Max! How wonderful to see you!" Anna von Steigert's face was a picture of pure delight as the elevator doors opened to the apartment's foyer. She stepped back to let her visitors enter. "This is, indeed, a pleasant surprise. We knew you were in Koropi. Your mother's letters keep us up to date. I'm so glad you decided to pay us a visit."

Anna's welcome was so heartfelt that Max experienced pangs of guilt that only utter desperation had brought him to her doorstep. Switching to Greek, he introduced Cassandra.

"I'm delighted to meet you!" Anna took both of Cassandra's hands, all the while hoping her amazement wasn't too apparent. Dorrit's letters had said nothing about a new romance, and where on earth had Max found this girl? She had a lovely face but was as unkempt as he, which was not at all becoming for a female.

Anna von Steigert was exquisitely groomed; her blond coiffure professionally arranged each and every morning and her garments were *haute couture*. Today she was wearing a navy dotted dress with a white pointed collar and wide belt. Anna adored designer clothes and wore them well, safeguarding a slim figure by indulging in a good deal of starvation. The consummate ambassador's wife, she was gregarious, equally comfortable in the company of a single person or a large crowd; all manner of strange languages notwithstanding, she conversed easily in five.

"Enno is tied up in a conference with some business men from Khios," she said, nodding toward the closed door to the library as she linked arms with her guests, now leading them into a large magnificently furnished living room, done entirely in shades of pink and pearl gray. "They're ship builders seeking German cooperation

on some new venture. I suppose it's a meeting of some importance."
She turned her head and winked at Max. "Of course, when Enno
heard that you were here, he promised to quickly dispense with
them." Her sensitive nose having detected a fish-like smell on her
visitors, Anna suddenly decided against the living room and instead
went out onto the terrace, which ran the length of the apartment and
offered an unobstructed view of Philopappos Hill with the Acropolis
rising majestically in the distance. The ancient columns of the
Parthenon stood veiled in the morning mist, lending the scene
surrealistic qualities.

The sight tightened something in Cassandra's chest. She
remembered visiting the sacred rock with her parents during their
one trip to Athens and recalled running among the ruins of the
Parthenon, her mother fretting she might fall while her father
laughed with the fun of the chase as he tried to catch a small girl
who could scamper over the broken blocks good as a mountain goat.

"In 1907 or thereabouts..." Max's voice broke through
Cassandra's bittersweet musings; "German archaeologists working
at Kerameikos discovered the cemetery of the ancient Athenians
who occupied the Acropolis during its glory days. I studied the site
two years ago. My thesis, which I have yet to organize, let alone
write," he grimaced admitting to some neglect in the matter, "deals
with the ancient Greek and Egyptian burial practices and their
conceptions of an afterlife."

Anna von Steigert who loved life too dearly to have the slightest
interest in any rituals associated with burials, reached for a silver
bell. A moment later, a maid appeared with a tray of assorted fruit
drinks.

"Let's sit down," Anna said once the drinks were handed out. She
pointed to some cushioned patio chairs. "So, what brings you to
Athens on a Monday morning?" she asked point blank and sat
down, her brow puckering with curiosity as she looked at Max.

He pretended surprise with the question.

She laughed and waved her hand as if swatting at a fly. "Come
now! Yesterday I wouldn't have asked because it was Sunday. A
day for visiting. But a Monday morning? That's unusual. And, my
dear boy, as delighted as I am to see you, I am not going to believe
you suddenly yearned for the company of people your parents' age.
I know you better than that. So what's going on? It appears as if the
two of you have been roughed up. Are you in some kind of
trouble?" Anna looked from one to the other. "Go ahead. You can
tell me. Speak up."

Cassandra pinched her lips together, leaving Max to explain and almost wishing he'd do it German so she wouldn't need to listen. She was too tired to relive last night, and she was afraid. Surely, once this elegant lady heard their story, she would regret having welcomed them.

"You're right, Anna. We're in trouble," Max admitted. "It's a long and shocking story."

"Shocking? What do you mean?" A worried frown spread on Anna's face, even as her blue eyes danced with delicious interest.

Max made a snap decision. It was better to wait and tell the whole saga once Enno joined them; he would be a stabling influence in case Anna's delicate sensibilities were rattled. "I'll tell you what. If we can first get cleaned up and if you promise us a meal we'll divulge all the bizarre details. We're not only dirty, we're starved."

Anna could barely contain herself. *Bizarre?* She licked her glossy red lips, thinking it was refreshing to entertain guests with troubles they weren't inclined to keep to themselves. Again ringing the silver bell, she went into action. "Katerina," she said the minute the maid appeared, "tell Georgiana to get two guest suites ready. Then alert the kitchen. We will want..." Anna consulted her watch and glanced at her guests. "It's ten o'clock. What would you like?"

"Breakfast," Max said, reaching over to squeeze Cassandra's hand.

Chapter Forty

Cassandra slipped into the warm, scented bath and let it buoy her tired body for a few minutes before reaching for the soap and sponge and scrubbing herself. Pushing the sponge under the water and squeezing it, she watched the bubbles rush to the surface. Again and again she dipped it and held it against her neck, the stream of water soothing her. Closing her eyes, she rested her head on the edge of the blue marble tub where a folded towel served as a pillow. Anna von Steigert must be a very special friend, she mused, to have taken them in as though they were family. She wondered if the ambassador would be as welcoming as his wife.

Georgiana knocked on the door and walked in with some dresses belonging to her mistress and from which Cassandra was to choose one that fit her. After hanging the lovely outfits on a brass hook near a full-length mirror, she bent over to pick up the pile of dirty, discarded clothing.

"I'll have these cleaned right away," she promised, eying the pretty embroidered silk vest and wondering why this guest had arrived in something that appeared to be a wedding dress.

"No! Don't bother." Cassandra could barely look at the wilted garments; she would never wear them again. "Throw everything away. Oh, and here..." she pulled Dimitri's ring off her finger, "take this as well." She realized she should have thrown it overboard last night, but had completely forgotten about it until now.

Georgiana felt the weight of the gold as the ring was dropped into her hand. "You don't want it?"

"No." Cassandra shuddered. "Please get rid of it. You can have it."

"Thank you!" Palming the ring and carrying the clothes, the maid left hurriedly before this guest could change her mind.

Chapter Forty-one

Half an hour later, dressed in one of Anna's expensive frocks, a yellow sleeveless eyelet batiste with a fashionable dropped waist, Cassandra was crossing the vestibule on her way to the terrace just as two gentlemen in dark tailored suits were shown to the elevator by the ambassador's assistant, who was making quite a fuss over them. Stepping into the lift, both men looked at Cassandra with bland curiosity, when one of them - the one carrying a large alligator briefcase - suddenly stiffened. His eyes narrowed and his complexion turned a deathly shade as if he had seen a ghost.

Smiling at his strange reaction, Cassandra watched the elevator doors close. No one had ever looked at her like that. This beautiful yellow dress must be very special. The ambassador's assistant disappeared down the hall and the hum of the elevator grew faint as it descended toward the lower floors. Experiencing a new level of confidence, Cassandra lingered a moment to admire her reflection in a mirror hanging above a black-lacquered console with brass lamps at either end and a crystal vase of pink roses in the middle. Her hair was still damp. She pushed it behind her ears and wished she had a rubber band to hold it in place.

"Ah, there you are!" Max jumped up from his chair the minute Cassandra walked out on the terrace. He was clean-shaven and was also wearing something borrowed. The clothes didn't quite fit, but he looked extremely handsome. Taking her arm, he drew her over to a stout, balding gentleman - similarly dressed in dark blue jacket and light trousers - seated on a chaise lounge.

"Enno..." Determined not to use the hated Vrachnos surname in the introduction, Max said, "I'd like to present Cassandra Helen Chandros."

"Well, it's a real pleasure!" The ambassador rose from his chair with some difficulty. "Welcome, my dear!" he said, his command of Greek as excellent as his wife's. Remaining in her seat, Anna decided that the girl had cleaned up rather well. She looked sensational and to her credit seemed unaware of it. Enno now took Cassandra's hand and put it to his lips. "You're the second Chandros I've had the pleasure of meeting today. I just had a fellow in my office by that name."

Cassandra experienced a twinge of curiosity but pushed it aside and uttered a greeting she hoped was appropriate; she had never before met an ambassador.

"I've been told that you and Max have had an adventure of some magnitude," Enno von Steigert remained standing and offered Cassandra his arm. "And if my wife and I hope to hear about it, we'd better sit down eat." With Anna and Max following, he led the way toward the far corner of the terrace where a round patio table stood covered in a sheer lace-bordered cloth set with heavy silver and wafer-thin bone china. A canvas awning stretched over the table, shielding the four occupants from the bright sun, which had finally burned off the morning mist. A profusion of red geraniums bloomed in a number of large urns standing along the stucco balustrade, and from the street far below one could hear the muffled sounds of traffic. Maids breezed silently in and out, replenishing dishes of grave lax, scrambled eggs and pastries, while a white-gloved steward poured orange juice and coffee.

From the moment they sat down, and once Max began outlining the events of last night, the von Steigerts were rendered speechless. Anna had come to the table, expecting a delicious scandal, never dreaming it'd be otherwise and when Max finally finished his story, her worried eyes implored Enno to say something comforting.

He didn't.

"The years escape me..." Enno ran a hand over his head where only a fringe of gray remained at the back. "You're in your mid twenties, aren't you, Max?"

"Yes. I'll be twenty-five in February."

"And you, Cassandra?"

"I'm sixteen."

"Sixteen?" The ambassador's eyebrows rose to where his hairline had once been. He looked visibly shaken and took a sip of coffee while his dismay subsided. "That...uh, that complicates the situation," he said. "You can be married with parental permission at sixteen, but you're a minor." He looked soberly at Max. "Running off with a minor is a very serious matter."

"Max didn't run off with me," Cassandra said. "I agreed to go."

"Your age, my dear, precludes you from agreeing. The authorities will disregard any consent on your part. As despicable as Dimitri Vrachnos no doubt is, you are still his wife. In the eyes of the law an abduction has taken place and the adult involved will be held accountable." Enno looked grimly across the table at Max. "I wouldn't be surprised if an arrest warrant hasn't already been issued. The Miranda's registry has your particulars even if your letters were discarded long ago. I suspect this embassy will be the first place the police will look. Of course you can claim temporary asylum, but the consulate will not be allowed to shelter a Greek citizen."

"Enno, after what we've just heard, Cassandra can't possibly go back to Aiyina," Anna said. "But that's what the Greek authorities will probably insist on. And they'll insist on detaining Max in some horrible jail." Anna's worried frown deepened. "Max has got to get out of the country while you try to work something out."

"Yes, we'll need to get an annulment," Enno said. "No question about that."

"How long will that take?" Max asked.

"Several weeks. First we need proof that the marriage contract was fraudulent and coerced. Then we file the paperwork and wait for a court date."

This was not what Max wanted to hear. "Maybe Cassandra and I can both make a run for the border. They are pretty lax at the crossing into Albania."

"After Albania? What then? There are several more borders to cross before you reach Germany. They, assuredly, will not let Cassandra enter without a passport."

"But Enno!" Anna cried. "You have such marvelous connections. Surely you can obtain a measly little passport."

"Not without a birth certificate."

"Couldn't you send someone to Aiyina to fetch it?"

"Time is of the essence, Anna. Suppose Max is arrested in the meantime. And, don't forget, we still need an annulment. While it might be wise for Max to get out of the country, Cassandra will have to remain and appear at the hearing."

"If Cassandra stays, I stay," Max said.

"Kidnapping is a capital crime," Enno reminded him.

"I'm convinced the marriage contract is bogus." Max dug in his heels. "So unless they can hang me for irresponsible behavior I'm willing to face Vrachnos in court."

"What if the contract turns out to be valid?"

Max shrugged. "Hanging is preferable to being stoned."

"*Stoned?*" Enno looked confused.

"If we'd been caught last night," Cassandra spoke up, "the mob would have stoned us."

"You believe Dimitri Vrachnos would have killed you?"

"I'm sure of it. He's done it before."

"He has?"

"Yes. Three years ago he and his cousin stoned an adulterous couple."

"The couple died?"

Cassandra nodded.

"No one investigated?"

Cassandra shook her head.

When Enno pressed her for details, she repeated everything Marie had told her, including the lies Dimitri and Pavlov had concocted for the respective families. "Pavlov buried his wife in a spot where nobody would think to look. Days later, when her family arrived from Poros, he had a funeral service for an empty coffin, burying it under a gravestone in the cemetery."

"That's sacrilege!" Enno sputtered. "I can't imagine the church being party to such a thing."

"I don't know if Father Stravos realized no one was in the casket he held prayers over."

Enno took a sip of coffee while his mind tested a whole new approach to a considerable problem. "Cassandra, do you know where this poor woman's body is buried?"

"Yes. It's on the south side of the island. I went there occasionally to pick wild herbs. One day I noticed a mound of loose dirt that hadn't been there before. It looked like a grave. I mentioned it to Marie. Swearing me to secrecy, she told me about the stoning."

The steward refilled the ambassador's cup and Enno drank the coffee without adding the usual two cubes of sugar and a splash of heavy cream, such was his preoccupation with what he was hearing. Of course, it was premature to raise expectations but, sure enough, shady characters usually had a skeleton in the closet. In this case, a skeleton in the hills, while a headstone marked an empty grave in consecrated ground.

"Cassandra, can you show us the location of this grave-like mound you saw?" She looked at the ambassador, shocked that he would ask. "On a map," he added hastily.

"Oh? Of course...yes. The area has long since become part of the landscape, but I'll never forget the spot. I know exactly where it is."

Glancing around the table with a glint of triumph in his eyes, Enno straightened in his chair. "It might behoove us to dispatch a coroner to Aiyina along with a judge and annulment papers. I suspect Dimitri Vrachnos will sign just about anything as long as no spade of earth is disturbed. I assume the man and his cousin are sufficiently clever to decide it's better to lose a bride..." Enno leaned over and patted Cassandra's hand, "even such a lovely one, than face a double murder inquest."

Max looked at Enno with some skepticism. "Will a coroner and a judge threaten Vrachnos, obtain his signature, then turn their backs and not investigate a crime?"

Enno shrugged. "I don't know what they'll do. Once I lean on them and things are set in motion, I ask no questions. They count on that. Otherwise they wouldn't accommodate me." The ambassador pushed his chair back and rose from the table. "Now, if you'll excuse me, I'd better get to work. No sense waiting for Vrachnos to strike the first blow and hit us with an arrest warrant."

The minute Enno left the table Anna began making plans. "Your mother is still in mourning," she said, looking at Max, her face crumbling as she remembered the funeral she and Enno had attended in Bernau this past July. "I'm sure she's not up to the task of planning a wedding. But if Enno can have the paperwork done quickly, why don't the two of you marry right here at the embassy? I have never been blessed with children. But I've always dreamed of hosting a wedding."

Chapter Forty-two

It was several weeks before Georgiana set about to clean and alter the dress a guest had discarded along with a gold ring on a day back in November. Georgiana had sold the ring but kept the dress and the pretty embroidered vest, again reveling in her windfall as she carefully turned the lovely fabric inside out to adjust the seams. Her fingers felt something in one of the pockets. Her hand dove in and fished out a small photograph, a picture of a man and a woman. It looked as if it had been pulled from a frame. Maybe it wasn't important; still, it ought to be returned. But how? The guest had married and left Athens weeks ago.

Georgiana brought the photograph to her mistress.

Anna glanced at it with little curiosity and walked into Enno's study, handing it across the desk to him.

"This must be Cassandra's," she said. "Georgiana found it. But it's no use sending it out to Koropi. She and Max are leaving for Berlin any day now. It might miss her."

Enno nodded. "We'll mail it to her at Heidelberg once Max resumes his studies there after the Christmas holidays." He put the photograph down just as his secretary came into the library with the day's mail, placing the pile on the desk for Herr Ambassador's perusal.

The picture was promptly forgotten.

Chapter Forty-three

Stepping from the train in Berlin, Cassandra had barely set foot on the platform before she was smothered in a luxurious sable coat. She heard Max's introduction, redundant as it were because she knew this was his mother.

Releasing her daughter-in-law, Dorrit uttered a prepared welcome in Greek before turning and pulling forward a tall, dark-haired individual wearing a tailored camel overcoat. "This is Fritz!" she said, exhausting her inventory of Greek words.

Cassandra tipped her head back in order to meet Fritz's gaze and was momentarily unnerved by the intense curiosity she saw in his slate gray eyes. He was staring at her as though she were an oddity; still, she managed to repeat the German greeting she'd just mumbled into the expensive fur, reproducing the words Max had taught her with more confidence the second time around. Fritz was not as demonstrative as his mother and didn't embrace her; instead he reached for her hand, kissing it in a formal gesture.

Schmidt was waiting curbside with the black sedan. He greeted the new Frau von Renz with a cool, polite nod, reserving his warmth for Max. "It's good to have you home again Herr Baron!" he said with a conscious effort to address the new heir with an old title before he opened the car doors, took the luggage from the porter and stowed it in the trunk.

Cassandra sank into the soft dove gray leather cushions next to Dorrit; Max and Fritz took the jump seats facing the women. Schmidt got in behind the wheel and pulled the car into the midday traffic on Saarland Strasse. Turning left at Potsdamer Platz, he crossed the Cornelius Bridge spanning the picturesque Landwehr Canal, and now continued on to the Kurfurstendamm, which would take them west toward Grunewald.

147

During the drive and in order to generate some conversation between Cassandra and his family, Max tried his hand as interpreter. However, after tedious repetitions the essence was lost in translation, the dialogue went flat and eventually the four passengers rode along, *sans parler*, each acutely conscious of the language barrier separating them. During this uncomfortable silence, Dorrit stole several sideways glances at Max's bride. Her son's hasty marriage so far from home had given rise to all manner of speculation. Since the day of his telephone call, and in spite of Anna's endorsement of the girl, Dorrit had pushed her fears aside with various degrees of success.

Stymied by her own inability to communicate with Max's family, Cassandra kept her head turned toward the window, pretending to study the busy streets where pedestrians were bundled in dark woolens and furs as they hurried along the sidewalks. This clothing, along with the architecture - massive brick structures with steep green copper roofs - was vastly different from anything she was accustomed to. Moreover, the trees were brown and bare; the grass in the parks they passed was dormant and dull. The lack of color depressed Cassandra almost as much as the lack of conversation. She wished she knew what Max's mother was thinking. She knew the baroness was appraising her because she felt her stealthy glances like prickly heat at the back of her neck, heat that spread until finally, suffering unbearably, she could no longer stand it. She tore off her wool scarf and removed her gloves. When that failed to make her comfortable, she unbuttoned her heavy coat and threw it back over her shoulders, freeing her arms. Next she yanked off her hat with its silly ostrich feather that Anna claimed was a necessary fashion accessory, shook out her mane of black hair, and was finally able to breathe. Not accustomed to wool coats, hats, gloves and stockings, Cassandra wondered how anyone could wear such constricting garments on a daily basis.

She wished herself back in Koropi where she hadn't been scrutinized or been obliged to wear fancy clothes. During the entire time at the dig, she had worn men's work shirts and slacks, slept in a tent, and had taken her turn at the stew pot like everyone else. She sighed with profound longing to be back there. Max's colleagues had made her feel comfortable, each incorporating her into the work they were doing. Franz gave her some Greek textbooks and Martin demonstrated how to brush a patch of dirt to expose the smallest buried fragment. Ernst - her favorite in the group - had shown her his journals from the Valley of the Kings, translating whole sections for her benefit. Professor Krugg had also been supportive and had taught her how to label and sort artifacts. She loved the work and had quickly learned many of the Latin names used in classifications. Best of all, there was no need to speak German. Everyone had a command of Greek and was happy for the daily practice she afforded them. She sighed. The past six weeks had been heaven. Of course, she would only be in Berlin for a short visit. Surely she and this uncomfortable wardrobe that Anna had insisted on would survive the week. She glared down at her high-heeled shoes. In spite of their enormous price tag, they hurt something awful. An instant later they suffered the same fate as the hat, coat, scarf, and gloves. Kicking them off, she granted her toes the freedom they deserved.

In order to keep a straight face, all the while wondering what clothing Cassandra would shed next, Fritz toyed with his wristwatch, winding it and tapping the crystal as if the clockwork was defective. With each passing minute, he was growing more and more intrigued with his uninhibited and exotic sister-in-law.

"So, darling, what do you think of our fair city?" Max said in Greek, having taken no notice of Cassandra's state of undress. He wore his usual khakis, boots, sweater and a suede jacket that had seen better days.

"It's pretty much how Anna described it," she said, rather than admit she wasn't bowled over. "She told me Berlin is the Paris of the north." But, having never seen Paris, Cassandra wasn't really sure what that meant.

"Hah! Paris is but a poor cousin. I'll have you know that Berlin is four times the size, has taller buildings and more lakes, rivers, canals, forests, and public parks. Our Zoo, our Aquarium and Botanical Gardens are the largest of their kind anywhere in the world. We even have our very own French Riviera."

Frowning, Cassandra asked how that was possible when Berlin was nowhere near an ocean.

"Who needs an ocean when we have lakes with white beaches, sand dunes, and cresting waves."

"Now you're trying to fool a newcomer," Cassandra grinned.

"Not at all. Wait till you see Wannsee Lake. Plus, I'll show you the biggest department store on the continent and the most beautiful theaters. Our stage and cinema productions set the creative tone around the globe. Berlin is the financial center of Europe and, as Fritz will confirm, has three opera houses, countless concert halls, a world acclaimed Philharmonic, and no less than thirty museums housing everything from the greatest collection of Rembrandts to the ancient Pergamon Altar from West Turkey. A Greek kingdom at one time."

"I'd love to see that altar," Cassandra said, finally impressed because since her experience in Koropi old relics appealed to her.

"It will be our first excursion," Max promised.

As the car drove through a large intersection, Cassandra craned her neck, staring at an enormous cathedral with a tall spire.

"That's the famous Kaiser Wilhelm Memorial Church," Max explained. "Not named after our last Kaiser...our exiled monarch, but after his grandfather, a more popular emperor. As you can see, it takes up an entire city block. People travel from all corners of the world just to hear the choir."

"So it's world famous?"

"The world and beyond." Max grinned. "When the choir sings, the angels in heaven turn green with envy."

Chapter Forty-four

Having celebrated a quiet family Christmas, Dorrit decided to invite a few close friends for supper on New Year's Eve so they could meet her daughter-in-law.

As Cassandra walked down the prodigiously polished flight of mahogany stairs with Max on this last evening of 1927, she was again profoundly moved by the splendor of his home. A magnificent chandelier with hundreds of faceted crystals hung from the high rotunda-like ceiling, exquisite paintings adorned the walls, and her steps were cushioned in thick Persian carpet runners. Maids catered to her every comfort, only Schmidt remained aloof, but it never occurred to her to wonder why. She did not know that the butler was not reconciled with the mixing of the bloods and that her dusky coloring troubled him. Keeping German blood pure was an attitude Schmidt had embraced after hearing a man of the people, Adolf Hitler, speak at Pharus Hall, where he had warned the audience about outside influences; a message Schmidt took to heart.

In a tailspin about the evening ahead, Cassandra worried about her ponderous mission, that of winning over a group of strangers whose language she didn't speak. "I wish the von Steigerts had come to Berlin for the holidays," she said as she and Max crossed the hall toward the library. "I'd have someone to talk to. My German phrases will run dry in three minutes."

"At that point, darling, just look bored. It works every time. My mother's guests will talk themselves into a stupor, trying to be clever. The less you interrupt, the more they will sing your prominence as a delightful conversationalist."

"They are that easy to fool?" Cassandra said, thinking his suggestion might have merit.

"Yes, and since they're bound to discuss politics I will look bored

151

as well."

"You don't like politics?"

Max shook his head. "I find that I'm equally irritated by conversations leaning toward reinstating Kaiser Wilhelm to those expounding the genius of a nonentity like Adolf Hitler." Max strolled over to the cart behind Johann's desk and poured a glass of port from a crystal decanter. "Fritz claims I have no convictions. Perhaps he's right. I admit to having no solutions to the problems that have dogged Germany since the Great War, so I prefer to distance myself and let others hassle it out. As long as no one starts another war, I'll sleep soundly."

Dorrit and Fritz walked into the library.

"Cassandra, how lovely you look!" Dorrit cried, so animated that it needed no translation. Cassandra had pulled her black hair back from her face and gathered it into a neat chignon, which gave her young face an air of maturity. "Your dress is stunning!" Dorrit came closer and admired the rose-colored velvet gown; its neckline enhanced by a double strand of luminous pearls Max had given her for Christmas.

"Anna helped in the selection. Before Max and I went out to Koropi, she took me shopping." Cassandra spoke slowly in fragmented German, all the while admiring Dorrit's green gown and wishing she had the vocabulary to compliment it. Dorrit had worn black the entire week, and Cassandra was wondering at the sudden change, when her mother-in-law explained herself.

"My husband liked to see me wearing green. Tonight I'm wearing it in his memory. He would want this particular evening to be festive. He proposed to me on a New Year's Eve and would w...want..." Suddenly Dorrit's voice broke and her face took on a strange far-off look while a cold mist blurred her eyes. They glimmered with torment for a moment before she spun around and walked briskly over to the fireplace, now turning all her energy on the hearth where an earlier fire had sunk into a small pile of smoldering ashes.

"Oh, dear! Where is Schmidt?" She wrung her hands. "The house will be cold as a cellar if he doesn't tend to the fires. Gerlinde has a bit of congestion. She and Karl-Heinz will be arriving any minute now. After the long drive from Bernau, a chilly house could be the death of her."

Schmidt heard his mistress from his station in the hall, one he immediately abandoned to attend to the fireplaces.

"Come!" Max took his mother's arm and left the library, walking toward the drawing room where servants were preparing for the pre-dinner hour, setting up buckets of ice holding champagne bottles. "Let's have a private toast to 1928 before your boisterous high hats intrude with their garish greetings."

"Max, please! Try to be civil tonight or those you so freely call high hats might be tempted to pity Cassandra for having married a tiresome bore."

"They wouldn't recognize a bore," Max grinned. "They've been associating with each other for years without catching on."

"Hush your mouth!" Despite the admonition, Dorrit's light laughter could be heard echoing in the hall.

Fritz turned to Cassandra and offered his arm. She took it and, crossing the hall, decided he looked particularly elegant in black evening attire. Only three years her senior, she had grown devoted to him during this past week. He was determined to learn Greek and at the same time help her with German. They had spent many hours, playing tug-of-war with a lexicon in the library while Max was at the university, organizing his thesis. Fritz had laughed at his own mistakes but never at hers, and he always politely turned away whenever she kicked off her shoes and pulled up her skirts to peel off her stockings in front of the fire, choosing comfort over convention.

During these language sessions, she had studied the various family pictures displayed in the library and was sadly reminded of the lost photograph of her parents. She didn't know what had become of it, but figured it must have fallen from her pocket during that desperate flight from Aiyina.

"Will you play for us tonight?" she now asked Fritz in broken German, remembering how much she had enjoyed listening to him playing the piano Christmas Eve.

"Only if you wish to chase the guests away."

"If the discussions get too political," Cassandra grinned, "I'm sure Max would be grateful if you could."

Chapter Forty-five

Athens...

Ari Chandros leaned forward in his chair, handing some papers across the ambassador's cluttered desk, documents that would ensure preferential treatment when his board of directors petitioned for access to the lucrative South American shipping routes now dominated by *Deutsche Sud*.

Reflecting on the astronomical fees these Greeks were willing to pay, Enno von Steigert leafed through the papers, delighted to deliver this boon to Berlin. This was a halcyon day in the life of a diplomat. "Everything appears to be in order," he said, silently tallying up the sums while moving aside some correspondence to clear a spot for this new important material. In the wake of this jostling, a long forgotten photograph slid to the edge of the desk.

Ari Chandros' eyes flitted across the picture with little curiosity. Suddenly the breath caught in his throat. Stunned, he leaned forward in his seat, his eyes peering down at a familiar face. *Peter...?* No. It couldn't be. He had been dead for years. But if not him, then who? The likeness was astounding. And who was the young woman in the photograph? Much as he tried, Ari Chandros couldn't place her. But he *did* recognize Peter. He appeared to be a few years older than when he'd last seen him, but there was no mistaking him. It was Peter. How on earth did Ambassador von Steigert come to have this picture? His mind in a maelstrom, Ari Chandros began to feel dizzy; beads of moisture collected on his brow. He reached into his suit pocket for a handkerchief, wiping it across his face.

Enno von Steigert noticed his visitor's sudden pallor. "Are you all right?" he inquired solicitously. "Can I get you something to drink?"

Ari Chandros shook his head and stuffed the handkerchief back into his pocket. The ambassador rose from his chair to open a window. "We need some air," he said. "It's stuffy in here. Rather warm for April." He sat back down and again eyed his guest. The man looked ill. Enno wondered if he might be changing his mind about the large sums he was agreeing to, sums that would have made King Croesus lightheaded. "Are you sure you're all right?" he asked again.

"Yes...yes. I'm fine." Ari Chandros waved his hand, dismissing the ambassador's concern. "The open window feels good. Thank you."

"Well, then..." Enno got back to business. "I'll have my assistant make copies of these documents." He touched a silent buzzer on his desk.

As the shock of seeing Peter with the strange woman slowly began to wear off, Ari Chandros was overcome with curiosity. "Tell me," he said after the ambassador's assistant had fetched the papers and left the office, promising to return shortly with copies, "where did you get this photograph?"

"Pardon?"

"This picture." Ari Chandros pointed to where it lay at the edge of the desk. "Do you know these people?"

"Oh, let me see." Enno picked it up and studied it. "Hmm, no, I don't recognize them. My wife might. I will be glad to ask her."

"No. That won't be necessary." Ari Chandros leaned back in his chair, suspecting he was imagining things. It had been a long day and he had slept poorly last night after being awoken at midnight from his suite at the Grand Bretagne by a false fire alarm that had roused the entire hotel.

"Come to think of it," Enno said, suddenly remembering something. "I believe one of our maids found this picture. Oh yes! Now I recall. It's Cassandra's. I assume this is a picture of her parents. They are both dead. Good gracious, I've been remiss. I was supposed to have returned it to her months ago. She was our houseguest last November. She married the son of very close friends of mine."

November? The girl in the yellow dress! As the memory of that brief encounter flooded back, Ari Chandros again fished out his handkerchief, wiped his face and asked, "Did she tell you the people in this photograph were her parents?"

"No. My wife and I assumed it when, as I said, a maid found this picture after Cassandra left. If you'll pardon me for asking, is there something about it that..."

"No! No!"

155

"Actually," Enno said, "and this is clearly a coincidence, of course, but Cassandra's maiden name was Chandros." He grinned at his guest. "I don't suppose she's some distant cousin of yours? Her birth name was Cassandra Helen Chandros. She came to us from Aiyina as Cassandra Vrachnos. It was her married name."

"She's no cousin." Ari Chandros shook his head. "But didn't you just say that she married the son of a close friend of yours? Was he Greek?"

"No, German. Max von Renz. We had the wedding right here at the embassy. However, when she arrived here with Max from Aiyina, she had just been married to a man named Dimitri Vrachnos. A despicable character. The marriage was annulled and we've had quite a time with the fellow. I won't go into details, but it has included exhuming bodies. He and his cousin are behind bars here in Athens."

Ari Chandros had stopped listening. He'd heard enough. There could be no doubt about it. This was a photograph of Peter. The woman was obviously his wife and they'd had a daughter. But what about the doomed trawler?

Noting the Greek's still furrowed brow, Enno made a suggestion. "We can clear up any question you might have regarding this photograph. I'll be glad to contact Cassandra in Heidelberg. Her husband is finishing his doctorate at the university there."

"No." Ari Chandros shifted uncomfortably in his chair. "For a moment I thought the man in the picture looked familiar. People occasionally resemble one another. There's nothing here but an uncanny likeness. Let's drop the subject. May I ask you a favor?"

"By all means."

"Don't discuss this with anyone. Especially not with the young woman in question. I certainly wouldn't want to trouble her with my silly notions. Suppose rumors begin to circulate that I'm seeing ghosts. It could jeopardize our South American venture." He winked at the ambassador, securing his silence by reminding him of the lucrative deal they were signing.

Chapter Forty-six

A key rattled in the door lock.

"Is that you, Max?" Cassandra called out. Curled up on the couch under a small dormer window with a book on conversational German, she didn't attempt to get up and open the door. It was too much trouble these days.

"I should hope so," Max grinned as he walked in, using his heel to kick the door shut behind him. He dropped a pile of books on a chair before he came over to give Cassandra a kiss and a playful pat on her bulging stomach. "You haven't given the key to someone else, have you?"

"I can't imagine who would want to visit me in this condition," she said, watching Max walk across the room to the sink.

He was finished for the day. There was a seminar tonight, but he might skip it. He glanced at his watch. Six o'clock. Half an hour till dinner. This boarding house catered to students and served supper early. The delicious smell of sauerbraten had tempted him during his climb up the crooked staircase to the garret room on the third floor.

"Something odd happened today, Max."

"Really?" He shrugged out of his jacket, tossed it over the metal bed frame, and washed his hands. "What, sweetheart?"

"Someone followed me."

"Followed you? Where?"

"All around. No matter where I was today, I kept seeing the same person."

"Ah-hah! A student with his hand over his heart and his tongue hanging out?"

"With this disgusting waistline?" Cassandra made a terrible face and adjusted her navy dress over her midriff. She'd been reduced to

157

wearing dark colors because maternity garments only came in shades of gray, brown and navy, the latter being the only one that didn't turn her complexion sour. She was not at all happy about being pregnant, had no interest in children, and was determined this would be her only one. In fact, at the very next opportunity she planned to speak privately with Anna von Steigert who'd managed to remain childless. There must be a secret. Cassandra intended to discover it.

"Waistline or lack thereof, you still turn everyone's head," Max said. "If not a student, who followed you?"

"A man."

Max laughed and fell into a chair. "I thought so. Just because you've lost your figure doesn't mean you've lost your charm."

"Really, Max, be serious. I'm trying to tell you something."

"All right. I'm listening. A man followed you. Go on..."

"He was Greek."

"Ah, a compatriot?"

"Yes. I was at the book café on Schloss Strasse when he introduced himself. I had just bought a cup of coffee and this." Cassandra held up the book she was reading. "Of course, I wasn't a bit surprised to see him because, like I just said, he was everywhere today. I first saw him outside our building when I left here around noon. That's why I felt he was following me."

"Hmm, I see how you might have gotten that idea."

"Still, I was surprised when he pulled up a chair and sat down at my table when the café was practically empty. He must have noted my startled look because he immediately apologized, explaining that he was visiting Heidelberg, strolling around the historic sites and hoping to find someone who spoke Greek and could tell him about the campus. His knowledge of German was poor. He figured me as a fellow citizen and had followed me, waiting for an opportunity to chat. I told him I knew very little about the university because I was not a student. Still, he stayed and talked. He must have had half a dozen cups of coffee. His hand shook a lot. From the caffeine, I guess. He asked where I was from and posed some rather personal questions."

"Really? Such as?"

"Oh, you know…what it was like growing up on Aiyina. He also wanted to know about my parents. *And* my grandparents. He asked if I had family anywhere else in Greece?"

"Perhaps he was one of those genealogy enthusiasts."

"Could be. If so, he didn't learn much. I explained that both my parents were dead and that I'd never known any of my grandparents because my father came to Aiyina as an orphan and my mother's parents died before I was born. He asked about the circumstances of my father's death, and I told him. Of course he soon realized he was being too nosy and apologized, saying he'd gotten carried away because it was so nice to speak Greek after days of struggling with the German language."

"Where was *he* from? One of the other islands?"

"No. The mainland. He runs a shoe business in Athens."

"What was his name?"

"He didn't give his name."

"What did he think of Heidelberg?"

"He liked the old historic buildings. The fortress in particular."

"That figures. It's a favorite with tourists." Max loosened his collar and rolled up his sleeves. "I'm starved. What do you say? Shall we go downstairs?"

Chapter Forty-seven

When Ari Chandros left Heidelberg and returned to his home on Khios, he was satisfied that his concerns had been addressed.

Peter, his younger brother, had not died in 1910 as the family had been told weeks after he left Khios in a fit of youthful rage following a bitter argument with their father. The two were constantly at odds. Peter's abrupt departure surprised no one. He had run away before, the first time when he was only twelve. However, he was always found and brought back home, until that last time when he disappeared without a trace. The family eventually learned that he had stowed away on a trawler that, tragically, went down at sea. That information, as it now turned out, had been incomplete. Peter must have been discovered during the voyage and put ashore - the common fate of stowaways - and when the trawler sank in a fierce storm days later, no one survived to tell that a young man had been set off on Aiyina. Had Nicholas Chandros known, he would have spent his fortune to woo his son back home. Unbeknownst to the family, Peter had remained on Aiyina, married a local girl, and by all accounts lived happily for a number years before the sea *did* claim him.

But why had Peter settled on Aiyina? Was freedom so sweet that poverty became an adventure? Did his foolish pride prevent him from returning home? Did his wife refuse to leave Aiyina? Did he ever wonder why no one came looking for him? Did he know that his father believed him dead? Of course, those questions didn't need answers. Too much time had passed for Ari to be curious about his brother's motives. More important issues were at stake, which was why he had single-handedly orchestrated the meeting with Cassandra. He could not risk hiring a private investigator; word might get back to Nicholas Chandros. Therefore, he had played it extremely safe, traveling under an assumed name, dying his hair gray at the temples, and wearing dark-rimmed glasses for his meeting with Cassandra to avoid any chance that she might remember him from the ambassador's residence last November, or in the future recognize his picture in some press release concerning his shipping line. All this was done in order to learn if she had any knowledge of her relatives on Khios and, if so, might try to claim her inheritance in due time. It was crucial that Ari deflect any ambition on her part because he had no intention of sharing his own birthright. The girl had a striking likeness to his mother, practically a carbon copy, and it rattled him that Peter had honored their mother's memory by naming his daughter after her.

In her day, Cassandra Helen Chandros had been a classic and acclaimed beauty. Peter and Ari were small boys when she died, but Ari remembered her well. How could he not? To this day, her portraits hung in every room of his father's house. Nicholas Chandros had never remarried because in his own eccentric way he lived with her still.

When Peter took off it hurt him to the point of illness and after tracing his youngest son to the lost trawler it nearly killed him. Despite their differences and many arguments, Peter was his favorite, and it wasn't until he was officially declared dead that Ari felt comfortable as sole heir. Today Nicholas Chandros, venerable patriarch, was a happy man, relatively speaking. Why resurrect old and painful memories with the sudden appearance of Peter's child? Peter was dead, nothing could change that, and Nicholas Chandros had long since been blessed with a grandson and two granddaughters. He didn't need another. In view of past wrongs, perceived or otherwise, he might decide to favor Peter's child, even though Ari's children had spent years doting on him.

Chapter Forty-eight

Following Max's final term at Heidelberg, culminating in his successful exams, he and Cassandra arrived in Bernau in August to await the birth of their child. Once there - and although Max talked about the advantages of Berlin hospitals - Cassandra refused to budge. This was where she wanted to spend the rest of her confinement, far from the glare of fancy city folk. Here she could go barefooted, trudge across lawns and meadows, dragging her ungainly body. She felt uncommonly ugly, couldn't wait to have this baby business over with and lived in the vain hope that Max hadn't noticed how swollen she'd become. She could only wonder at Fritz's respectful glances and the frequency with which he appeared out of thin air to accompany her on her long walks. Dressed in neat slacks and a shirt rolled up to the elbows, he casually fell into step with her just as she was about to start down the tree-lined driveway or across the fields. She suspected he found the slow pace tedious and would have preferred to be out riding with Max. But he never let on. He adjusted his longer strides to her inelegant duck walk, practiced his Greek, and appeared not the least bit embarrassed to be seen with a whale. In fact, he often suggested that they stop in at the Black Wolf in the village, where he lingered over a beer while she drank apple cider.

Cassandra was resolved to have her figure back once the baby was born, even if it meant starvation. And she also intended to go along with Max on his next expedition. She hadn't yet figured out what to do with the baby and didn't dwell on it because it'd be premature to plan before the child was born. It might not survive; a possibility that didn't trouble her.

Except for leaving delicate surgery procedures to those with steadier hands, Ben Tarnoff never exhibited signs of slowing down. Therefore, it was no surprise that he arrived in record time the night in late August when Dorrit telephoned him in Berlin to report that Cassandra was in labor and that Max had raced to Ladeburg for a midwife.

Ben arrived in Bernau with hours to spare and helped Cassandra deliver a healthy boy. Gertrude came by train the following day with Fraulein Heller, an experienced nurse with recommendations from a dozen discriminating clients, which clearly gave her airs. She had barely set foot inside the barony before instructing the kitchen staff that she wished to have all her meals served in her quarters and required mint tea with lightly buttered *schoonbrot* brought up to her room every afternoon at three o'clock. She also demanded fresh flowers on her night table, explaining that she was not particular about the blooms available, as long as they were changed every three days. Once these demands were spelled out, she seemed to remember that she was an employee and climbed the stairs to the nursery.

As Dorrit watched the rail thin middle-aged woman, her silver blond hair fastened in a tight bun, walk up the wide staircase, she questioned Gert's judgment. This nurse appeared much too stern to be caring for a baby. However, after unpacking and donning a white uniform and cap, Fraulein Heller looked less severe.

The next morning as Ben prepared to return to Berlin, Dorrit convinced Gertrude to remain behind for a few days. No sooner had the cloud of dust settled behind his car, when the two women decided to visit Gerlinde.

"We'll surprise her," Dorrit said, linking arms with Gertrude as they walked over to one of the cars parked in the courtyard. Dorrit climbed in behind the wheel of the convertible.

"When did you learn to drive?" Gert asked in amazement, as she settled into the passenger seat.

"A few weeks ago. I wanted to be free to go visiting and not always depend on Heinrich. Especially now that he needs to be available for Nurse Heller when she shops for baby supplies."

Gerlinde was delighted with the impromptu visit of dear friends. The weather was sunny and warm, and the three women settled down on the patio, where Karl-Heinz shortly joined them for the midday meal. As he stepped onto the terrace in a burst of masculine presence, Dorrit half expected to see Johann coming up behind him, a happy anticipation that lasted only an instant. Karl-Heinz greeted the ladies with his usual gusto and, grinning broadly, walked around the table toward Bernau's newest *Oma*.

"I'm surprised you left the nursery long enough to come visit us," he said and bent down to plant a big congratulatory kiss on her cheek. "How's the little scion? I hear he's to be named Peter Johann."

"Yes..." Dorrit's throat tightened. Karl-Heinz had come directly from the stables and the familiar scent of horses and old leather triggered a desperate loss inside her. She felt chilled as if the sun had suddenly ducked behind a cloud, leaving the terrace enveloped in a gloomy shade. Although surrounded by her dearest friends, loneliness cut through her like a cold blade. She sagged in the chair under the weight of her memories.

Oh...Johann...only last summer...

Realizing Dorrit was grappling with heartbreak, Gerlinde eyed the decanted Gewurtstraminer on the table. "Karl-Heinz," she said a little too loudly. "We need a toast!"

Taking his cue, Karl-Heinz filled four wine glasses and filled the environs with a string of bountiful salutations to the newest little citizen of Bernau. By the time the first course - herring in cream sauce with pearl onions - arrived at the table, Dorrit's mood was restored.

"Nurse Heller suspects that Peter is the most precocious infant she's ever had the pleasure to care for," Gertrude told everyone; further lifting Dorrit's spirits.

However, as pleasant as the subject of a newborn was, the conversation eventually shifted from a baby's sweet gurgles to the fire and brimstone speeches of a slightly built man with brown hair and a ridiculous narrow mustache.

"Herr Hitler has left the dark beer halls and come out into the open," Karl-Heinz remarked, leaning back in his chair while a maid removed his empty plate. "But his oratory makes no more sense in broad daylight than it did below ground."

"And it's not enhanced by constant repetition either," Gert added. "He delights in circling around a small core of primitive ideas. Of course, I suppose his promise of full employment bears repeating."

"I doubt he'll succeed where other politicians have failed," Gerlinde said. "And, let's face it, joblessness is just one of many, many problems. He has yet to spell out how he plans to cure any one of Germany's ills."

"Yes, the list is long," Dorrit agreed. "So far he's only making lavish promises and reminding us that the entire world is suffering. As if that's supposed to make us feel better."

"He'll have to come up with some concrete ideas to help solve our economic mess or he'll fade into obscurity like all the other wannabes," Karl-Heinz sniped. "Promises won't do it. Promises don't provide jobs."

"But it draws crowds," Gertrude said. "Last week people stood spellbound on Leipziger Platz for hours, listening to him."

"You went to hear Herr Hitler speak?" Gerlinde asked.

"No, I just happened to be in the area. I was meeting a friend on Voss Strasse. We were planning to have lunch at Kruse's but changed our minds and left the area rather than fight the multitudes. I've never before seen so many people gathered in one spot. Some were so moved by his words that tears were streaming down their faces."

"The man's a born actor," Karl-Heinz snorted. "He should be playing Hamlet. Not politics."

"I'm sure the tears stemmed from the music, not the message," Dorrit suggested. "He never begins a speech until everyone's been whipped up with a lot of colorful marching bands. Germans are fond of entertainment and Herr Hitler provides it."

"Which explains the crowds," Gerlinde said.

When lunch was over and Dorrit and Gertrude got up to leave, Karl-Heinz and Gerlinde walked them to the front of the house where both were astounded to see Dorrit climb into the driver's seat and turn the key in the ignition.

"Where's Heinrich?" Karl-Heinz shouted over the roar of the engine, impressed with her newfangled prowess. "Don't tell me you've fired him?"

"No. His job is safe."

"Then why are you driving?" Karl-Heinz was scratching his head.

"For amusement." Dorrit grinned, tying a scarf securely around her head. "In Berlin it's becoming quite common to see women behind the wheel. Of course I only plan to drive here in the country."

Karl-Heinz looked askance at his wife, hoping she wouldn't get any ideas. Reading his expression, Dorrit worked the clutch and winked at Gerlinde. "If you feel like giving it a try, I'll teach you." Her foot hit the accelerator.

Gerlinde and Karl-Heinz jumped clear as the large touring car lunged forward.

Chapter Forty-nine

When a premature and freak cold snap threatened the harvest, farm machinery was quickly primed and Max and Fritz joined Klausen along with two-dozen field hands working from dawn to dusk to bring in the wheat before the stalks snapped from the shock of the weather. The speedy and decisive action saved the crop and, disaster averted, the family returned to Berlin.

Once there, Max made no mention of resuming his fieldwork. Instead, he moved his family into a spacious apartment on Unter den Linden near the university where he took a position as assistant professor at the College of Archaeology. However, settling into a lecture routine was not in his nature. By November he was corresponding with Howard Carter and shortly received a wire inviting him back to the Valley of the Kings. Since Cassandra was adamant about going along, they discussed the idea of leaving Peter at home in the care of Nurse Heller and Frau Berenstahl, their housekeeper. Cassandra had no qualms about the baby remaining in Berlin. In fact, she frequently had to trouble herself to feel any maternal love, which was not to say that she was displeased with him. He was quite cute and didn't cry much; still, she'd never dream of staying behind with him.

In mid December, Dorrit and Lillian Eckart met for lunch in midtown at the trendy Hotel Eden, afterwards browsing in the expensive boutiques on Tauentzienstrasse, where some exquisitely embroidered Madeira tablecloths in the display windows at Mosse & Grunfeld caught Lillian's eye.

"A perfect Christmas gift for Elsie!" she cried, pulling Dorrit inside the store. "She'll need several sets for her trousseau." Lillian's eyes fairly danced, seeing a case full of the lavish linen. "Once she is the wife of a diplomat, she'll be expected to entertain."

166

The Eckarts had recently announced their daughter's engagement to a dashing French consul ten years her senior. Elsie and Jean Paul were introduced at a Friday night embassy ball, found each other in the same pew during Sunday services in the Franzosischer Dom, and were betrothed the following Wednesday. Of course, in view of Elsie's age, Lillian would have an entire year in which to plan an extravagant wedding.

From Tauentzienstrasse, the two ladies rounded the corner on Kurfurstendamm, stopping in at Friedlander's where Dorrit picked up several pieces of the von Renz jewelry she'd had reset for Cassandra. While she was inspecting the workmanship, Lillian impulsively bought diamond cuff links for Kurt. "They'll have to be his only Christmas present," she said, mortified with the hefty price tag.

At a children's shop a few doors down, Dorrit became as impulsive as her friend, purchasing several costly outfits for Peter, each more frivolous and dainty than useful or appropriate. "But after all," she shrugged, "a grandmother is *supposed* to spoil the child."

"I couldn't agree more," Lillian said, stroking a blue satin bonnet with three rows of ruffled lace. "Come to think of it, when do I get another peek?"

Dorrit took the hint. "Let's stop in now. I'd like to drop off these clothes right away. The way Peter is growing, he'll soon resent wearing ribbons and lace."

"Are you going to give Cassandra the jewelry now as well?" Lillian pointed to the long narrow box tucked securely under Dorrit's arm.

"Yes. I want her to have it before Christmas. Not that she needs precious stones to sparkle, mind you, and Max has bought her some nice pieces, but his taste in jewelry is much too conservative. This holiday season I want Cassandra to outshine every female in Berlin. With the exception of your Elsie, of course." Dorrit laughed, a smile lingering on her lips as she recalled a New Year's ball of long ago where an insecure girl in the company of a much too handsome escort had worn a homemade gown and pearl earrings so small that no one noticed them. Among the haughty and bejeweled women that night, only Lillian had befriended her. Remembering the occasion as if it were yesterday, Dorrit put her arm around her friend's waist, squeezing her fondly as they left the store and crossed the sidewalk to where Schmidt was waiting with the car.

Taking a shortcut along the Ost-West Achse through Tiergarten, that vast city woodland in the center of Berlin, Schmidt drove the ladies toward Unter den Linden, soon leaving the park and passing under the Brandenburg Gate. Spotting the French Embassy on Pariser Platz, Lillian smiled inwardly, pleased that Elsie had made such a good match. Of course, once she was married, the Eckart's townhouse would become intolerably empty. It was already lonely. Kurt was often late for dinner; sometimes he didn't show up at all. Since resigning from Wirchow and devoting himself full time to politics, his hours were erratic.

"Kurt's so frightfully busy these days," she mused out loud, turning toward Dorrit with a petulant expression. "But I suppose it comes with being one of Germany's new power brokers. His schedule is as brutal as back when he was a young resident."

"That's what he gets for affiliating himself with the Nazis," Dorrit said. She had known for years that Kurt hankered for a role in public life, but was surprised earlier today when Lillian told her that he had joined the National Socialist German Workers' Party; a questionable coalition attracting the unemployed and disgruntled blue collar workers. "I still can't imagine what Kurt has in common with them."

"Initially, I also thought his choice was odd," Lillian admitted. "But he claims it's the only political party where he can get in on the ground floor. All the others are top heavy with managers. Of course, we both realize the membership is not exactly...well, whatever..." She shrugged and continued. "But that's not what's important right now. Our country's recovery is vital. We mustn't lose sight of that. We've suffered far too long with a sick economy. With no end in sight, people are tired of strikes, bread lines, and hyperinflation. The fact that Germany is still floundering ten years after the end of the Great War is scandalous." Listening, it was clear to Dorrit that Lillian was simply paraphrasing Kurt. She could never initiate such rhetoric herself; political elocution did not fit into her realm of conversation. "It's high time we bury the long-festering misery," she droned on. "Rid ourselves of foreign demands for our lifeblood and get on with some real reconstruction. And for that purpose we must try new methods. New leadership! New ideas!"

Dorrit held up her hands in mock surrender. "I hear you," she said. "I just can't abide Adolf Hitler. Your own cousin, Karl-Heinz, calls him a second-rate actor."

"Is that so?" Lillian raised her finely penciled eyebrows. "Well, we can't take Karl-Heinz seriously. He's lived in the country his entire life. He's out of touch. Did I tell you that I met Herr Hitler?"

"No."

"I must have. Didn't I tell you during lunch?" When Dorrit shook her head, Lillian grinned, saying, "Well, I guess I was saving the best for last. I met him and I can report that he is gracious, warm, and intelligent."

Dorrit gave her a dubious look.

"He *is*. I spoke with him. Kurt and I attended a reception on Prinz Albrechtstrasse a few nights ago and Herr Hitler was absolutely charming. He greeted all the ladies with gallantry and asked such sweet and considerate questions. He's concerned about our children. He adores children. It's a pity he's a bachelor. Of course he may not remain one for long. A dozen women fell in love with him on the spot." Lillian dug into her purse and was suddenly fanning herself. Hot flashes, Dorrit suspected, or else she was one of the besotted and the memory of Herr Hitler's charm brought heat to her cheeks.

Lillian folded her fan and put it away. "Before the evening ended he gave a clever speech. Witty and grave at the same time. He spoke so sensibly. Nothing at all like the loud rhetoric one hears at his public appearances. On our way home, Kurt explained that I'd seen the man as he truly is. Soft spoken and knowledgeable. His rousing speeches, the music, the marches are staged for the press and for foreign consumption."

"And for people wanting free entertainment," Dorrit said, slipping her hands into her gloves trimmed in black Persian lamb, which matched her coat. They were nearing their destination and she gathered her packages together. "Our tottering economy has pushed a huge percentage of the population to the brink of poverty, which begs the question: if they all thirst for Herr Hitler's message why is his coalition such an insignificant bloc?"

"I don't know. But Kurt says they will soon take control of the Reichstag."

"God forbid! I can't imagine it'll come to that. I certainly hope not."

"Maybe if you met him, you'd change your mind."

"*What?*" Dorrit turned to stare at her friend.

"Why not? Kurt can arrange it. There are lots of receptions. You can come with us. Once you speak with Herr Hitler, you'll see how charming he is."

"I already know he's charming. How else can he make young women swoon and old women cry? But do you really believe he'd want a middle-aged Russian Jew to darken his doorstep? Let alone drink his champagne? He talks a great deal about the advantages of being pure German."

169

"Really, Dorrit! You're only half Jewish and your other half is blue-blooded Russian. Anyway, your origins are not important. When you married Johann you became German and titled beyond doubt. Herr Hitler will be flattered to meet a baroness."

Woe be it for me to flatter the lowborn Adolf, Dorrit thought and dropped the subject.

Chapter Fifty

"This expensive building really ought to install an elevator," Lillian grumbled a short while later, leaning on the banister to catch her breath after walking up two flights of stairs.

"We're just getting old," Dorrit suggested with a grin.

Lillian's eyes flashed and she immediately found the fortitude to attack the last set of stairs.

The housekeeper opened the door and smiled broadly the minute she recognized the baroness. "Come in! Please!" She stood aside to allow the women to enter.

"How are you, Frau Berenstahl?" Dorrit walked into the apartment ahead of Lillian and put her parcels on the telephone table in the hall.

"Very well, thank you." While the housekeeper busied herself, hanging their coats in the closet, Dorrit and Lillian glanced through a door that stood ajar to a pantry leading to the kitchen, where they saw Cassandra sitting at a utility table, drinking tea with Nurse Heller. Lillian pursed her lips and raised an eyebrow, making it crystal clear what she thought of socializing with the help. Dorrit ignored her. She'd bite off her tongue before uttering a word against Max's wife.

Cassandra rushed into the hall the minute Frau Berenstahl announced the visitors. After embracing Dorrit and shaking Lillian's hand, she explained that Max was not at home and apologized for his absence. "I'm awfully sorry," she said. "He was here for lunch, but dashed off to a meeting having to do with the expansion of the Egyptian Museum. The board is picking his brain about his experiences in the Valley of the Kings. They're hoping some of Tutankhamen's treasures can be loaned to Berlin."

"My dear girl," Dorrit patted her daughter-in-law's cheek. "We

171

didn't come to see Max." It was obvious that in Cassandra's life only Max mattered and it didn't occur to her that they had come visiting, never expecting to find him at home. "We just stopped in to see you and little Peter. And to give you these." Dorrit pointed to the parcels on the hall table. "The long box is for you. It's the necklace and earrings I showed you a while back. Everything has been reset and polished. The other packages are some outfits for Peter. You can open everything after we've had our visit. Now, tell me, how is the little darling?"

"Sleeping, but I'll wake him."

"No, don't disturb him."

"Actually…" Cassandra consulted her watch, "he has slept long enough." She turned to Frau Berenstahl. "Please tell Nurse Heller to get Peter up."

The housekeeper scurried back to the kitchen and Cassandra took her guests into a large but empty living room. The four tall windows, each with a Juliet balcony, allowed for a wonderful view of Unter den Linden, but the room itself begged for thick carpets and plump sofas and chairs. Walking across the floor, their steps echoing plaintively on the bare parquet, Lillian immediately offered the services of her decorator. Cassandra didn't pick up on it, merely explaining that the bedrooms and Peter's nursery were furnished, which was all they needed at the moment.

Frau Berenstahl came back, carrying two small spindly chairs, which she arranged near one of the windows where a lone coffee table and one upright chair stood in dire need of company. She told the ladies that the lights on the royal palace across the street would soon be lit and be a pretty sight. Then she hurried back to the kitchen, promising to bring refreshments. On her way out, she switched on a ceiling light; it was only three-thirty but dusk came early in December.

Dorrit sat down on one of the spindly chairs with a bright pink cushion; she figured it'd been fetched from one of the bedrooms and smiled inwardly, wondering what had possessed Cassandra to chose such an extravagant color. Dorrit had learned some time ago that her daughter-in-law liked plain, unpretentious things, and was not surprised today to see her wearing basic gray slacks and a blue shirt like the ones Max wore.

Good as her word, Frau Berenstahl shortly rolled in a tea cart and a plate of delicious almond butter cookies, evoking raves from the two visitors. A while later when Nurse Heller brought Peter in, dressed in his Sunday best, Cassandra told her to hand him directly to Dorrit; it was clear she was itching to hold him. Indeed, her eyes grew misty the minute he was in her arms. Dorrit loved this child with all her heart and decided that Cassandra could drink whiskey with the scullery maid if she so chose. Anyone who could produce such a precious child and make a profligate roué like Max behave himself, need not add the observances of certain social sanctions to her accomplishments.

"Cassandra needs the company of young women her own age," Lillian suggested tactfully when the two friends left the building an hour later, Lillian still struggling with the kitchen *tête-à-tête* that had greeted them upon arrival. "Now that she speaks German she can socialize. I'll tell Elsie to call her."

"I don't expect she will be in Berlin long enough to make friends," Dorrit said pensively.

"What do you mean?"

"I mean that she and Max will soon be off. Didn't you notice how animated she became during tea when she told us about Max's association with that British archaeologist."

"Howard Carter?"

"Yes. I'm sure they're planning to go to Egypt."

"They? You mean Cassandra will go along?"

"Of course."

"What about the baby?"

"They'll leave him home."

"*What?*" Lillian was shocked.

"Why not? For generations the British have gone abroad and left their children behind."

"Yes, but Peter is so young!" Lillian protested. "Smart as he is, he's not yet ready for boarding school."

Lillian had forgotten her silk scarf in the apartment on Unter den Linden. It was discovered on the hall table among Dorrit's gifts when Max returned home from his meetings.

"She'll think she lost it," Cassandra said. "I better call her."

"Don't bother. I'll return it. I need some exercise after being cooped up in that stuffy museum all afternoon." Max grabbed the scarf and was out the door.

The Eckart's townhouse was only a few blocks away. He returned shortly but returned looking troubled and went directly to the telephone.

"6170," he said into the receiver.

Cassandra recognized Dorrit's number and watched Max

173

impatiently shift his weight from one foot to the other while the operator connected the line. When Dorrit picked up, his hand tightened on the receiver and he all but shouted, "Mother, did you know that Kurt's a Nazi?"

Max's lips formed a tight line as he listened to Dorrit's response. "Oh, I see," he said. "No, Kurt's political affiliation is of no importance to me. I'm surprised, that's all. I just ran into him in front of his house. We had a little chat. He's completely bewitched by Adolf Hitler. I told him the Nazis strike me as a bunch of extreme types. Even so, he tried to recruit me. Huh? Really? An invitation? Hmm…well, of course, it might be interesting but don't rush to take him up on it."

Chapter Fifty-one

Early January, the very thing Dorrit had predicted came to pass, and no sooner had Cassandra and Max left for Egypt, when she moved Peter and Nurse Heller to Grunewald, leaving Frau Berenstahl behind to tend the apartment. Mailing a letter to Luxor, explaining the new living arrangement, she apologized for overstepping her boundaries; a redundant apology, as it were, because in their reply both Max and Cassandra wrote that they had hoped she would take Peter under her wing in their absence, but had not suggested it for fear he might be a burden.

A burden? Dorrit put the letter down. On the contrary. It was pure joy to have a baby in the house. For the first time since Johann's death, she began to face each day with happy anticipation. Peter lent new meaning to her life. Her days became busy and left her with little time to dwell on the past.

However, there were still the long winter nights, nights when she couldn't sleep, couldn't escape her pain. After tossing and turning endlessly, she invariably got out of bed, put on a warm robe, stuffed her feet into comfortable slippers, and plodded down the stairs to the kitchen to fix herself some warm milk.

Choked in the absence of noise, the dark house seemed onomatopoetic of her mood. Peter and the staff were asleep. Fritz was still out, and the large home echoed in a midnight silence that lay heavy on Dorrit's chest.

Holding the glass of warm milk between her hands against involuntary tremors, she left the kitchen, crossing the hall to the library where a light was always left burning until Fritz returned. She walked into the wonderful room; embers in the fireplace still gave off some heat along with a cozy glow. She looked expectantly towards Johann's favorite chair and no matter how involved he was in his reading, he looked up the minute she entered, took off his glasses and smiled, igniting that silvery glint in his eyes that beckoned her to come and sit with him.

She sat down in the red leather chair opposite his and they immediately fell into conversation, touching upon a great number of things. Lately Dorrit talked mostly about Peter. She told Johann that his grandson had Cassandra's coloring and Max's strong build and like a little prince commanded everyone's attention.

Speaking with Johann soothed Dorrit more than the warm milk. Eventually, she put the glass down on the table next to her chair - Frau Schmidt would remove it in the morning - and prepared to go back upstairs, knowing she would be able to sleep now. The ache in her heart had dulled; an ache that often made her chest heave for air as though she were surfacing after being under water for too long.

Those who presume that time works a cure are wrong, she thought bitterly as she took off her robe and climbed into bed. Shivering, she pulled the down comforter up to her chin. Time heals no wounds. It merely serves as a dressing…a splint on a broken heart.

Chapter Fifty-two

Having exhausted every political science course offered at Berlin University, Fritz was growing bored and began looking for a new challenge, such as a year's study abroad at Columbia University in New York. Of course, as long as Max roamed the world, it was no secret that Dorrit counted on him to remain at home. If he suddenly announced that he was going to America, she would probably go into shock. But it was either that or he would lapse into mental moratorium.

That said, he was floored the day he told her.

"New York?" Dorrit showed no signs of buckling knees. "Why, that's a splendid idea, Fritz. Tell me more later. I want to get to the playground with Peter while the sun is out."

Flabbergasted, Fritz watched a radiant grandmother march out of the house and across the street to Grunewald Park, Nurse Heller pushing Peter in the stroller.

Fritz remained in the United States for two years. After completing a year at Columbia University, he and his roommate Robert Grantham spent another on a cross-country motor trip. Robert hailed from Chicago, was an engineering student majoring in aeronautics and alert to the fact that America was developing new and fast planes. He not only aspired to help design them, he wanted a seat in the cockpit. Upon graduation, he committed himself to the air force, deferring for a year in order to see all the nooks and crannies of the country he would serve.

Throughout his college years Robert had changed roommates with the same frequency he changed socks. However, the door to his Morningside Heights apartment stopped revolving once Fritz moved in. Toward the end of his senior year, Robert had decided that his

177

roommate from Berlin was possibly the only individual on the face of the earth with whom he could spend twelve months in an automobile and not be tempted to commit murder. Fritz rolled with the punches, never argued on a personal level, and was so well read that they never ran out of material. More importantly, he attracted women. His upper crust European manners worked like flypaper on American girls, and when more than one adhered herself, Robert helped out; a small kindness among friends.

Standing at a better than average height, Robert Grantham weighed-in a tad above average as well, the excess due entirely to muscle. His eyes were an everyday blue, his hair community brown, but to compensate for the colloquial coloring, he refined his appearance by wearing the *parure et mode* of the day: natty jackets, wide ties, and suspenders. In addition, he lifted weights and endured grinding workouts on the handball court. Still, in spite of corded biceps rippling beneath jackets that didn't need shoulder pads, whenever he and Fritz frequented the usual college hangouts or the Cotton Club at 142nd and Lenox Avenue, where they listened to jazz and drank prohibition gin, it was the conservatively dressed German who spoke English with a British accent - the very same who couldn't tell a joke to save his life - who attracted the prettiest females; something that earned him Robert's undying respect.

Dorrit enjoyed Fritz's letters from New York and, later, his detailed accounts as he and Robert crossed America in a Ford sedan Fritz bought in New York and planned to sell upon returning there. He spent several days in Chicago with Robert's family, and told her about the informal American lifestyle in the suburbs where everyone was immediately on a first name basis. Food was served on paper plates when dining in the out-of-doors, which was done quite often because cooking on an open fire and charring the meat black seemed to be an American summer ritual.

Weeks later, Dorrit read with gruesome curiosity as Fritz described the migrating cicadae he and Robert came across in Texas, where for miles their car crunched over live carpets of insects crossing the roadway. His account was so vivid she felt a need to scratch and was glad when his next letter arrived with no talk of crawling critters, only delightful descriptions of the unusual adobe structures in New Mexico and the compelling colors of Arizona. Soon he wrote about the majestic Rocky Mountains, which he compared to the Alps.

Once he and Robert reached the west coast, Fritz devoted volumes to California, chronicling the remarkable weather and the Pacific

Ocean that he didn't think lived up to its name because of its turbulent surf. He described the tall palms in the southern part of the state, where pink and turquoise homes were the rule rather than the exception. He wrote detailed accounts of Los Angeles, adding an amusing anecdote about the time he and Robert had dined at the Brown Derby at a table next to Greta Garbo and John Barrymore. A young woman had walked over to the famous film stars and after securing their autographs approached Fritz, mistaking him for a screen personality as well. Smiling shyly, she handed him her autograph book and, of course, he obliged her by signing right below John Barrymore's prominent scrawl. The entire episode kept Robert howling for a week.

There were times when Fritz's talk of California was so enthusiastic that Dorrit worried he'd put down roots. However, at long last she received a cable informing her of his arrival back in Berlin.

Chapter Fifty-three

It was a markedly different son Dorrit embraced at Lehrte Bahnhof on an October day in 1931. His shoulders were broader than she remembered; there was a notable firmness in his posture along with a breezy élan in his general demeanor. His resemblance to Johann was so pronounced that she experienced a moment of *deja vu* when he stepped from the train, flashing that same glamorous smile and nonchalantly raking a hand through that same dark brown hair.

That evening, sitting down to a cornucopia of his favorite dishes that Frau Schmidt had prepared for his homecoming, Fritz raised his wine glass in a salute to the huge country across the Atlantic Ocean.

"I intend to go there again," he said, putting his mother on notice. "Perhaps you'd like to come along the next time?"

"Good heavens, no! America is much too far away. I have no interest in traipsing around the globe." Dorrit reached over to stroke Peter's chubby cheeks, a gesture that spoke volumes.

Inasmuch as tonight was a special occasion, the three-year-old Peter was present at dinner. He had been in the park with Nurse Heller when Fritz arrived home and, after being bathed and dressed, was brought down to the dining room, where he immediately began playing with his food, all the while eying the strange man at the table who had invaded his small, secure world.

"Papa?" he tried haltingly, pointing a sticky finger at Fritz.

"No, Peter," Fritz smiled, "I'm not your papa. I'm your Uncle Fritz."

"Unca Fiss..."

"That's right," Fritz laughed, then sobered and turned to Dorrit. "When were Max and Cassandra last in Berlin?" he asked.

"About four months ago. This past June to be exact. They stayed for six weeks and spent most of the time in Bernau. Max was so determined that Peter learn to ride that he bought him a miniature pony."

"Poey's all mine!" Peter piped in.

"He sure is, darling. Tell Uncle Fritz what you named him."

"Aba...a...ham," the boy stuttered.

"Abraham?" Fritz raised a dark eyebrow questioningly.

The boy nodded happily.

"That's a very special name," Fritz agreed.

"And thank goodness, the animal turned out to be extremely slow and patient," Dorrit said.

"That must have irritated Max." Fritz grinned and took a second helping of the delicately seasoned Wiener schnitzel Frau Schmidt was passing around. "How is Cassandra?"

"She's fine. She has an amazing amount of energy. It's quite extraordinary how she has taken to the rigorous routine and the tiresome travel. I'm told she is in the excavating pits, scraping and digging with the best of them. Max says Heidelberg ought to give her an honorary degree. Heat, snakes, and insects don't bother her. I would never have guessed it. I thought the novelty would have worn off by now and that she would want to settle down and raise her child. "Perhaps…" Dorrit suddenly looked wistful, "perhaps if there was another baby."

"I don't suppose that's out of the realm of possibility," Fritz said.

"I don't know." Dorrit put some more food on Peter's plate. "I have the feeling Cassandra is not particularly fond of motherhood."

"She didn't have much of a childhood," Fritz said softly. "That might have something to do with it."

"Could be." Dorrit nodded. "Did you know that Max has let the flat on Unter den Linden go?"

"Why? It was such a nice place."

"*Why*, you ask? My goodness, Fritz, you *have* been away a long time. There's a terrible housing shortage in Berlin. The bad economy dragged its feet for too long. There's been no new construction. People are clamoring for apartments. Max couldn't justify letting that big place stand unoccupied for so many months at a time. In fact, the housing authority began questioning his right to do so."

"And he knuckled under?" Fritz laughed. "You're right, I have been away a long time."

After dinner Fritz got up from the table and, lifting Peter from the booster seat, noticed a veritable smorgasbord under the chair. Shaking his head, he flung the boy over his shoulder like a sack of potatoes.

Hanging upside down, Peter squealed with delight.

"Be careful, Fritz!" Dorrit warned. "He'll throw up and you'll have his dinner running down your back."

"I doubt it. He didn't eat much. Everything is on the floor." Fritz nodded toward the mess, but realized the value of his mother's concern and put Peter down, took his hand and marched him across the hall into the library.

Seating himself in the sofa, he put the boy on his knee and let him fiddle with his tie clip until his wristwatch caught the lad's attention.

"Now then, young fellow," Fritz removed the watch and gave it to Peter to play with, "let me tell you a story about a wonderful place called America..."

Chapter Fifty-four

"Hello! Fritz?"

"Robert? Is that you?" The long distance connection was poor.

"Yeah! It's me old man. Can you hear me?"

"Barely."

"Okay. Listen up! I'll make this short." Robert Grantham was shouting above the static on the trans Atlantic wire. "I got a two-week furlough and a free ride on a cargo plane to Paris. We leave in an hour."

"Paris?"

"Yeah, I'm looking for some nightlife."

"You might try Berlin. The express train from Paris runs every hour."

"Is that an invitation?"

"No. It's an order."

"Yes, sir!" Robert did some quick calculations, allowing for several refueling stops and time zones. "Okay, I'll be there tomorrow...mid afternoon."

Fritz hung up, smiling. In the eighteen months since returning to Berlin, he and Robert had exchanged letters regularly. Robert's were usually a grocery list of complaints with the air force. "I've yet to fly solo," he had groused in the last one. "So far I've worn out my ass sitting in a classroom. I might as well have gone to graduate school. And, *damn!* It's only April, but hot as hell in San Antonio."

Fritz had no complaints about his own pursuits since returning home. He was taking journalism courses at the university and, using his notes from Columbia, outlining a book about New York's governor Franklin D. Roosevelt, now campaigning for the White House with slogans for a new "great society," ideas that ought to generate curiosity among Germans fed up with their own ineffective leaders.

Fritz met Robert's train on a glorious April day. The city parks were ablaze with red and pink tulips and ornamental fountains were bubbling with dancing waters. After a week of showing his American friend the sights and every imaginable nightspot Berlin had to offer, Fritz suggested some R & R in Bernau. Once there, and though Robert was skeptical, Fritz convinced him to try riding.

"There's nothing to it," he insisted, strolling the stables on their first day in the country and after a groom had outfitted Robert with some riding boots.

"Okay, I'm game." Robert eyed the large snorting animals in the stalls. "But maybe we ought to wait until tomorrow once I'm used to the altitude."

"Altitude?"

"We're at sea level, right?"

"Approximately."

"Well, I just crossed the Atlantic at a whopping 30,000 feet."

Fritz laughed. "My intrepid American friend is afraid of horses?"

"Me? Hell no!"

"We'll see..." Fritz managed to maintain a straight face as he stopped in front of the stall of a chestnut brood mare long past its prime. He clucked to the animal. It approached eagerly, softly frupping its nostrils as it poked its head over the enclosure. Robert noted this animal didn't snort. "Of course, riding does pose a risk of injury," Fritz said, patting the horse's coarse mane. "Head and spinal trauma are common in the steeplechase. And polo is as dangerous a sport as any." Robert flinched. Fritz turned away from the brood mare and walked over to a black stallion pacing in an oversized stall. "This is Satan's Son. Long in the legs and fast. He's the grandson of the great Asmodeus." As he was saying this, Fritz knew his American friend was hooked; Robert could never pass up a challenge. "On the other hand you might enjoy a jumper."

"This black devil or a jumper? That's a helluva choice!"

"You're right." Fritz returned to the chestnut mare, hoping it wouldn't display its worn and yellowed teeth, in which case even the Chicago-bred Robert might suspect its age. "This one will probably suit you better."

"A jumper?"

"No."

"Is it related to...to whatchamacallit?"

"Asmodeus?" Fritz shook his head and tried not to laugh. "Not even a distant cousin."

"Okay, sold!"

Robert watched with interest as a groom led the chestnut from the stall. Once it was saddled and out in the yard, he was given a leg up on what was obviously a well-mannered creature compared to that descendant of Asmodeus being readied for Fritz.

Breathing easy, Robert settled into the saddle and patted the chestnut's shiny neck in a friendly fashion, letting his mount know that the rider was an amicable fellow who expected the same consideration in return.

Suddenly the horse began to move. "Whoa...take it easy!" The animal kept going. "*Whoa!* Wait a minute!" Robert instinctively pulled back on the reins and much to his surprise the animal stopped. "That's the ticket," he said and stroked the horse's mane. "That's a good boy. Good boy."

"Her name is Gooseberry," Fritz said, swinging lightly up into his own saddle. "She'll give you no trouble. She's a follower."

"What did you say?"

"I said she's a follower."

"No, I mean, what's her name?"

"Gooseberry." His shoulders shaking with muffled laughter, Fritz quickly turned his horse and led the way from the stable compound, now riding along a bridle path.

Behind him Robert was groaning. "Gooseberry? *Geez!* Pray this never gets back to my squadron. I'll be laughed off base and clear out of Texas."

Hours later when the riders returned to the stables and dismounted, Robert's legs refused to come together. His muscles were tight and aching.

"Do you actually enjoy this sort of thing?" he wanted to know as they walked up to the house, heading for the terrace and the comfort of some garden chairs.

"Riding?"

"No. Inflicting pain on unsuspecting foreigners?"

"Only if they're American," Fritz grinned.

Robert collapsed into a chair. Heinrich, who'd watched his clumsy approach, immediately brought out two cold Steinhagers and announced that lunch would follow.

"Ah, thanks, Henry!" Robert accepted the beer and swatted at a fly that had followed him up from the stables. Foregoing the glass, he saluted Fritz and drank straight from the bottle. "I thought we were supposed to exercise the horses," he said a moment later, "not the other way around." Grimacing and massaging his sore leg muscles, Robert noted that his friend suffered no ill effects from the morning workout. "Something's rotten in Germany," he muttered.

"Rotten in Denmark," Fritz corrected, leaning back in his chair and stretching his legs out in front of him. "If you're quoting Hamlet."

"Yeah...whatever. I never could figure out all that literary stuff. Math's my game. I like numbers. You can count on them."

"Pardon?"

"Forget it, old man." Robert twisted the sleek amber bottle in his hand. "Hey! Henry!" he said to the butler bringing their lunch. "I'll have another one of these." Remembering Heinrich had no command of English, Robert pointed to the bottle before turning back to Fritz, saying, "I have to admit your beer is almost as good as what we brew in Milwaukee."

"Aren't most of those breweries run by Germans?" Fritz cocked an eyebrow.

"Yeah, I guess so. Okay, let's call it a draw."

Despite sore leg muscles, Robert was up early the next morning and headed for the stables with rejuvenated resolve.

"I take it you are finally enjoying yourself?" Fritz said, turning in the saddle as he waited for Robert at a fork in the trail; the latter was again lumbering along on Gooseberry.

"Not yet. This is basic training. By week's end I intend to ride a brute like the one you're on. That'll be fun."

Chapter Fifty-five

Cassandra and Max came to Berlin in June for the birth of their daughter. They named her Sigrid, and no one was more delighted with this new infant than Dorrit, for surely now Cassandra would stay at home and raise her children. But that was not to be. She seemed indifferent with the appearance of another child and as soon as she was able to travel, went off with Max. The work in Egypt was finished, and their new project was in a remote corner of Tunisia, where they were joining Ernst Horstmann and a team of international archaeologists on the excavation site of a newly discovered two thousand-year-old village.

Peter was happy with his new baby sister, if only because Nurse Heller was now too busy to bother with him. He quickly shifted his allegiance to Mademoiselle Morisot, a governess employed to teach him French. Much younger than Nurse Heller, Mademoiselle was also much more fun. She let him play in the park on windy days, and had yet to complain about brittle bones. She laughed a great deal and could be coaxed into pushing the swing so hard that Peter flew higher than any of his friends. In short, all was well in Peter's world. His parents' long absences from home didn't bother him; he had never known anything else. His grandmother was the mainspring of his existence.

Fritz's book, *Roosevelt, A Revolutionary With Common Sense*, was published and soon became required reading for political science majors across Germany and, judging from brisk bookstore sales, struck a chord with the general population as well. Citizens, bone-weary with the discord in the Reichstag and footsore from years of standing in unemployment lines while inflation evaporated their savings, wondered how other governments overcame depression and financial ruin. Would the newly elected American

187

president set a course that Germans could follow? Their patience worn razor thin, they clamored louder than ever for the powers-that-be in Berlin to alleviate the suffering.

Adolf Hitler had his ear to the ground and his political fortunes grew overnight the day he promised that if he were elected chancellor, every man would be guaranteed a job with a pension indexed to inflation.

"I want nothing for myself except the honor of serving the German people!" he bellowed in town squares across the country. "Give me your vote and I will give you a future." His eyes flashed and his fists pounded the rostrum as he also vowed to cleanse the country of foreign enemies lurking among decent citizens, squarely blaming them for Germany's inability to recover from the Great War. "Give us back our identity!" he shrieked. "Give Germany back to the Germans! Then watch and see what we can do!"

On January 30, 1933, Adolf Hitler captured an astounding ninety-two percent of the vote. Germany had a new chancellor.

With the success of his book, Fritz was offered a position as a political writer for the Berlin Zeitung, the city's largest newspaper. Before long his editorials were syndicated in publications throughout Germany. He was fast becoming a respected journalist.

Chapter Fifty-six

In May of that year, Robert Grantham returned to Berlin with his bride, Linda. Growing up, they had been neighbors in Chicago, but he had never paid her any attention. However, when she showed up at a party at his parents' house during one of his leaves from the air force, he couldn't help take notice. She stood out among a sea of old friends and new acquaintances, helped by a pair of high heels and a red sleeveless dress that displayed the perfect symmetry of her white shoulders strafed by a long blond pageboy. Her waistline was as slim as her ankles, and the entire package gave wedlock a good name. After the cocktail party ran out of steam, Robert took her out for a steak dinner.

Their affair burned across the telephone wires between Chicago and San Antonio. However, once Robert entered his final training and was assigned to Edward's Air Force Base in California, Linda grew impatient with the long-distance romance. In open defiance of her Presbyterian upbringing, she upped and drove herself out to the Mojave Desert, site of Robert's new and super secret assignment. Once there, in the interest of national security, circumstances required that they be married.

The ceremony was held in a hot and dusty chapel on base. Robert was given a short leave. The newlyweds hitched a ride on a cargo flight and touched down in Berlin the same day their respective families back in Chicago received letters notifying them of the nuptials.

Fritz met Robert and his bride at Tempelhof.

"We sure appreciate you scrambling to accommodate us on such short notice," Robert said, greeting his friend on the tarmac with a back-thumping male hug. "I promised my bride a European honeymoon before realizing my military stipend wouldn't cover it."

He pulled Linda forward to meet Fritz.

"Hi, handsome!" she said, her blue eyes flirting with him. "Robert told me you were a lady-killer. I see he was right."

Fritz smiled and offered his hand, which she ignored, instead raising herself up on tipped toes and kissing him smack on the lips, leaving a smudge of fire-engine red lipstick. Reaching up and wiping at the mark with her thumb, she said, "I have a sister you ought to meet. She's drop-dead gorgeous! Your kids will be movie stars. I guarantee it."

"Welcome to Berlin," Fritz mumbled, chagrined with her kiss and fast talk before he remembered that irrepressible American informality.

"Thanks, we're sure glad to be here. I can't believe we arrived in one piece." Linda took Fritz's arm as they made their way along the tarmac to the plane's open cargo door where their luggage was being unloaded among crates and packages. She gave the plane a once-over and frowned. "This obsolete piece of scrap metal is going to Madrid, Lisbon, and Milan from here. It'll be a miracle if it comes back next week to pick us up."

"The ride was free," Robert reminded her.

"We will pay with our lives going back," she countered.

"Sweetie, when you see Bernau, you'll know it's worth it."

Linda looked up at Fritz. "Bernau...that's where Robert rode Satan's Son?"

"Uh..." Fritz was about to clarify an obvious misunderstanding when Robert stopped him with a withering look.

"I just *love* horses," Linda continued dreamily, missing the look that passed between the two men and saving Fritz from concocting a response that wouldn't damage Robert's ego. "When do we go out there?"

"Tomorrow," Fritz said. "It's early in the season so you'll have the place all to yourself. I've put the staff on notice. They'll take good care of you." He gave Robert a conspirator's wink and added, "Don't ride Satan's Son. He's had a bit of a...uh, a hoof problem."

"Okay. He's off limits. I'll remember," Robert said and knowing that he and Linda were about to wallow in luxury such as the finest resort on the continent couldn't match, he landed an appreciative blow on Fritz's shoulders. "It's sure good of you to put your place at our disposal. I can't thank you enough."

"You might try by suffering some of my friends at dinner tonight."

"Germans?" Robert asked.

"Of course."

"Linda and I don't speak a word."

"No problem. They speak English."

"Geez! Talk about putting us in our place." Robert reached for a piece of luggage after handing a small bag to Linda.

Taking the other suitcase, Fritz led the way toward the gate where the Americans' passports were checked and beyond which Schmidt was waiting with the car.

"You know something," Linda said, smiling shrewdly at Fritz as she got into the back seat. "My sister took two years of German in high school. She could hold her own among your friends anytime."

Chapter Fifty-seven

Helmut Niemann had been Fritz's close friend since their early days at the prestigious Verdersche Preparatory School, and both had continued their education at Berlin University. Helmut eventually went on to study law and was now a barrister with his father's law firm. The minute Fritz learned of Robert's marriage and arrival in Berlin, he called Helmut to secure his company for dinner. Helmut's English was excellent and he was already acquainted with Robert, having met him during his first visit to Berlin. Fritz asked Helmut to bring a date who could, likewise, converse with the Americans. Little did he know that this small request forced a reluctant suitor's hand.

Helmut had met Julianne Siemers a few months earlier at the Charlottenburg Social Club when he joined a bridge group. He soon discovered that he didn't particularly like playing cards, but stayed with it because he found himself attracted to his bridge partner. He took her out for dinner a few times, which was quite pleasant, and to the opera once, which turned out to be a fiasco. In fact, he had just about decided to give up on bridge *and* Julianne when Fritz telephoned him about having dinner with the Americans. Helmut remembered Julianne telling him that she'd spent a year in London. He called her.

For the party honoring the Granthams, Fritz also included a friend of shorter duration, a colleague at the Zeitung, Ulrich von Ritter. He had a good command of English as did his steady companion, Edith Harsen, a research assistant at the paper.

The dining room shimmered in a sea of tall candles and the sconces on the cream-colored satin walls brought the magnificent paintings to life. The room, though large, seemed intimate on this festive evening and conversation flowed easily. Dorrit officiated as

192

hostess and with graceful timing alerted the kitchen staff when to serve each course. She was enjoying herself in her role tonight, her pleasure dampened only by the fact that Fritz was without a date. She wondered why he hadn't invited Claudia Holderlin. Her mother was American, Claudia spoke English and according to the scuttlebutts, she and Fritz were regularly seen at various nightspots around town. Perhaps Claudia had another commitment? This party was put together on extremely short notice.

Dorrit noted that Helmut Niemann's eyes repeatedly lingered on Julianne Siemers, which didn't surprise her; Julianne was a lovely girl. Her dark hair was cut in a short modern bob with bangs that reached her brows. Her eyes were dark as well and slightly almond shaped, leading one to believe that there must be some Asian blood in her ancestry. She looked bewitching in a burgundy satin dress with three-quarter length sleeves and a shirred ecru lace collar. Linda and Edith were both blondes and, as it happened, were both wearing blue dresses - different styles - but with strings of pearls that were almost identical. Linda's hair hung in a pageboy while Edith's longer mane was swept back and held in place with large rhinestone clips.

"Robert tells me you're planning a trip back to the States," Linda said to Fritz at one point during dinner. "May I ask when we might reciprocate this wonderful hospitality you're showing us?"

"I'd get on that plane with you and Robert next week," he said, a warm gleam in his eyes, attesting to his partiality for America. "If only I had job security. I'm afraid to take time off for fear the paper will decide it can do without me. I'm not particularly popular at the moment."

"Why not?" Robert couldn't imagine Fritz being unpopular. Back in the States he'd been the cat's meow.

"It seems I'm annoying the editors."

"Which is not smart," Ulrich von Ritter said. "You've got to play ball. Especially with those fellows strutting around with a Nazi badge. They can make or break you. And, believe me, they prefer to do the latter. Now me? I refuse to give them that satisfaction and write in the vein they fancy."

"That's not giving them satisfaction?" Fritz said, frowning.

"Who cares?" Ulrich shrugged. "As long as I am retained on the payroll. The streets are littered with stubborn journalists looking for work."

Studying a flaw in her nail polish, Edith Harsen nodded, saying, "Whatever department you work in nowadays, Fritz, you have to play along. The new people in charge of my division, for example, don't care about accuracy as long as we make the government look good. Once you learn that, you'll never be fired."

Fritz's eyes narrowed and he was about to say something, when Robert jumped in.

"If you guys want job security, join the military," he said cheerfully. "I'm as safe as the gold in Fort Knox. Uncle Sam has invested a bundle in me. The air force can't afford to cut me loose."

Linda looked around the table and proudly divulged that Robert had been tapped for the test pilot program. "As soon as we get back home, he'll be flying a brand new experimental plane," she said.

"What kind would that be?" Fritz asked while giving attention to the whipped cream being heaped on his apple strudel; it resembled the Matterhorn before he held up his hand, signaling the serving girl to retreat. "Anything like the British Camels?"

"Sorry, pal. Top secret. My lips are sealed."

"You Americans aren't planning to inflict your mechanical muscle on us, are you?" Helmut said. "We're still smarting from the last time."

"Hell no!" Robert put his coffee cup down so hard it clattered in its saucer. "What do you take us for? Warmongers?"

Helmut laughed. "No, I'm afraid that's our claim to fame."

"Well, your new chancellor seems to be a peace-loving man," Robert said. "Most of our papers back home, including the influential New York Times, endorsed his election. By and large Americans are pleased with the turn of events in Berlin. Herr Hitler promises stability in Germany, which will be good for all of Europe. And now that he's declared himself a pacifist, I don't suppose anyone need fear the kind of aggression your Kaiser dished out?"

"It'll be a cold day in hell..." Fritz mumbled.

Dorrit withdrew at the conclusion of dinner. Fritz and his guests were going to a nightclub, but since Ciro's didn't open its doors until ten o'clock, they had time to kill and retired to the library for cordials.

Ulrich and Edith, fanatic bridge players, corralled Julianne and Linda for a game, the four of them settling down at the felt covered card table in the far corner of the room, while Robert and Fritz bent over the alabaster chess board. Not one for games of any kind, Helmut lit a pipe and perused the glass-fronted bookcases, occasionally opening a door and reaching for a rare volume.

Julianne kept one eye on her bridge hand and the other on Helmut Niemann. She watched him examine titles and study prologues. The smoke curling from his pipe made him squint as he read. Tall and well built, his hair was the color of wet sand. He was wearing a dark gray suit tonight, which made him look every inch the attorney, complete with the trademark tortoiseshell glasses.

Thinking about the pleasant prospect of going to a nightclub, Julianne wondered if he would prove to be a good dancer. She hoped so. She loved to dance, but he had never suggested it. He had taken her to dinner and to one excruciatingly boring opera, an experience she'd like to forget. Even now her cheeks flamed in humiliation with the memory of her head lolling on his shoulder as the audience leapt to its collective feet, applauding wildly as the curtain fell. And, as if dozing at the opera wasn't bad enough, she discovered she had lost a shoe to the sloping floor.

Long after the hall emptied out, she and Helmut along with a surly usher holding a flashlight, searched under countless rows of chairs before locating the trampled remains of black satin. Limping out of the elegant opera house on a broken heel, her eyes puffy with sleep, Julianne figured she'd never see Helmut again. She was surprised when he called yesterday.

Chapter Fifty-eight

Sigrid was ill, not an unusual situation; she'd been ill several times during the past winter, but now as her first birthday was approaching she ought no longer be so vulnerable. Dorrit's heart ached for her frail little granddaughter and, although Nurse Heller was on hand, at the first sign of Sigrid's fever, she canceled all engagements including the last opera of the season, one she hated to miss.

Not thrilled with the prospect of attending the opera alone, Fritz telephoned Helmut Niemann with the offer of box seats. But it turned out that his friend was committed to more enticing pleasures, explaining that he was taking Julianne to Roma, a trendy Italian restaurant with singing waiters. "As close to opera as she cares to get," Helmut said. "Tannhauser is out of the question." Laughing, he added, "It's about four hours too long."

Replacing the receiver, Fritz thought of calling Claudia but rejected the idea. He enjoyed her company, though never at the opera where she persisted in talking during the performance. Pacing the floor in the library, he strolled over to the windows, pushed at the red velvet drapes, and peered through the leaded glass panes. It was still raining, a warm spring rain; nonetheless, he shivered. The drooping limbs on the birch trees just outside the windows, and the soggy grass and dripping wisteria clinging to the fence along the sidewalk, all looked dispirited in the gray mist. Suddenly he felt as gloomy as the weather, his mood plummeting for no apparent reason. Again a shiver ran through him. Cursing under his breath, he left the library, stopping a moment to adjust his tie in front of the hall mirror. Confounded by the black mood that had enveloped him, he grabbed his trench coat from the closet with unnecessary roughness, sending several wooden hangers crashing to the floor.

196

The noise brought Schmidt running into the hall. Fritz glanced at the umbrellas at his disposal. *To hell with them!* He turned on Schmidt, told him to bring the car around and, rolling up his collar and thrusting his hands into his pockets, left the house.

Half an hour later, fingering the gold-tasseled libretto, Fritz settled into the loge his family had subscribed to for generations. He scanned the program for cast changes. There were none. The conductor, as expected, was Maestro Boehm of Vienna. Tossing the reading paraphernalia onto the empty seat next to him, some commotion in the adjoining box drew his attention. He leaned forward and glanced past the partition into what had formerly been the imperial *parterre.* After Kaiser Wilhelm's exile to Holland, a string of presidents and chancellors had used the box, their presence always signaled by the German flag hanging from the balustrade. There was no flag tonight. But just as Fritz was settling back into his chair, he saw the red, white, and black Nazi banner being unfurled over the railing. A moment later, Germany's new chancellor strolled into the loge of the Kaisers, followed by Josef Goebbels and his wife, a pretty blond woman. They took their seats on Herr Hitler's left, Frau Goebbels smiling and chatting with the chancellor. Josef Goebbels had failed at several professional pursuits, including a stab at being a novelist, but lack of credentials notwithstanding had recently been appointed leader of the Nazi Party in Berlin.

Rudolf Hess, Hitler's chief adviser and a man known for some intellect, entered the loge next. His wife took the other coveted seat next to Herr Hitler, greeting him effusively before acknowledging Josef and Magda Goebbels. Herr Hess sat down next to his spouse, leaning across her lap to whisper something in Adolf Hitler's ear. The chairs behind this notable cynosure were soon filled with various officials whose expensive uniforms did little to hide their low birth.

Herr Hitler's presence in the *parterre* was immediately noted and a hush fell over the opera house. However, the silence lasted only a moment, giving way to a round of applause that grew in intensity the minute he rose and executed the ancient Roman salute that he and his party members had adapted as their own. Many on the floor below returned the straight-armed gesture, some shouting "Heil Hitler!" His personal retinue behind him nodded to each other, basking in the warm tribute their Fuehrer was receiving.

Fritz's hands lay motionless in his lap as he studied the man, noticing his rigid posture and the awkward way his hand repeatedly pushed at the flap of brown hair falling across his forehead. His manner tonight was a far cry from the animated politician Fritz had observed at the midtown rallies he covered for the Zeitung. Assigned to attend and report on Herr Hitler's speeches, Fritz rarely found fault with the man's message. Herr Hitler spoke of law and order, children's health, education, and prosperity for all. He promised to rebuild city infrastructures, put up new housing, and restart idle factories. These were issues no journalist could take to task. However, one could question the messages in his book, *Mein Kampf*, and Fritz never missed an opportunity to encourage his readers to buy a copy. He occasionally wondered if Herr Hitler was pleased with the free plug. *Mein Kampf* had never sold well, but Fritz was anxious to draw attention to it because he found it to be a chilling eye-opener. Within its pages, Herr Hitler suggested that people were more likely to swallow a big lie than a small one, and he held the opinion that the average worker lacked the ability to think for himself and could therefore be manipulated into total dependency on the government. The book contained a virtual blueprint for the destruction of the middle class, followed by an arms buildup and a conquest of the modern world only a certifiable madman dared dream about, let alone put into print. Fritz suspected that Herr Hitler's first step toward this systematic undermining of the old order came that night this past February when the Reichstag mysteriously burned to the ground. In a few short hours Germany's symbol of power was reduced to a smoldering ruin. Berliners were stunned with the disaster but were appeased days later when the arsonist was arrested, discovered to be a communist, and summarily executed, giving proof that the new government of law and order worked as promised.

Chapter Fifty-nine

The dimming of the twelve immense pear-shaped crystal chandeliers suspended from the gold dome of the opera house, brought Fritz back to the impending performance. Dismissing Herr Hitler, he glanced around the opulent hall, his gaze drifting up toward the balcony curving around on his left where he spotted Herr Professor Weber from Berlin's Music Conservatory. Director Weber was an old friend, the von Renz family had been patrons of his fine institution for many years and, catching his eye, Fritz nodded a cordial greeting to the stout man, whose pink elf-like face was topped by a helmet of white hair. Herr Weber sat among several faculty members and the rows behind them were filled with conservatory students. For the lack of other diversions, Fritz's eyes roamed over this latter group in their predictable Bohemian attire. He reached the end of a row when his head snapped back a few seats, returning to an unusually angelic face he had passed over much too quickly.

Ignoring the distinct possibility that he might be accused of staring, he lifted his opera glasses to study her in more detail. Her hair, a riot of blond curls, was carelessly combed, but as if in defiance of the unruly mop, her oval face was finely boned and her features tidy. Her nose was small and straight and her lips were full and well defined, turning up at the corners, suggesting a sunny disposition, while a slightly prominent chin bespoke of stubbornness. Her eyes - he couldn't make out their color from this distance - but how they sparkled when she laughed at a comment from a fellow student. Fritz watched with continued interest as the girl tilted her head in order to catch another remark. Again she laughed, the bell-like tones of her voice floating down a tier to where Fritz sat, sufficiently charmed to forgive her the motley attire:

199

a hideous black and yellow polka dot blouse with a tacky green scarf wrapped around the collar. The huge glittering earrings she wore were clearly paste and part of some theatrical costume. Still, he was so mesmerized by the pretty picture her face projected in the lens of his binoculars, that he forgot his rudeness until she suddenly blew him a kiss.

Damn! She had caught him spying and was mocking him.

Fritz dropped the opera glasses into his lap and, molding an expression of cool indifference, leaned back in his seat and reached for the libretto on the chair next to him. Picking it up, he pretended to study it. Several moments passed before he realized he was holding it upside down. Thankfully, he was spared further embarrassment when the hall fell into complete darkness, and Maestro Boehm entered the orchestra pit under a low beam of light that followed him to the podium, where he bowed to a round of applause before raising his baton for the overture.

During the first intermission, sincerely hoping he wouldn't run into the blond Bohemian blower of kisses, Fritz left his seat and walked out on the grand mezzanine. Strolling along the gilded hall, he was waylaid by several of his mother's acquaintances; one and all surprised at her absence. Fritz kept his comments brief, quickly moving on till he spotted Isabel and Philip von Brandt at the champagne bar. As he walked up to them, Philip immediately ventured a wry comment about the chancellor's presence tonight.

"I'm surprised the little man has an understanding of opera," he said, speaking louder than was necessary, causing Isabel to look uneasy. "Tannhauser yet. Not the common man's dish."

"Actually, I've heard that Herr Hitler is a Wagner enthusiast," Fritz said, reaching for a glass of champagne just as the ninety-year-old Count von Beckstein, recently widowed and leaning heavily on a gold-tipped cane, shuffled up to the bar. Nodding his greetings all around, the elderly man lifted his cane, poking it unceremoniously against Fritz's leg.

"So tell me, young man, what do you *really* think of our fire-breathing chancellor? Surely you have an opinion other than that watered-down stuff you write in the Zeitung." The count's eyes bore into Fritz, his advanced age giving him license to be blunt.

Fritz smiled at the crusty old gentleman. "I think he's an aberration," he said, taking a sip of the champagne.

"Yes...and?" Count von Beckstein grunted and looked impatient; on doctor's orders he could no longer partake of spirits, which only added to his petulance. "Go on! Go on!"

200

Fritz complied, saying, "I believe he's a dangerous egotist. Although Germany needs government stability, I sincerely hope he'll be a one-term chancellor. A revolving door is preferable to a blustering narcissist."

"Well, now that's more like it." The count seemed satisfied. "So why don't you say that in your editorials?"

"If I did, my columns would be scratched in the copy room and I'd be fired."

"That wouldn't be a calamity. I knew your father. He left you well off. You don't need to make a living. At the Zeitung, yet! I hardly recognize that paper anymore."

"Perhaps a watered-down voice is better than none," Fritz suggested before realizing he sounded an awful lot like Ulrich von Ritter.

Count von Beckstein appeared to digest the statement. "I suppose there's some truth in that. I shudder to think who would take over your column if you left."

"One of those." Philip nodded toward several men strolling the mezzanine, wearing the black uniform that had recently replaced traditional evening wear for individuals in high government positions.

"Yes," Count von Beckstein said darkly and turned back to Fritz. "You would be replaced by a card-carrying Nazi. No doubt about it."

Fritz shrugged. "For a while."

"A while?" Isabel asked. "What do you mean?"

"I mean that they can't last. Mediocrity never does. Since January our paper has been flooded with new and incompetent writers. Our editorial department will eventually sink under the weight of too many Nazi badges."

"I hope you're right," Count von Beckstein said. "But don't make any extravagant bets." Clearing his throat noisily, he leaned closer and whispered to the group. "There are dark days ahead, my friends. Dark days for Germany. Worse than any we've seen. Worse than the Great War. Worse than the misery that followed. I can feel it in my old bones. On your advice, Fritz, I read that abominable book our chancellor has written."

"You read *Mein Kampf?*"

"Yes. It scared the living daylights out of me. And after that ghastly fire at the Reichstag, I honestly can't say that I want to be around to see what else our chancellor is capable of."

Philip von Brandt held his empty champagne glass across the bar for a refill. "There's no doubt about it," he agreed. "The Reichstag fire was deliberately set. But not by the poor wretch they executed for the crime. The real arsonist is among us tonight."

"He won't be among us for long," Fritz said. "Certainly by the next election..."

"Election? Bah!" The count interrupted and wiped his flushed face with a handkerchief he pulled from an inside pocket. "There won't be any. Herr Hitler will see to that."

"Surely parliament and the public won't go along," Isabel ventured.

"Of course they will go along," Count von Beckstein snorted. "The man has a bizarre hypnotic appeal. Such an individual can't be stopped. His followers become fanatics. And why not when he promises them the moon on a silver platter."

The five-minute warning lights flickered. Fritz took leave of the old widower and the von Brandts as everyone headed back to their seats. Before reaching his loge, Fritz spotted the Eckarts along the corridor, his brows snapping together at the sight of Kurt in the black uniform with its preponderance of silver regimentals that other government officials wore tonight. He wondered if he would ever get used to Kurt being a Nazi. Of course he had known the Eckarts his entire life and exercised some tolerance, greeting Kurt with his usual *éclat* and embracing Lillian who gushed that Elsie and her French diplomat husband were expecting a baby.

Once back in his seat and before the hall fell into total darkness, Fritz glanced up toward the balcony on his left. A number of conservatory students had not returned from the intermission. Apparently Tannhauser was too long even for them. He noted that the blond blower of kisses was still there and, in spite of the embarrassing moments that had passed between them earlier, he felt oddly happy that she had remained. He decided to attend a performance at the Music Conservatory at the first opportunity. He hadn't been there in a while, not since Herr Weber twisted his arm and emptied his wallet for a benefit production last year. Perhaps Herr Weber could now show his gratitude by making an introduction.

Chapter Sixty

It was a week later when Fritz attended a conservatory production of Don Giovanni. Performances were free and an hour before the curtain went up the sidewalk was already milling with people waiting to get in. Once the auditorium doors opened, a mad scramble ensued.

Fritz arrived on the heels of this stampede and, being late, had to be content with a seat at the rear of the hall where he squeezed in next to some restless youngsters rustling paper bags of candy their parents believed would keep them quiet. Bribery occasionally fails. Fritz gave the children a stern look. It didn't help. He glanced around for another seat. There were none. The auditorium was packed to capacity. He accepted his lot. If it became unbearable, he'd simply get up and leave.

However, once into the second act and despite the fidgeting youngsters, it never occurred to him to leave. Mozart himself would have enjoyed this spirited interpretation of what some claimed was his greatest opera. Adding to Fritz's pleasure was the fact that the blond Bohemian - the very person he'd come hoping to meet - played the part of Zerlina, the peasant bride seduced by the powerful Don. She had a splendid soprano voice and her whimsical capers were brilliantly timed as she succumbed to the Don's charms one moment, only to persuade her offended groom of her innocence the next. Fritz found her name in the program. Lisbet Lundgren. He figured she was a student from one of the Scandinavian countries.

Once the final curtain fell, he quickly left his seat before being trampled by the caramel-covered kids clawing a path toward the exit. Walking to the front of the auditorium, searching for Herr Director Weber, he found him standing at the foot of the stage.

"A magnificent display of talent," Fritz said, squeezing through the crowd and finally pumping his fleshy hand. "I don't believe the State Opera has any better."

"Only the ones they've plucked from our school," Herr Weber laughed, his pink face turning red. "As you know, we train our students for the finest opera houses in Europe."

"The one who played Zerlina tonight shows particular promise," Fritz said.

"*Ach!* Indeed, yes. She's a first year student from Denmark and though the role of Zerlina is traditionally reserved for a senior, her audition won over the faculty." Herr Weber was obliged to turn away from Fritz for a moment to acknowledge several people pushing through the crowd to shake his hand. "Look," he said once he'd extricated himself, "why don't you come backstage. If you'd like I could introduce you around. Perhaps there's a particular member of the cast you'd like to meet?" He jabbed an elbow into Fritz's ribs, for although he was a confirmed old bachelor, he was not so old that he couldn't guess what was on a young man's mind. Signaling Fritz to follow him, he now plowed through the crowd, working his short stubby arms like a swimmer.

From across the disorderly prop room, giddy in the knowledge that opening night had gone off without a hitch, Lisbet looked up from a costume bin and caught sight of a tall man entering the melee with Herr Director; obviously an esteemed individual, or Herr Weber wouldn't be bringing him backstage. As she watched the dark-haired stranger being introduced to Gustave Riener, who'd played the part of Don Giovanni, she thought he looked familiar but didn't know why.

Lisbet wasn't the only one observing Herr Director's guest. A third year student, who had distinguished herself as Donna Anna in tonight's production, noted him as well, moved closer, and as he was being introduced to the set designer, overheard Herr Weber say that he was a generous patron of the conservatory, carrying on in the tradition of his late father, the Baron von Renz. Donna Anna immediately pulled off her cloche, shook out her mane of black hair and after a provocative toss let it cascade over her shoulders in the hope that she might attract an introduction.

Her maneuver paid off. Herr Director Weber singled her out. But although Herr von Renz kissed her hand and commented graciously on her performance, he appeared anxious to move on. Donna Anna uttered a few clever comments but couldn't hold his attention; his eyes were already elsewhere and his feet followed all too quickly. Swallowing her disappointment, she watched him plant his feet near where Lisbet Lundgren was rummaging through a cloak rack. Envy raised its ugly head, but was instantly replaced by delicious mortification when she saw Lisbet laugh in the man's face as he put her hand to his lips. One never, positively *never*, ridiculed such a chivalrous gesture. Donna Anna watched with continued glee for signs that the frothy Dane would disgrace herself further. She knew that Lisbet always suffered a reverse case of butterflies and on the heels of tonight's success was probably airborne. Pretending to peruse a box of costume jewelry, Donna Anna inched closer to eavesdrop on her giddy friend.

"Forgive me..." Lisbet was bubbling, "your old-world gallantry is not practiced where I come from. I'm still trying to get used to it."

"Where are you from, Fraulein Lundgren?" Fritz asked, although he already knew. Reluctantly he let go of her hand.

"Copenhagen."

"How do you like living in Berlin?"

"It's wonderful. I love it!"

"*Ach*, there's Andrei Drubetzov!" Herr Weber grabbed Fritz's arm, interrupting the pleasant eye contact he had established with the effervescent star. "Come! You must meet our new choreographer, Andrei Drubetzov!" Weber pointed above the crowd, no small thing for a short man. "He hails from Moscow. Honed his skills with the Bolshoi. We are extremely fortunate to have him." Suddenly Herr Weber remembered why Fritz had come backstage. It was not to meet a Russian expatriate. "Come to think of it, Andrei Drubetzov can wait. We're all going next door to Alois'. You can meet him there. I always treat the cast and production team to supper after opening night. It's a tradition. How about it? Will you join us?"

When Fritz hesitated, Herr Weber held up his hands to fend off any rebuff. "Let me put it a different way," he said. "I *insist* that you join us. Perhaps you'll show your appreciation by arranging a little praise for our production in your newspaper. Eh?"

Fritz laughed at the old fox. "Fair enough," he said.

205

Chapter Sixty-one

Lisbet Lundgren sat down in the chair Fritz was holding out for her when, much to his irritation, the bearded fellow who'd played the part of Leporello in tonight's performance, plunked himself down in the seat Fritz had eyed for himself. Biting down his annoyance, he took another spot at the long table between the Bolshoi choreographer and a female member of the chorus. Donna Anna, two seats down, leaned forward and gave Fritz a decidedly pleasant smile, indicating she was perfectly willing to talk around the illustrious Russian separating them.

Director Weber seated himself at the head of the table where he could hold court over the cream of Europe's talent pool. With the wave of his hand he immediately got the attention of an adipose serving girl in a dirndl costume and blond braids wrapped around her head like a crown. She wore wooden clogs, but moved fast in spite of them. Within minutes, pitchers of beer, miles of spicy wurst, and buckets of steaming sauerkraut arrived at the table.

One came to a smoky underground environment such as Alois' to get indigestion and lend an ear to rising talent down on their luck, singing for their supper. Except for having taken Robert Grantham to a number of *rathskellers,* Fritz generally avoided them. Tonight, however, and although Leporello exercised proprietary rights by keeping his arm draped around Lisbet's shoulder, he was enjoying himself; due in large part to the fact that amid fragmented conversations, laughter, and loud background music, he periodically caught Lisbet's eyes on him and found that she was in no hurry to look away. Thankfully, she gave no indication of remembering him from that night of the Tannhauser production. The opera glasses must have obscured his face sufficiently.

Though thoroughly charmed, in the days following, Fritz tried to put Lisbet Lundgren out of his mind. He was not sure he wanted to complicate his life with an actress...a singer, albeit a very pretty and gifted one. Plus he could not entirely discount Leporello whose attention she appeared to welcome. Fritz figured there was something of a romance between the two of them, an idea that was a source of great aggravation on the one hand and a hesitation to proceed on the other.

However, after a week of cooling his heels, he returned to the conservatory for a repeat performance of Don Giovanni. In order not to show his hand this early in the game, he deliberately took a seat in the very last row and left before the final curtain to avoid being spotted when the house lights came on.

Once outside on the street, he felt oddly depressed and remained standing for a moment, his hands thrust into his pockets, while listening to the applause and watching the lights from the auditorium flood through the windows and cast golden puddles onto the dark sidewalk. He wanted nothing more than to go back inside and seek out the pretty Zerlina. From his seat in the last row, she had looked like a Dresden doll, an exquisite porcelain figurine come to life. And like a thief perusing a jewelry display, he had wanted to reach out and snatch her.

Damn! I'm being absurd!

Fritz kicked a pebble across the sidewalk.

He got into the car and snapped at Schmidt.

"Nach Hause!"

Chapter Sixty-two

Like Lorelei - nymph of the Rhine - whose voice lured sailors to shipwreck, Lisbet's siren song proved stronger than Fritz's reserve. Barely a week passed before he went back to the conservatory.

The sign on the door said tonight would be the final performance of Don Giovanni, yet there was no crowd on the sidewalk. Puzzled, Fritz strolled into the auditorium, expecting a poorly attended production and was surprised to find a rehearsal in progress. He remained standing in the back of the hall for a few minutes, wondering if he had misread the poster, at the same amazed that a delightful show could evolve from this chaos. Paint was being applied to some cardboard sets while a foursome practiced a dance step on the stage, clicking their heels and counting out loud even as a soloist, none other than the bearded Leporello, wrung a different tune from an upright piano on wheels. Several students sat in clusters in the front rows of the auditorium, talking, while backstage someone was hammering and chains were grinding.

Fritz took a seat, stretched his legs out in the aisle and decided that in lieu of any performance he might ask Fraulein Lundgren out for dinner...if she was here. If not, he'd go home and have Frau Schmidt warm up some leftovers and play cards with Peter; a pleasant enough alternative. He had taught the boy a number of games and discovered him to be sharp and cunning.

Fritz had waited only a few minutes when a glint of gold near the stage caught his eye. Straightening in his seat, he craned his neck and searched the students, now recognizing the back of Lisbet's head. With considerable annoyance, he also recognized that his heart was suddenly racing. Apparently, she'd been hunched over a libretto with an instructor and had not been visible when he first came in. He saw the teacher stand up and signal another student.

Lisbet gathered some sheet music together and as she did so, turned and spotted the lone figure in the middle of the auditorium. She dropped her music books on the seat and walked up the center aisle as if she'd been expecting him.

"Hi Fritz!" she said, cocking her head in a flirtatious manner. "I hope you didn't come expecting a performance?" On the strength of their short acquaintance she'd used his first name. A Bohemian lifestyle has its compensations, he decided, delighted with this American-style informality.

"Actually, I did," he said. "The sign outside said Don Giovanni would have its final performance at eight o'clock."

"Oh! Someone forgot to take the poster down. Sorry about that. We closed the show last night."

"I see. What are you working on now? I don't recognize the number that fellow at the piano is playing."

"It's brand new. We're taking a stab at originality. The score is modern but with a few old-fashioned melodies borrowed from the masters."

"And the theme?"

"Star-crossed lovers. What else?" Lisbet grinned and spread her hands. "But, contrary to traditional complicity, our *menage a trois* has a happy ending. Our heroine doesn't cough up her lungs and the leading man is not obliged to fall on his sword."

"That's a new wrinkle, all right. I'll make a point of attending opening night to see how you pull it off."

"Please do! Herr Director will no doubt invite you to supper again in the hope of getting another nice write-up in your paper. The last one is turning yellow on our bulletin board."

She had brought up the subject of food. Fritz seized upon it. "How about tonight?" he said. "Would you care to have dinner?"

"I'd love to!" she cried without bothering to conceal her eagerness. "But, please, not at Alois'. My stomach is becoming intolerant to wurst. The cook in our dormitory has a hundred different ways of serving it. He calls it Boarders' Beef."

Fritz laughed. "I happen to know a restaurant that disclaims any knowledge whatsoever of that fine old German fare. But it's not in the immediate neighborhood."

"That's all right as long as we can get there by bus. My feet have been pinched in these wretched boots all day. I can't walk another step." Lisbet stuck out a scuffed ankle boot before clamping her lower lip between her teeth and asking with a worried frown, "Is it terribly far away? The dormitory locks us out at ten thirty on weeknights and I don't relish sleeping on a park bench. I tried it once."

Fritz checked his watch. "Time should be no problem unless your rehearsal runs a lot longer."

"It will. But they'll just have to get along without me. I'll die if I don't have a decent meal. Wait here. I'll get my jacket and sign out."

Lisbet went backstage, returning a moment later wearing a beige jacket over her blue shirtwaist dress and knotting a multi colored silk scarf around her neck. As she walked out of the auditorium, the soloist at the piano fell silent.

Chapter Sixty-three

Schmidt was waiting at the curb.

"Gatow's on the Lake!" Fritz said, touching a button raising the glass partition once he and Lisbet were seated.

"A chauffeur?" she blurted as the car pulled into traffic. "What a delightful convenience. Don't you drive?"

"I do. But never at night. Poor night vision," Fritz lied smoothly because Schmidt was capable of reading lips in the rear view mirror. His senses were sharp, only his bones were frail; he was too old to do much work but too proud to admit it, and Fritz was hard pressed to invent duties that would preserve an old butler's pride without straining his back. Driving was one of them.

From force of habit Schmidt took the direct route along Unter den Linden and was soon near the university on a collision course with a spectacle Fritz had already seen and had no desire to revisit. But it was too late now to tell Schmidt to take a detour.

Earlier, when rumors of a bonfire on Opernplatz across from the main gates to the university began circulating at the Zeitung, Fritz left his office, notebook in hand, and arrived at his alma mater sickened by what he saw. Although students occasionally in the spirit of celebration burn texts after completing exams, this was entirely different. This appeared to be an orchestrated destruction of literature. "Barbarism has its rituals," he jotted down in his notebook as he stood on the square, watching the leaping flames. "On this evening in May 1933 we bear witness to primitive instincts carried out by a government determined to debase an entire nation." Of course, even as he was formulating his scathing report, Fritz realized it would never pass the censors. Freedom of the press was a thing of the past. There was less and less a journalist could say and he often wondered how long he would keep his column. Returning to his office in a foul mood, he wrapped up a revised bland report, turned it in, and decided to go to the music conservatory in the hope of seeing a ray of sunshine.

Now glaring out the car's window at the fiery spectacle, he was grinding his teeth. The bonfire had been burning for more than two hours. Traffic was hopelessly snarled, and to seek escape by rounding a corner would serve no purpose. As far as he could tell, the side streets were congested as well. The large beautiful square facing the Humboldt Gates, flanked on one side by the gothic-columned State Opera House and on the other by the Library and National Archives buildings, had become a parade ground of riot proportions. Motor vehicles passing the area were the least of it. Hundreds of pedestrians dashing indiscriminately between cars and buses in their quest to cross the street were causing the real gridlock. Some spectators were coming to view the blaze while others were in a great hurry to retreat from it.

As the car crawled along, Fritz saw that Josef Goebbels, Berlin's Nazi Party Chief and now newly appointed Minister of Propaganda as well, was still on the scene. Bullhorn in hand, he was tirelessly encouraging students and brown-shirted individuals - whom Fritz had referred to in his article as *book burning bureaucrats,* to toss boxes of books into the inferno. Literature deemed unacceptable to the regime and the German mind was disposed of. Works by Thomas Mann, Albert Einstein, H.G. Wells, Zola, and Proust, were devoured by the leaping flames to a chorus of pagan chants and under the innocuous eye of the police standing by without interfering. Fritz noted that they were not armed. One of Herr Hitler's first decrees upon taking office was to make gun ownership a crime, a law that apparently applied to police officers on foot patrol but not to Herr Goebbels' private security detail. They were heavily armed.

Also peering intently through the car's windows, Lisbet was lost in thought and for the time being remained as quiet as Fritz.

"What was that back there on Opernplatz?" she asked after they were finally free of the traffic jam.

"A fire," he mumbled morosely.

"I could see that." She swatted his arm playfully. "Were they really burning books?"

"Yes."

"Why?"

"They believe certain books will drive Germany into moral decay. They've got some warped idea that they're saving the German soul.

Tonight they are burning the great literature of the world. A few months ago they burned the great hall of the Reichstag. God knows what will be next."

"They? Who?"

"The Nazis."

"You think your chancellor knows about this?"

"I'm sure it's being done at his direct order."

"Really?" Seeing the sudden and appalling frown on Fritz's brow, Liebet realized his mood had hit rock bottom rather suddenly. She became determined to lift it.

"Do you think they're burning your book?" she asked with a coquettish grin.

Surprised with the question, Fritz turned to stare at her. "Pardon?"

"The one about President Roosevelt. I saw it in Menzel's bookshop the other day. It was displayed in the window. I figured it was yours because I didn't think there were too many writers with the name Frederick Alexander von Renz. I would have bought a copy but I was flat broke."

Fritz smiled. "I'll see that you get one *gratis*."

"Will you autograph it?"

He laughed. "Isn't it enough to flatter me by suggesting my book is sufficiently controversial to be burned?"

"In view of the prominent spot Menzel's gave it, I can draw no other conclusion," Lisbet said, glad his humor was restored. "But tell me, why would students be involved in destroying books on such a large scale?"

"As an extremist act it appeals to them. Students are quick to embrace radical causes. Herr Hitler is popular with them because he promises change. The word resonates with them. The Nazis know it and are skillfully guiding them in a rebellion against the established order of their parents' generation. What you saw back there was a deliberate stab at the intellectual community. Not a mortal thrust but a nasty wound nonetheless."

Chapter Sixty-four

Well-known clients did not need reservations at Gatow's. The maitre-d immediately made one of the best tables available for Herr von Renz and his guest.

"Um...this is heaven!" Lisbet sighed, running her fingers over the smooth white tablecloth shimmering pink in the candlelight. She was glad she had borrowed a silk scarf from the prop room; it gave her navy dress some pizzazz. As she leaned forward to inhale the fragrance of the exquisite rosebuds in the center of the table, a cameo dangling on a gold chain slipped from her open collar. Fritz smiled inwardly at the sight of the pricey ornament. Perhaps Lisbet Lundgren was not totally committed to a Bohemian lifestyle. He signaled the waiter for the wine list.

While Fritz was studying the list, Lisbet gazed through the window; no table in the restaurant had a better view. The dark surface of the lake rippled gently in the light of lanterns marking the shoreline and illuminating some decorative trees drooping with yellow blossoms and bending gracefully over the water's edge as if admiring their own reflection. On the far side of the lake, buildings along Koenigs Allee were silhouetted against the night sky, sprinkled with the first stars of the evening.

"What a sight," she murmured, turning her attention back to Fritz, surprised he'd picked such a romantic place because he appeared far too studious and serious to have a soft spot. Along with his conservative dark jacket and slacks, he was what she and her friends at the conservatory would normally call *a stiff*. "I have never been in a prettier setting."

"Then let's hope the food doesn't disappoint you," he said.

"You *did* promise there'd be no wurst on the menu."

"The chef has never even heard of it."

Lisbet laughed. "My parents warned me about German food. They said it'd make me fat as a porker within a week. They tried everything to keep me home. Including appealing to my waistline."

"They didn't want you to study in Berlin?" Fritz said, surprised.

"That's right. Copenhagen has a very respectable conservatory. I applied to Berlin in secret."

Fritz cocked an eyebrow. "Your own rebellion?"

Lisbet nodded and gave him a small acquiescent grin. "If wanting to leave Denmark constitutes a rebellion."

"Well, I can't imagine anything short of anarchy would cause people to leave. It's such a pleasant little country."

"That's just it. It's too pleasant. Too little. Too homogenized. I needed a break from the monotony of a society where everyone is poured from the same bottle." Lisbet reached for her glass and took a sip of the chilled wine the waiter had just poured. "Oops...sorry! *Skoal!*" she grinned, belatedly clinking her glass against Fritz's. "Of course in case Berlin rejected me, I had applications for both Paris and London ready to mail." She took another sip of wine. "Umm..."

"You were that determined to study abroad?"

"Absolutely. But I was in for a surprise when I got an audition."

"You didn't expect one?"

"Oh, I figured I'd get an audition, but I never figured my parents would be good sports about it. Such good sports, in fact, that they decided to come along for a bit of a holiday in Berlin. That alone should have made me suspicious."

"They don't like to take a holiday?"

"My father *never* takes a day off. Let me give you an example of the Lundgren treachery. From the time we drove across the German border, and once it finally stopped raining, he rolled down the car window so he could smoke a vile cigar without annoying my mother. Of course I knew perfectly well that he was simply hoping I'd get laryngitis and blow the audition."

Fritz laughed.

"Once I was accepted and preparing to move to Berlin, my father was so sure I'd be homesick that he bet my brother a small fortune I'd be back within a month."

"You have a brother?"

"Yes. Torben. He's three years older than me and I've always been a thorn in his side. He was the only one in the family glad to see me go. My absence, along with winning the bet, made him so deliriously happy that he lost his head and squandered his winnings on a ring for his girl. The stone was so enormous it tipped the scales in his favor and she agreed to marry him. He quit the university and took a job in my father's business."

"What kind of business?"

"Publishing. Mostly trade books. You know...professional stuff. Plus a tabloid my father is forever upgrading in order to compete with more respectable newspapers. The silly thing has more pictures and gossip than serious text. But people love it. Its circulation keeps growing."

"Then I'd leave well enough alone."

"That's exactly what Torben says."

"I'm sorry to agree with your nemesis."

"That's all right. Torben and I get along better now that I'm no longer underfoot."

"How long will you study in Berlin?"

"Two more years. The conservatory is the finest in Europe. It's important to graduate from here if I expect to be taken seriously. Besides, I fell in love."

"You did?" Fritz stared at her. Leporello reared his bearded head.

"Uh-huh," Lisbet nodded dreamily and took another sip of the wine. "I fell in love the day I arrived. The noise...the hubbub, the fast pulse of the city was in perfect sync with mine."

"Copenhagen is not exactly a sleepy hamlet," Fritz said, putting Leporello to rest for the moment.

"True. But, as I just told you, it had gone flat. I knew every street...every building...every landmark."

"Familiarity breeds contempt?"

"Precisely."

"Like sauerkraut and sausage?"

"Yes." Lisbet laughed and pushed some wayward curls behind her ears. "My only complaint about Berlin. You're so sweet, Fritz, to spare me tonight." As she said his name, she caressed it as if saying *darling*.

His gray eyes narrowed against a sudden heat flaring in his body. He picked up the menu. "Shall we order?" he said, chagrined with his male weakness.

It was two hours later when Fritz told Schmidt to circle the block while he walked Lisbet across the sidewalk to the door of the student residence on Landsberger Allee within minutes of lockout.

Stopping in front of the doorway, Lisbet pulled up the sleeve on her jacket, extending her wrist and smiling up at Fritz. "You may kiss my hand," she invited with a teasing glint in her eyes.

"I'd rather not."

"Oh...?"

"I had something else in mind."

Lisbet's heart skipped a beat. She knew what he meant.

Grinning, his teeth glinting in the light of the lamp hanging over the door, he slipped an arm around her and pulled her so close that she became aware of the clean scent of his clothes. For an instant she worried that - after a day of high jinx on the stage, - hers might offend him. The borrowed scarf, though pretty, reeked of the stale perfume residue from others who'd worn it. However, a moment later she became aware of nothing except being held in a lover's embrace. Her palms against the smooth cloth of his jacket, Fritz drew her further into the shadows of the doorway before his lips found hers, touching and exploring the soft contours of her mouth in what was an excruciatingly tender kiss. Lifting herself up on tipped toes, Lisbet wound her arms around his neck, her lips moving under the increasing demand of his.

On the other side of the door, the shuffling footsteps of the dormitory matron rattling a key chain reminded Fritz of the time. Releasing Lisbet, he fanned his hands into her hair, the yellow curls springing between his fingers.

"I think you need another square meal tomorrow," he whispered, pressing a kiss on her forehead, his heart taking a bruising, slamming in an unsteady rhythm against his ribcage.

"You know of another place with no wurst on the menu?" Her dreamy eyes turned up to meet his.

He grinned. "I know a thousand and one."

A smile curved Lisbet's lips. She slipped from his embrace and disappeared through the door just before the key turned.

Chapter Sixty-five

Fritz was never home anymore. Dorrit was reminded of his presence in the house only on nights when she was awakened as he stumbled down the hall toward his rooms, too tired to remember to be circumspect. She smiled to herself, turned over, and went back to sleep. Something was afoot. She had never before heard him whistle at one o'clock in the morning.

Over the summer he barely spent two weeks in Bernau, and only when Cassandra and Max were home for their visit with the children. And, short as his stay was, the entire time he looked as if he couldn't wait to return to the hot pavements of Berlin. The day he did, a casual remark thrown over his shoulder puzzled Dorrit far less than it did everyone else who'd come out to the courtyard to see him off.

"By the way..." Fritz said as if reporting on some trivial matter as he gave Dorrit a quick peck on the cheek, "I forgot to tell you that I'll be going to Denmark next week." He turned to Max, saying, "But don't worry, I'll be back in time to help with the harvest." After giving Cassandra and the frail Sigrid a kiss, he gave Peter a manly handshake - something the boy appreciated, then he got into his car and was gone in a cloud of dust before any questions could be raised.

"Ah-hah! So Frederick Alexander is finally serious about someone of the opposite sex," Max announced with a sly gleam in his green eyes, watching the car disappear down the long driveway. "He's in love with a Danish damsel, is that it?" Max looked at Dorrit for confirmation.

"I don't know. He hasn't said a word to me. Did he tell you anything during these past two weeks?"

"Nothing."

"That's odd," Dorrit said, shaking her head.

"Why is he so tightlipped?"

"I honestly don't know, Max. I haven't wanted to pry. Frankly, I haven't had a chance. He's out so much and comes home late. And in the mornings his nose is always buried in the newspaper during breakfast."

Max frowned. "I wonder what's wrong with her?"

"Wrong?" Cassandra bent down to pick up Sigrid who was collecting some pebbles from the gravel and was about to put them in her mouth. "Why should anything be wrong?" She pried the stones from Sigrid's small fists.

"Because he's keeping her under wraps. Why not bring her out here to meet us? You suppose she has thinning hair and warts?"

"Don't be ridiculous!" Cassandra laughed. "I'm sure Fritz's girl is lovely."

"If she's so terrific why can't she wrangle an invitation to meet his family?" Max dug a handkerchief from a pocket in his jodhpurs and wiped at the perspiration around his neck. It was brutally hot in the courtyard under the glaring noon sun. "It appears he's managed to get himself invited to meet her folks."

"Well, never mind." Dorrit turned to go into the house; the heat was getting to her. "We're not going to solve anything standing here. If it's a serious relationship we'll meet Fritz's lady friend in due time. Besides, he could have a hundred different reasons for going to Denmark. Maybe he's preparing a story for the Zeitung?"

"I doubt it," Max said, but dropped the subject and put an arm around Cassandra. She and the children were in their bathing suits and about to go to the river for a swim. Cassandra looked particularly fetching in a red smocked maillot with a small skirt that did little to conceal her cute bottom.

"Darling, can you wait for me to change out of this riding gear?" he said, deciding to tag along. Everyone was suddenly watching him closely, Peter and Sigrid because they were eager for his company, while Nurse Heller, who'd just stepped from the house with Mademoiselle Morisot carrying the picnic basket, was eying him with her usual disapproving frown. She had long ago come to the conclusion that her employer, baron or no baron, did not fit the mold of a proper parent. He was too flamboyant to be a good influence and too much in absentia to claim any. Of course, she was decidedly thankful for the latter, so much so that she stiffened with the threat of his company at the river.

"On second thought, don't wait," Max said. "You all go ahead. I'll join you shortly."

"Papa! Come! Papa! Swim!" Sigrid struggled so fiercely in Cassandra's arms that she put her down on the gravel where the child hopped up and down on her spindly legs; she was frail but compensated with a surprising vocabulary; something Cassandra felt was due in large part to the many books Dorrit read aloud to her.

Max picked Sigrid up for a kiss and as he put her down, gave her small behind a gentle pat. "Now, run along. Test the water. When I get there you can warn me if it's too cold."

"She'd better not scare the fish away," Peter muttered under his breath as he untangled some fishing line and bent down to pick up his bucket of bait.

"Just go upstream a bit. Away from the beach and any splashing." Max ruffled his son's dark hair. "Pick a shady spot. You'll catch plenty of fish."

The swimming party left, walking single file across the lawn, Nurse Heller leading the charge; Peter, loaded down with his fishing gear, pulling up the rear.

Max turned and went into the house with his mother. It was cool inside, thanks to the heavy drapes pulled across the windows, keeping out the midday sun. Heinrich had made himself scarce, something he routinely did on hot days - a small inconvenience which meant that Max had to fetch his own beer. He had worked up a powerful thirst, riding this morning, and once inside the hall, the smell of horse sweat along with his own was overly persuasive. He realized he would need a shower before joining the party at the river or risk attracting flies and spoiling Nurse Heller's antiseptic environment.

Dorrit stopped at the foot of the stairs. "I'm going up to change my dress, Max, then I'm off to the Konauers. Gerlinde and Karl-Heinz are expecting the Eckarts this afternoon. They'll be visiting for a few days. I'll stay and dine with them tonight."

"How's our esteemed Nazi friend?"

"Kurt?"

"Yes. Unless you've cultivated another Nazi?"

"I most certainly have not!" Dorrit laughed at the very idea. "Did you know Kurt's been named head of the Medical Examiners Board?"

Max nodded. "I read about it in the papers."

"Well, I don't need to tell you that Lillian is ecstatic with his new prominence. She raves about the intimate parties they now attend at the chancellery. A far cry from the large receptions she used to delight in. I attended one of those a while back and to tell you the truth I didn't enjoy it. It was awfully noisy and crowded. But last month Lillian managed to get me an invitation to a small intimate dinner for twelve."

"Which you declined, of course."

"No, I couldn't. She would have been devastated. I went just to please her. But, believe me, I was totally unimpressed with our chancellor and his uniformed aficionados."

"Did you speak with Herr Hitler?"

"Of course. We had a nice chat. We discussed you, Max."

"You did?"

"Yes. He's quite keen on archaeology. He saw Tutankhamen's exhibit while it was in Berlin. When I explained that you were responsible for getting the artifacts here from Cairo, he indicated he'd like to meet you."

Max rolled his eyes.

"I know," Dorrit said. "I don't like him either. Can you imagine Lillian actually believed Herr Hitler was enamored with me? *Me?* A Russian with Jewish blood."

Max looked at his mother, an uneasy feeling pricking the back of his neck. "Did you mention your ancestry in the course of your little chat with the Fuehrer?"

"No. The subject never came up." Dorrit touched Max's cheek tenderly with the back of her hand before turning toward the wide flight of stairs. "Even if it had, I know enough not to flatter myself by talking about myself. I may be getting old, Max, but I'm not yet foolish."

Max grinned. "Obviously not. You didn't swoon at Herr Hitler's feet like most women."

"Swoon? Good heavens, no! He is quite homely with his tight little mouth under that silly patch of a mustache. And his loyal henchmen are about as attractive as mud. Herr Goebbels' face reminded me of a rodent. Herr Goering is horribly overweight and wears make-up. Only Albert Speer was genuinely charming and good-looking."

"The new city architect?"

"Yes. His wife was lovely too. She has great poise. Most of the other women were guessed-up in gaudy silk dresses and hideous fake jewelry. As I told you, I only went because Lillian was so persistent. Funny though, for all her pleasure in my being there, I sensed Kurt was on edge the entire evening. I don't think he felt it was the right place for me. And, of course, I won't accept another invitation. I'd much rather remember the glamorous affairs during the Kaiser's time. In view of what we have now, Germany would be well served to bring Wilhelm home from exile."

"Mother, you sound like a Monarchist!"

"I suppose that I am."

"Well, don't admit that within earshot of any Nazi. I've heard one can be arrested for expressing loyalty to Kaiser Wilhelm."

Dorrit laughed. "Arrested? For goodness sakes, Max, where do you get such ideas? Besides, since when do *you* take rumors seriously?"

"I don't know." Max shrugged. "I'm probably overreacting. But be careful just the same."

Chapter Sixty-six

Sigrid was frequently ill during the autumn, and winter came with various childhood diseases. Along with Nurse Heller, Dorrit spent many a night comforting the feverish child, which put a crimp in her social life. Her friends, however, visited and kept her informed about the goings-on in town, which was how she learned that Fritz was consistently seen in the company of a blond woman, a Danish student at Berlin's Music Conservatory. She and Fritz made a handsome couple and were regularly spotted attending the opera, dining at Horcher's, Gatow's, the Adlon, and a number of other popular eateries. They were also sighted at Ciro's with Helmut Niemann and Julianne Siemers; the foursome drinking champagne and dancing till dawn. Some of Dorrit's friends reported with delicious outrage that they had seen Fraulein Lundgren take the stage when the musicians went out for a smoke. She belted out racy ballads and, oh yes, Fritz accompanied her on the piano. Apparently, he spent enough money in the place for the management to overlook union rules regarding entertainment.

Spring arrived, spreading a soothing balm over winter-weary Berliners. Garden furniture was brought up from damp basements, dabbed with a fresh coat of paint, and set out to dot the greening lawns behind the stately homes along Lindenstrasse. Lilac scented the air, Gertrude's apple trees bloomed, and happy voices once again rang out in Grunewald Park where nannies took their charges for romps in the fresh air.

Tagging along with Nurse Heller and Mademoiselle Morisot, Dorrit rarely missed an outing in the park. She hovered over Sigrid playing in the sandbox and watched Peter and his friends race their bicycles on the forested paths.

Peter was a handsome, strapping boy with his mother's black hair and brown eyes. He had Max's breezy personality, made friends easily, and was always surrounded by boys eager to follow him in the games he invented on the spot. He had started his formal education at the Koening's Allee School, and it appeared that he had a great capacity for math computations, something his teacher thought unusual enough to comment on. He was also captain of his soccer team.

In direct contrast, Sigrid was timid and her social development was slow. Some might call her dull, but Dorrit knew better because at home Sigrid's hesitant ways were less conspicuous and her vocabulary was astonishing. The fact that the child was thin and small worried Dorrit less with time, especially with Ben Tarnoff's assurances that she would outgrow her frailty. Sigrid certainly surpassed her more robust contemporaries in beauty. Her reddish hair was abundant and a pair of enormous green eyes dominated her small face. Romanov eyes, Dorrit mused, knowingly.

Peter was not immune to the charms of his pretty sister, and at the risk of losing face among his friends, repaired her sand castles and rushed to her aid whenever necessary. If she fell and skinned her knee, he was first on the scene to inspect the mortal wound before marching her over to the bench where Nurse Heller had a bottle of iodine ready. After receiving medical attention, Dorrit whisked Sigrid up on her lap and kissed the child's face, wet with frightened tears brought on by the sight of blood.

"Don't cry, my precious," Dorrit murmured. "Save your tears. Save them for tomorrow. You never know when you might need them."

Oma's words invariably made Sigrid forget her injury. She stared at her grandmother, wondering how she might go about saving her tears. Dorrit winked, and soon Sigrid was giggling. She ran back to the sandbox, her scrape forgotten, her tears saved for tomorrow.

Chapter Sixty-seven

During his second year in office, clearly a martinet about making good on his promises, Adolf Hitler continued to infuse life into the economy. Formerly idle factories hummed with activity, absorbing the jobless as vast economic programs were launched, including the manufacture of the Volkswagen, a car for the common man. Infrastructures were being rebuilt and an autobahn system soon connected major cities with wide, straight lanes designed to accommodate heavy traffic at high speeds. New currency replaced the old, further stabilizing the economy, and an optimism of euphoric proportions beat in the German breast. Evidence of the regime's success was everywhere. New apartment buildings were rising for workers who were no longer shuffling their feet in the unemployment lines. Back lots of industrial plants were turned into cheerful little parks where this new army of wage earners could enjoy their lunch amid flowering shrubs; another sign that Herr Hitler was concerned with the well-being of blue-collar workers. Those who had initially felt uneasy with his dogmatic personality were reassured with his accomplishments. After all, only fools were inclined to argue with success. The future looked brighter than at any time in people's memory, and the crisp parades and marching bands - regular sights on German streets nowadays - were a welcomed display of discipline and harmony.

Of course, there were still those who spoke of their mistrust of Herr Hitler and questioned the assortment of misfits propelled into positions of authority. Some began to suspect that he was gaining too much personal power. But all spoke in private because as time went by it was becoming risky to voice an opinion. Government officials and military personnel, who sought accountability from the Fuehrer, vanished. Other individual protests were silenced with jail

225

time. "A temporary cooling-off period," families were told when a loved one was incarcerated. The press went along, agreeing that it was necessary to remove dissidents attempting to sabotage the chancellor's good works. Soon many citizens languished at Lehrtestrasse Prison. Those who were tried faced immediate execution for treason. Never before had treason been so broadly interpreted. Eventually, it became difficult to raise any public opposition whatsoever.

"We are completely muzzled at the Zeitung," Fritz told Helmut Niemann during one of their regular weekday lunches at Café Maitre on Kurfurstendamm, their respective offices were only blocks apart. "Never before has so low a premium been placed on content and substance. Every word I write goes through the Nazi wringer. If one of my editorials survives in a quasi-original form, it's because the editor who checked it was illiterate. Other articles are reworked to a point where they no longer resemble the original. It's madding!"

Helmut looked glum. "Can I give you some advice?"

"Go ahead."

"Think about what Ulrich once said."

"About not testing the editors' patience?"

"That's right. They're bound to get cranky and decide it's easier to get rid of you than be troubled rewriting your columns."

"Frankly, I no longer care if I'm fired."

"I'm not talking about being fired, Fritz. I'm talking about retribution."

"Arrest?"

"Exactly."

"Don't worry. I'll watch myself."

"Good. I'd hate to see you buy a one-way ticket into obscurity."

"I'm already there. I have no voice anymore."

"Well, at least you are still physically present."

"I'll remember to be grateful. Actually, I've never known you to give in under pressure. What's happened to the fearless prosecutor?"

"You can't fight the Nazis." Helmut took a quick glance around for anyone in uniform who might be within earshot. "Our only hope is to vote Herr Hitler out of office."

"I used to believe that was possible. Now?" Fritz shook his head, "Now I don't know. People are happy. They are working. Why would they want to throw out the party that delivered the goods?"

"Because there's a lot of strange stuff going on. What do you make of it? All those mysterious disappearances, for example. Now

Frau Baden's son has dropped off the face of the earth."

"Frau Baden?"

"My housekeeper. Her son's gone. She hasn't heard from him since he called Herr Hitler an Austrian refugee with a personality disorder."

"That's a pretty good description. Frau Baden's son is an astute fellow."

"No. Unfortunately he chose to sound off in a public café. The next day on his way to work he vanished. He rounded a corner and disappeared into thin air."

"Any witnesses?"

Helmut shook his head. "I've been talking to some of his friends who were at the café, but they weren't with him the following morning when he disappeared. His mother is desperate. She's a widow and he's her only son. Her pride and joy. Just nineteen years old, for God's sake! Why would the Nazis care about his frivolous talk?" Helmut looked grim as he stirred his coffee. "If I don't locate him in a prison cell soon, we might as well start dragging the rivers."

Fritz shuddered. Berlin's rivers and canals had yielded an unusual number of bodies lately; all officially declared suicides or victims of accidental drowning.

However, as sinister as individual disappearances, jail, and executions without due process were, by the middle of 1934 the entire nation felt true and collective terror. It happened the night of June 30th.

While the country slept, blood flowed in its four corners. Thousands of influential citizens, those who had openly rejected Herr Hitler or were determined to block his ambitions, were systematically killed as they slept in their beds. The following morning the German people awoke not yet aware of the blood purge but aware that a different wind was blowing.

The day dawned to a balmy warmth and citizens set out for their places of work, thankful they had jobs and gratified they'd had eggs for breakfast, thick slabs of bacon, and rich cream in their coffee. However, by midmorning and in spite of the warm sun overhead, an unexplained chill permeated the air. An eerie anxiety seeped into every conscious Berliner, causing their usual brisk productivity to wane. Why, people asked one another, were soldiers encamped in Tiergarten and across town in city squares? Why were truckloads of special police units with rifles and bayonets cruising peaceful neighborhoods?

227

Was Berlin under siege?

Housewives at home turned on their radios. There was no news; no announcements; soothing chamber music and broadcasts of Herr Goebbel praising the works of the Third Reich greeted their ears. The morning papers sold out rapidly, readers leafing through the crisp pages but finding nothing out of the ordinary. Texts of Herr Hitler's speeches as well as excerpts of the accolade he regularly enjoyed in the foreign press dominated the text. In the opinion of the United States, Great Britain, and France, Adolf Hitler was the new hope of a depressed nation, which had at long last attained competent leadership.

Two weeks passed before Herr Hitler gave a public explanation of the blood purge. "For the benefit of all the good people of Germany..." he bellowed at Krull Hall on July 15th, "it became necessary to rid the country of traitors. Those singled out for punishment were dangerous spies deserving the maximum penalty allowed by law."

Herr Hitler continued to speak for another hour while the aging President Hindenburg, beloved by the people, stood beside him; his presence on the podium effectively endorsing the bloody maneuvers.

"One must not shrink from the extreme in response to harmful elements," Hindenburg said after Herr Hitler had spoken, and might as well have called him a courageous man. Hindenburg's words helped soothe the German conscience.

Chapter Sixty-eight

That summer Fritz finally brought Lisbet to Bernau to meet his family.

Parking his car by the front steps, he reached into the back seat for Lisbet's valise and strolled up to the house, introducing her to his mother who'd been planted by the front door ever since receiving his call earlier in the morning; a short, concise call that included the announcement that he and Lisbet were engaged.

"My dear Lisbet!" Dorrit cried and in the heat of the moment clutched the young woman in a warm embrace. "Welcome! Welcome! I'm so delighted to finally meet you." Never before had Dorrit uttered words with more conviction.

Lisbet made a number of equally effusive comments.

From upstairs Cassandra heard the happy commotion in the hall and was amazed Fritz had gotten to Bernau so fast; his call had come barely an hour ago. She ran a comb through her hair, tucked her shirt into her slacks and with Sigrid trailing behind, raced down the stairs, as impatient as Dorrit to meet Fritz's mystery woman.

After being introduced to Lisbet and carefully sizing her up, Cassandra threw her arms around Fritz and whispered, "She's a living doll! I'm so glad we're here for the announcement."

"I planned it that way," he admitted with a grin.

Having worked her way down the stairs, holding the banister with both hands, Sigrid immediately retreated behind Dorrit, where she could eye the strange woman from a position of safety. No amount of coaxing dislodged her. Fritz pretended to be heartbroken not to have his usual kiss from his little princess, and Cassandra scolded, but the child only clung closer to *Oma*, her face turned inward, her small fingers kneading the fine green linen of Dorrit's skirt. Nurse Heller saved the awkward situation when, returning from her

229

morning constitutional, she came into the hall and took charge of the timid youngster with the promise of a trip to the flower gardens.

"Well," Fritz turned to his mother and Cassandra, "I'll let you get Lisbet settled in." Carrying his jacket over his shoulder in the hook of his thumb, he loosened his tie as he made his way up the stairs to change.

No sooner was he gone when Cassandra turned on her heels and without a word of explanation flew out the front door. Dorrit watched as she ran down the steps and across the courtyard, her long black hair flying in the wind. Closing the door Cassandra had negligently left open, she turned to Lisbet with a smile of apology.

"I believe my daughter-in-law has run off to find her husband and son to inform them of your arrival. They had already gone out riding when Fritz called and have no idea that you're here." She took Lisbet's arm. "Come, let me show you to your room so you can unpack." Heinrich came into the hall, took Fraulein Lundgren's suitcase, and followed behind the baroness as she led the way up the wide staircase.

"Oh, how lovely!" Lisbet exclaimed moments later as she was shown into a bright room with two large dormers. Suddenly, as impulsive as Cassandra, she scooted across the floor, threw open a window and leaned out. Climbing roses and ivy clung to the brick walls, and endless green lawns sloped gently away from the house toward rolling fields of yellow wheat. A wide river meandered though the countryside, the sun on its surface making it appear like slow moving mercury. In the far distance a pine forest rose tall and black against the blue sky. Directly below her, Lisbet spotted Nurse Heller and Sigrid strolling along the paths of an exquisite flower garden. She took a deep breath of the summer air, scented with a mixture of clover and roses, and was ecstatic at the prospect of spending an entire week in this beautiful setting.

Putting the suitcase down, Heinrich turned to leave when a maid came in to inquire if she might help the visitor unpack.

"Yes, Lotte," Dorrit spoke up and walked over to pat Lisbet's arm, saying, "I'll leave you now, my dear. You'll want to rest and see to your things. We'll have lunch at one o'clock. On the terrace. After last night's rain, the weather is so agreeable today..." Dorrit was interrupted by the sound of booted footsteps and Max's voice.

"Well, what do you know," he said, stopping in the doorway and pretending to knock on a column of air before entering. "So Frederick finally decided it was safe for you to meet his family. We were beginning to think he was ashamed of us." Max walked into the room in a couple of swift strides, took both of Lisbet's hands in his and stood back, boldly appraising her, a cagey glint in his green eyes. "Hmm, you are a treasure!"

"This…" Dorrit interjected, looking at Lisbet with mock exasperation, "is my oldest son, Maximilian."

"Max," he corrected without taking his eyes off Lisbet.

"It's nice to meet you, Max," she said, returning his stare and deciding that she'd never before seen anyone quite so virile. Blond and deeply tanned, he was wearing riding breeches with a blue shirt open halfway down his chest. It required conscious effort to draw her gaze away and over to a dark-haired youngster standing indecisively in the doorway. Max saw her eyes stray.

"Fraulein Lundgren," he said, turning and motioning for the boy to step forward, "may I present my son, Peter. A future contender on the equestrian circuit."

"And a sharp card player, I've been told." Lisbet smiled and offered her hand. "Perhaps we can have a game sometime?"

"Sure! That'd be great." Peter wondered if Uncle Fritz had shown her some of the same card tricks he'd taught him. "Do you play whist?" he asked.

"Certainly. It's my favorite."

"Mine too."

"All right, now. Everybody out!" Dorrit herded her son and grandson from the room. "There will be plenty of time to talk later." At the door she turned around. "Your arrival has made it a very exciting morning for us. I hope we haven't overwhelmed you."

"Not at all," Lisbet assured her.

Dorrit smiled with great pleasure in her guest and, closing the door quietly behind her, followed Max and Peter downstairs.

Chapter Sixty-nine

While Lotte attended to the contents of the suitcase, Lisbet flopped down on the soft eiderdown bed, her eyes studying the lace canopy overhead before perusing the walls of the room papered in a charming pattern of tiny flowers. A pair of parson's chairs stood near the windows, the tasteful fabric matching that of the yellow-striped drapes. She kicked off her shoes, which fell soundlessly into the soft carpet, and now watched idly as the maid hung her clothes in a mirror-lined armoire.

When Lotte was finished, she curtsied and left.

Alone, and from her prone position on the bed, Lisbet again looked around the beautiful room. She had grown up in a large villa in Gentofte, an affluent suburb of Copenhagen, and had always believed that her parents were rich. But this was a different kind of rich, and she giggled with the realization that her parents and coterie of aunts and uncles and hodgepodge of cousins were in for a surprise. Teacups would rattle across Copenhagen. From birth, Danes were ingrained with class-consciousness and titles made them positively quiver. Last summer her family had immediately approved of Fritz and during the long winter had wondered why no announcement was forthcoming. Lisbet, too, had wondered, but had consoled herself with the fact that Julianne Siemers was in the same boat, lamenting that Helmut Niemann was procrastinating and not getting around to the subject of marriage.

Pushing a pink satin pillow behind her back, Lisbet recalled Fritz's odd proposal yesterday. They had planned to go boating and have a picnic on Pfaueninsel - a small island on the Havel River flowing through the center of Berlin - a park complete with a twin-towered castle, iridescent peacocks, and four hundred-year-old gnarled trees shaped like trolls.

In preparation for her final evening recital before the August recess, Lisbet had to rehearse the entire morning; she and Fritz only had a few hours in the afternoon to call their own. But she planned to make the most of it by wearing some cute shorts for their outing on the river; no man was immune to shapely ankles and pretty knees, and sooner or later she figured she'd wear him down.

However, at noon when she saw him stroll into the auditorium, wearing a dark blazer and gray slacks, she left the stage and completely forgot about changing into the cute shorts. Fritz was not dressed for a picnic; it looked more like he was on his way to a funeral.

"Hi!" She walked up the center aisle toward him, wiping her suddenly moist palms in the folds of her skirt. Was he about to break their date?

"Would you mind skipping the picnic?" he asked, tonelessly.

"N...no...it's all right." Her fears were being realized, but she managed to appear indifferent, which was difficult when he looked so devilishly handsome. He also looked nervous, something she'd never seen before. In addition to canceling the picnic, was he about to end their yearlong relationship? Her sense of drama went into high gear. She envisioned herself floating facedown on the Havel, a modern day Ophelia.

"How about lunch at Café Maitre instead?" he suggested, interrupting Lisbet's plans for a jilted heroine's demise.

"Maitre?" she croaked. Café Maitre was a supremely elegant restaurant on the Kurfurstendamm. The perfect spot to end a relationship. No girl, emotionally inclined or not, would dare throw hysterics at Maitre.

Half an hour later, while eating open-faced Westphalian ham sandwiches smothered in tiny shrimp, Fritz took a gulp of wine and in an almost offhand manner suggested that they ought to get married, his tone as cavalier as if he were recommending the cucumber salad.

A fork arrested halfway between the plate and her mouth, Lisbet responded with a surprised, "Huh?"

"It was just an idea," he said and went back to his food. "I know you're committed to a stage career. Marriage would probably interfere with your plans. Anyway, think about it. Take as much time as you want."

"Time?" She leaned across the small bistro table and kissed him squarely on the lips. "I don't need time. Of course I'll marry you. I would have married you last year after our dinner at Gatow's."

This time it was Fritz who uttered, "Huh?"

"You know...the night they burned the books. You took me to Gatow's on the Lake."

"Oh..."

"Don't look so surprised. It was my first square meal in Berlin. I would have followed you home like a starved puppy."

Fritz laughed, glanced at his watch, and suddenly dug into his pocket, throwing a handful of bills on the table. "Come on!" he said.

"What? Where are we going?"

Figuring her stunned expression was regret at leaving the food behind, he grabbed her hand, saying, "Don't worry. We'll come back and eat. Maitre stays open all day. Friedlander's doesn't."

They left the restaurant and sprinted across the street. "I want to buy you a ring," Fritz shouted above the sound of angry motorists leaning on their horns. "Friedlander's closes at one o'clock on Fridays. But once we're inside the door they can't throw us out."

Now stretching lazily on the bed, Lisbet held up her hand and for the umpteenth time admired the large diamonds in her engagement ring. The flawless faceted stones caught the sunlight in the room, sprinkling the lace canopy with mirror-like reflections that jumped and skipped with the slightest movement of her hand. Smiling, she thought about the people she'd just met. Compared to her own large family, Fritz's was small, but decidedly interesting. Max positively looked nothing at all like the stuffed-shirt scientist she'd envisioned. She knew nothing of archaeology - science bored her to tears - and she hoped he wouldn't corner her with shoptalk because despite her stage training she wouldn't be able to feign the slightest interest. Cassandra, on the other hand, was a different matter entirely; no pretense was needed. She looked like a sultry film star, which intrigued Lisbet. The baroness intrigued her as well. Lisbet guessed she was in her fifties, but she certainly hadn't let herself slip into the frumpy mold associated with her age. Tall and thin, she was a graceful woman, her features mirroring a youth of extraordinary beauty.

Bolting from the bed, Lisbet glanced at the porcelain clock on the nightstand and panicked. Time had slipped by. Only another fifteen minutes until lunch. She suspected punctuality was of some value around here. She ran to the closet and flicked through her clothes with more than a hint of desperation. Everything looked much too plain for these grand surroundings. And to think that these very same outfits made her appear overdressed at the conservatory.

She finally settled on a periwinkle cotton *pique*, recalling that Fritz had complimented her on it when she'd worn it on a previous occasion. It had small cap sleeves, a round collar, and a row of tiny buttons down the front. As she put on the dress, she decided to wear open sandals to display her pretty red pedicure.

There was a soft knock on the door.

"Come in!" Lisbet hollered, working impatiently with the buttons; in her hurry getting them hopelessly looped in the wrong places.

"Hi!" Cassandra said, walking in. Lisbet saw that she had changed her plain slacks and simple shirt for a navy flared skirt and a dotted Swiss blouse. A beautiful gold herringbone necklace hugged her throat. "I came to see if you're ready for lunch."

"Yes, I am. As soon as I finish with these stupid buttons...ugh!" Lisbet groaned and turned back to the mirror to face her ordeal.

"Here, let me help you." Cassandra came to stand in front of her and began tackling the tiny pearls. "In my line of work I handle small things all the time. Objects far more delicate than these." While Cassandra worked, Lisbet glanced around for her comb and brush. She didn't see them and figured the maid had put them in a drawer. With no time to go rummaging around, she simply ran her hands through her hair, fluffing the curls.

"Thanks! You're a lifesaver," she said once Cassandra had finished all the loops. Quickly stuffing her feet into the white sandals, Lisbet followed her into the hall. "If I didn't know better," she said, closing the door to her chamber, "I'd think this was a hotel. I've never seen so many rooms."

"You'll get used to it," Cassandra smiled, leading the way along the corridor and down the stairs, now crossing the center hall to the back of the house where the French doors stood open to the terrace.

Lisbet heard children's voices outside and she heard Fritz laughing.

Never before had she heard anything quite so pleasant.

Chapter Seventy

The following day, walking up from the stables, Cassandra and Lisbet shared some amusement, sending peals of laughter into the air and all the way to the front door where Dorrit was watching their approach, thinking what a pretty picture they made. Wearing similar tan slacks and white linen shirts plucked from Cassandra's closets, they ran across the courtyard, their carefree voices beguiling the senses. Dorrit was filled with an unfathomable tenderness for these two young women.

"Hi!" Lisbet waved, first to spot her as she and Cassandra stopped at the fountain to hold their wrists under the refreshing spray of water. "Are you waiting for us?"

"Yes."

"You should have come down to the corrals," Cassandra said. "You missed all the excitement."

"Excitement?"

"Lisbet was riding Buttercup and there must have been a burr under the saddle because the poor creature suddenly took off like a crazed colt. It required both Max and Fritz to catch her. But not before Lisbet was thrown. The men are still trying to calm the horse."

"Calm the horse? What about you, Lisbet?" Dorrit had never lost her fear of horses and could only imagine the scene.

"My vanity got a bruising. Everything else survived."

"Well, thank God for that," Dorrit exhaled and remembered why she was standing by the door. "Can you two come into the library for a moment?" she said. "I need to consult with you right away. I'm thinking of hosting a party."

"A party? Uh, what fun!" Lisbet cried, shaking her hands dry as she ran up the steps.

"Can we stand up while we consult?" Cassandra grinned, coming up behind her. "I don't think Lisbet feels like sitting down yet."

"Fritz will have to be more careful when choosing a horse for you," Dorrit said, crossing the hall with a puckered frown. "Are you sure you're not hurt?"

"My backside is probably black and blue," Lisbet said, brushing at some grass stains on the seat of her pants. Craning her neck to inspect the area, she added, "And green."

"I will speak with Fritz," Dorrit said in all seriousness.

"It wasn't his fault." Cassandra came to his defense. "Buttercup is the most docile animal in the stables now that Gooseberry is too old to ride. If anything, someone ought to speak to the groom who saddled her."

"Hey, let's change the subject." Lisbet would much rather hear Dorrit's plans for a party than discuss her fall from grace. "I'm fine and I'm riding Buttercup again tomorrow." She tossed her head, walked into the library behind Dorrit, and sat down on the sofa and on her bruises without cringing. Cassandra took a seat next to her, pulled off her boots and curled her legs up under her. Dorrit settled down at the desk where she had pen and pad ready.

"I'd like to host an engagement party next Saturday," she said, looking over the rim of her reading glasses at Lisbet. "I have already made a list of my own friends. Now I need a list from you. And from you, Cassandra. I haven't had a large gathering in the years since my husband died and I probably don't know how to go about it anymore. Still, I'm willing to give it a try. Since we have less than a week, I must call everyone right away. Lisbet, do you think your parents can make the trip on such short notice?"

"Sure. My brother and his wife Karin will want to come as well. They can all drive down together." Lisbet rattled off their phone numbers before catching herself. "Actually, I guess I'd better call them. Their command of German is at grade school level."

"That's still better than my Danish." Dorrit smiled and dipped her pen into the inkwell. "I'll leave it to you to call them. But I'm sure I'll manage to communicate with them once they're here. Now, who would you like to include from the conservatory?"

Lisbet thought a moment. "No one," she said. "If I ask one, I'll have to ask them all and that would be an unmanageable number. Of course, we must invite Julianne Siemers and Helmut Niemann. Plus Ulrich and Edith. Fritz and I attended their wedding a couple of months ago."

"All right." Dorrit turned to Cassandra. "Who would you like to

237

invite?"

"Just the Horstmanns. Everyone else is in Tunisia. Too far away. Ernst is in Hamburg with his family. It'll be easy for him and Ellen to get here."

Dorrit came to the table an hour later, reporting that those she'd been able to reach had accepted, and since no one was expected to attend a celebration in Bernau and depart the same night, the next task was to assign guest rooms. After lunch the three women put their heads together again. It was shortly decided that Helmut could use the day bed in Fritz's room and Julianne would share with Lisbet. Ulrich and Edith von Ritter, Ellen and Ernst Horstmann, Torben and Karin Lundgren were assigned chambers on the third floor, which left enough guest suites on the second floor for the senior Lundgrens, the Tarnoffs, and the von Brandts. Dorrit would count on Gerlinde to accommodate Lillian and Kurt Eckart, the von Steigerts, and Anna's widowed brother, Georg Schellenberg.

Chapter Seventy-one

The Horstmanns were the first to arrive, pulling up to the barony early Saturday afternoon and parking their car in the far corner of the courtyard to leave room for others.

After a lengthy courtship by correspondence, Ernst had some years ago married the long-suffering Ellen. But, except for the fact that they now had two sons, little else had changed. Ernst still went on foreign digs while Ellen stayed in Hamburg to await his letters and holiday visits. "Ernst will soon be offered a professorship at Hamburg University," she declared after her first son was born, repeating the same belief when the second child arrived. Ernst didn't have the heart to contradict her on either occasion, but he knew that he wanted to work in the field, discover new things, not stand in a lecture hall and talk about the accomplishments of others. As it were, he finally made a decent living. His articles were regularly translated into several languages and he had two textbooks under his belt.

As others began to arrive, Dorrit discovered that Kurt Eckart would not be the only Nazi under her roof tonight. Ulrich von Ritter had apparently also joined ranks, displaying his newfound loyalty to Herr Hitler with a badge in his lapel. Anna von Steigert's widowed brother Georg Schellenberg wore a badge as well, plus a swastika armband. Since being widowed two years ago, Georg had moved to Dresden to be near his grandchildren but came to Berlin most weekends and always when Anna and Enno entertained at their home in Wannsee, where he invariably managed to be Dorrit's dinner partner. Dorrit suspected Anna was playing Cupid and in case Georg was in on it, was mindful never to offer him the slightest encouragement. For although Johann was no longer with her, he took up every inch of space in her heart, leaving no room for

239

another. Therefore, it was with little enthusiasm that she had included Georg Schellenberg in the festivities this weekend. However, she couldn't distress Anna by excluding him. She would simply manage to keep him at arm's length; a distance that widened considerably the minute she saw his affiliation with Herr Hitler.

Chapter Seventy-two

That evening the house was humming with laughter and animated conversation in the drawing room as everyone sipped champagne and nibbled on canapés before dinner. Soon the crowd moved into the salon where Lisbet delighted one and all with renditions from Die Fledermous. Fritz accompanied her on the Bosendorfer and when the applause refused to die down, the duo responded to shouts of encore.

Sitting among her dearest friends on the high-backed chairs along the mirrored walls in the salon, Dorrit wiped at a stray tear. The music affected her profoundly, swelling her heart with pure joy one moment only to burst with sorrow the next. Johann would have enjoyed this gathering, she reflected, bitter in his absence and while inconspicuously dabbing at yet another tear, she prayed that somehow the magic in this room tonight might reach him...touch him...wherever he was in God's celestial realm.

Johann, she whispered inwardly as Lisbet's clear voice filled the room with yet another sweet melody, *you and I will soon have another daughter-in-law. Had you handpicked her yourself, you couldn't have done better.* Drawing air into her lungs to ease a tight constriction, Dorrit again made discreet use of her handkerchief and suddenly felt Johann's presence like a gentle, comforting caress. It cheered her. By the time the dinner bell sounded, her eyes were dry and she managed to smile convincingly as she led her guests from the salon and into the dining room.

Despite the number of people gathered around the table, the setting was intimate, the soft glow of candles reflecting their flickering light in the mottled mirror hanging over the alabaster fireplace. Ancient tapestries graced the walls, the French doors stood open to the garden, and the heady breeze of the August

241

evening mingled with the fragrance of an abundance of red and white roses - Denmark's colors - displayed on the long table in Lisbet's honor. Maids in starched black uniforms walked around the room, serving up one delicious course after another.

The toasts offered to Lisbet and Fritz were as wordy as they were plentiful. Max proposed the first, Helmut went next, countless followed, and although Dorrit laughed merrily with each hilarious and outrageous remark, the melancholy mood she'd experienced in the salon returned. She picked at her plate, forcing down small mouthfuls of succulent lobster drenched in a delicious lemon butter sauce, all the while wondering at these peculiar bouts of sadness when tonight was such a happy celebration.

Was it because this party reminded her of bygone days? Did she simply miss the past, or did she fear the future? Germany was changing; no doubt about it, but everyone was reluctant to discuss it, an anomaly that alone was troubling. The political climate in good times as well as in bad had always been regular fodder for this crowd. But nowadays any meaningful discussion was deliberately avoided and this hesitation to talk freely was unsettling. For some time already, Dorrit had felt that the Germany of grace and kindness she had known and loved since the day she and her father found refuge in Berlin was being swept away by an ominous tide. She sensed that amid the country's newfound prosperity a perverse mistrust was growing among the people. New acquaintances eyed one another with suspicion and old friends were circumspect.

She reached for her glass and sipped the chilled sauterne with more resolution than was her habit in the hope it would loosen the pressure in her chest. Her eyes roamed the dining room where, as expected, everyone was now engaged in inconsequential and frivolous conversations as if by some unspoken covenant. Her gaze settled on the guest of honor and instantly her mood changed for the better. Lisbet, sitting next to Fritz, looked bewitching in a pink strapless gown from Cassandra's closet. Dorrit smiled, recalling this morning when chaos had reigned within these centuries-old walls.

"Ball gowns?" Lisbet gasped when, during breakfast, Dorrit happened to mention that tonight would require formal attire. "My parents have already left Copenhagen. They were starting out at the crack of dawn." She checked her watch. "It's too late to call and have them bring a dress from home. Oh, God!" Before Lisbet panicked further, Cassandra suggested that they run upstairs and take inventory of her closets.

"I wear nothing but slacks and shirts most of the year," she explained minutes later to a rapturous Lisbet, whose eyes were as big as her outburst when she saw the bounty, "so Max insists I keep plenty of these silly things around to wear when we're home."

"Silly? These are gorgeous!" Lisbet was in seventh heaven as they both tried on the fabulous gowns, pivoting in front of the mirror and in front of each other. "I have never before seen so much stuff in one place except in the wardrobe at the conservatory where everything is shopworn and smells of mothballs."

From her own rooms down the hall, Dorrit heard the happy chatter and was pleased when she was summoned to help make the final decisions. She immediately agreed that the pink tulle was perfect on Lisbet, and there could be no question about the fact that the yellow chiffon was stunning on Cassandra.

Smiling secretly, Dorrit left, returning moments later with two heirloom necklaces to put the final touches on the dresses. Diamonds and lotus pink padparadscha for Lisbet. Diamonds and yellow demantiod garnets for Cassandra.

Chapter Seventy-three

Reliving the happy scene of this morning, Dorrit's spirits were raised a notch and, glancing around the dinner table, she verified that the servants were not neglecting anyone's plate or glass.

Lisbet's parents, her brother Torben and his wife Karin, were handsome and delightful people, she mused, having immediately formed that opinion the minute they arrived this afternoon. Their command of German was respectable, the exception being Torben who seemed unwilling to try and, moreover, had an air of surliness about him. Perhaps he was uncomfortable among so many strangers?

Dorrit's eyes fell on Kurt Eckart. Uniquely among her guests tonight, his mood was as mercurial as her own. He seemed jovial one minute only to scowl the next. She saw his brow darken when Lillian shared a bit of gossip with Gertrude, which made both women giggle. Dorrit recognized his hostile glare because she'd seen it earlier this evening in the drawing room where it had been directed at Ben. Was it possible that the two old friends had argued? No, she refused to believe that. They had been friends and colleagues for over thirty years and never in all that time had there been a hint of acrimony between them. Even if there'd been a recent quarrel, any anger would have been put to rest before tonight. Kurt's mood was simply due to exhaustion. He was tired after too many late nights at political meetings. He would sleep half the day tomorrow and be himself again. He was past sixty and according to Lillian pushed himself like a young man. His demanding responsibilities in the government were bound to manifest themselves in his disposition, same as the years were manifested in his expanding girth, sagging jaw line, and graying hair. Only his blue eyes remained as clear and compelling as on that New Year's

Eve long ago when Dorrit first met him and thought him extremely handsome.

Where have the years gone? she wondered, but before sinking into another bout of suffocating sadness, forced herself to pay attention to the conversation between Anna and Philip at this end of the table. She didn't worry if Georg Schellenberg sitting on her left felt excluded. A Nazi was not to be indulged any more than absolutely necessary, and so far she'd managed to give a disproportionate amount of her attention to Harold Lundgren sitting on her right.

"Is Enno lobbying for another assignment abroad?" Philip was asking Anna.

"I'm afraid not." She shook her head. "He's been frozen out."

Listening to the conversation, Georg leaned forward so he could talk past Dorrit's cold shoulder. "My dear sister, as I've said before, Enno only has himself to blame. If he wants another ambassadorship, he's got to join the party in power. It is absurd for an ambitious man to remain loyal to an obsolete coalition of Prussian Junkers."

"Hindenburg is a Prussian Junker," Philip reminded Georg.

"Hindenburg is senile," the latter said without thinking.

"That's right," Karl-Heinz agreed, having overheard the remark from his seat next to Lisbet's mother. "He proved it by standing on the platform with Herr Hitler when he explained the blood purge."

Frowning, Georg was about to comment when Anna, fearing the discussion was veering onto thin ice, rescued the moment. "Actually I'm glad Enno has been forced into retirement," she said lightly. "It leaves us free to travel. Philip, when you were in Portugal last month, did you get down to Estoril and the Algarve?"

"Yes, but only for a few days. We cut our stay short."

"Really. Why?"

"We had no luck with the weather," Isabel chimed in from across the table. "After a week of rain, and although the shoreline was quite spectacular, we'd had enough."

"Hmm..." Anna appeared to reconsider the lure of the Algarve. "Well, perhaps Enno and I will go back to Greece in the fall. Or to the west coast of Spain. La Coruna is lovely. The weather is dependable to a fault. Dorrit, it's been a while of course, but didn't you and Johann go there occasionally?"

"No, we preferred San Sebastian. After honeymooning there we returned with the boys when they were little. Before the Great War."

"La Coruna? San Sebastian?" Suddenly Karl-Heinz's belligerent voice rose above the din at the table. "How about we try a subject closer to home?"

Gerlinde paled; short of raising her own voice, which she'd never dream of doing in polite company, she had no hope of controlling her husband when he was drunk or quarrelsome, and it appeared that he was now both. She did the only thing she could. She ignored him, hoping everyone else would as well. Turning toward Lisbet's mother, Gerlinde benignly asked about the weather in Copenhagen.

Her diversionary tactic didn't work.

"My friends!" Karl-Heinz's bloodshot eyes raked the entire table. "We discuss travel, the weather, the price of cigars, but not the price of prosperity or the price of freedom lost."

The dining room fell silent, everyone was waiting for someone to respond.

"That's a ridiculous statement," Kurt finally muttered, cutting through the pall.

"Is it?" Karl-Heinz jabbed his fork rudely across the table at Kurt. "What's ridiculous, my friend, is the fact that intelligent people are acting like brainless sheep letting that buffoon, Herr Hitler, herd them toward disaster."

Kurt stiffened, the stem of the crystal goblet in his hand snapped like a dry twig. He mumbled a few unintelligible words of regret while a servant rushed over with a new glass and a napkin to mop up the mess spreading on the tablecloth, a mundane activity that nonetheless held everyone's attention.

"After years of turmoil..." Karl-Heinz thundered ahead while Kurt's new glass was being filled, "we're told that all is well in the Fatherland. The clouds of despair have magically been lifted. We're suddenly living in a utopia. Well, I'd like to ask someone here tonight, especially you, Kurt, since you're so well connected. Why does Herr Hitler run a propaganda campaign for his good works? Why does every newspaper sell us bliss, harmony, affluence, and other hogwash? Why the constant and fanatic need to convince us that we're the envy of the civilized world?"

"Are you questioning Germany's new prosperity?" Kurt said evenly, determined to contain his composure; he regretted the incident with the glass and casually took another bite of food.

"Prosperity?" Karl-Heinz chuckled grimly. "The prosperity Herr Hitler sells is nothing but the pretty wrapping on a shoddy present. The tranquility he vaunts is nothing but fear. We don't dare take him to task. Those who do, vanish."

Kurt looked up from his plate as if he'd been poisoned. He took a sip of wine but couldn't decide whether to swallow or spit. Staring across the table at Karl-Heinz, he finally swallowed and with a bristled voice said, "I urge you to stop this crazy talk at once. Our Fuehrer..."

"That's another thing! Fuehrer?" Karl-Heinz barked. "What the hell...ah, pardon me ladies, what's that supposed to mean? Is Reich Chancellor not a big enough title for such a small man?"

"The moniker sets Herr Hitler apart from our former and sadly ineffective chancellors."

"I beg to disagree."

"It won't be the first time." Kurt grinned and looked around the table. He nodded affably to the visitors from Denmark, making it clear that he was exercising patience and had not lost his sense of humor.

"Compared to what we have now," Karl-Heinz reached for his glass, his throat was parched from so much use, "any one of our former chancellors was a giant. Herr Hitler is a charlatan. A charmer in private, I'm told, as benevolent as a daft uncle, but God help those who question his agenda."

Kurt leaned his elbows heavily on the table. "You are mighty quick to throw terms around," he said. "As quick as you are to forget the past. Have you forgotten a few years ago when five million Germans were out of work?"

"Of course not."

"Then tell me, what did the powers in the Reichstag do?"

For the lack of a ready response, Karl-Heinz emptied his wine glass.

"All right. I'll refresh your memory," Kurt said when his opponent remained silent. "They bickered like others before them and split into various factions so even more opinions could be aired. The end result being scores of political parties, few of which put forth a single noteworthy domestic improvement. My friends..." Kurt's gaze swept the gathering as he pressed his point, "surely we all remember the soup lines. The bloody riots. The ruinous inflation where we paid twenty thousand marks for a bottle of milk and a loaf of bread. Our currency was so worthless we used wadded-up money instead of kindling. For the love of God, Karl-Heinz, have you forgotten those grinding hardships?"

"Of course I haven't forgotten," Karl-Heinz acknowledged grudgingly.

"Well then...look around. Come to Berlin. You'll find no bread lines, no unemployment lines, no beggar with a tin cup. Visible improvement is everywhere. Instead of bellyaching you should be

247

thanking our Fuehrer on bended knee. He, and only he, has shown the courage to make the hard decisions. Bickering never put food in the mouths of the hungry nor did it open a single factory. Under Herr Hitler's guidance, Germany has joined the industrial world once again. The jobless have been absorbed into the work force. Our factories are again productive."

Karl-Heinz straightened in his chair. "Actually, now that you mention it, I have been wondering about all those humming factories. I suspect a number of them are being converted into...into..." Karl-Heinz rotated his glass between his fingers and appeared to be searching for the right word. "Well, I don't suppose anyone knows for sure. Secrecy is the order of the day. But I can tell you one thing. They sure as hell aren't cranking out farm machinery."

Stunned, Kurt stared at the drunken fool. He never imagined such dangerous innuendoes circulated in Karl-Heinz's sleepy Bernau crowd, and the realization that it apparently did, caused him a moment of hesitation, all the motivation Karl-Heinz needed to proceed. "What about the chronically jobless these new factories can't absorb?" His eyes were boring into Kurt. "The misfits in our society. Rumors abound that they're being inducted into a home defense echelon...the so-called Schutz-Staffel. Perhaps you'd be good enough to explain why we need armed peacekeepers to watch law-abiding citizens?"

"Some people need to be under surveillance," Georg spoke up when Kurt hesitated. "The bloody riots of the past have taught us something."

"Precisely what?" Karl-Heinz demanded, stubborn soul that he was. "What have we learned from the past that justifies deploying a police force comprised of hoodlums? The worst elements in our society are strutting around in uniform. They, not the average citizen, ought to be supervised. God knows they are a weird bunch. I've heard that the SS..."

"And I have heard enough!" Kurt found his voice and cut him off; it was time to stop Karl-Heinz. "You'd be well advised to keep gossip to yourself," he cautioned icily. "Hearsay is not rooted in fact. Your conclusion about the Schutz-Staffel proves that. But since you are too obstinate to admit it, let me suffice to say that you'll eventually see the error of your thinking. And when you do, you'll wonder why you didn't embrace Herr Hitler earlier."

"I can't embrace a man who attempts to solve unemployment by putting people in uniform. Our last Kaiser tried that. Look what it got us. War! And I cannot embrace sadistic officers with license to do as they please."

"You're ignoring an important difference between our Fuehrer and Kaiser Wilhelm," Kurt said. "Wilhelm delighted in provoking Europe. Herr Hitler abhors confrontations. Of course, he realizes that we must be armed, but only as a deterrent to any foreign power attempting to test our borders."

"Yes…" Enno von Steigert joined in, "on that we can all agree. Even those among us who don't endorse the Nazi party."

"Well, I suppose if…if it'll guarantee peace…" Karl-Heinz mumbled, sinking in his chair, remembering his son Hans.

"It will," Ulrich von Ritter vouched from down the table. "As Herr Doctor Eckart said a moment ago, our Fuehrer's heart and soul is in maintaining peace in Europe."

"And preserving our German heritage. Our way of life," Georg added.

"Which is precisely why we need the SS," Ulrich said. "Our prosperity, our domestic peace could be at risk from citizens within our own borders. People whose personal agenda is contrary to the good of the country."

"Exactly." Kurt gave the younger man a kind look. "Malcontents within our society can be a more menacing evil than any foreign power. Nettles in the flower bed, if you will, that must be weeded out so the soil can flourish and be fruitful."

"Oh, come now," Fritz smiled. "Surely you don't believe that assigning a bunch of *buch brauner bonzen* to embark on a witch hunt among German citizens is productive. Beating the bushes for trolls and goblins at a substantial cost to the tax payer seems a highly questionable mission."

Helmut Niemann could be heard chuckling.

Kurt looked at Fritz with a controlled expression. "This is not a joking matter, Fritz. I'm talking about people cloaking themselves in citizenship and proclaiming to be exemplary Germans when their true aim is to cause dissent and by insubordination attempt to destroy the core of what we hold dear. Our Germanic blood. Our identity. Until these insurgents have been identified and purged, Germany cannot aspire to her inherent greatness."

Max decided this dinner discussion had hit a new low. In spite of the vivacious Karin Lundgren sitting next to him, he could no longer contain his boredom. He rolled his eyes at Ernst, who rarely saw this much rich food, ate accordingly, and paid little attention to the conversation.

"Our exiled Kaiser, for all his faults, never purged his own citizens," Fritz said soberly, addressing no one in particular. "Was our blood less pure back then? Was our identity less sure? Were the communists less vocal?"

Reaching for his wine glass, Kurt chose to ignore the remarks; this was Fritz's evening and Kurt's sense of fair play did not allow him to argue directly with him tonight.

Karl-Heinz perked up at the mentioning of communists. He harbored no fondness for Bolsheviks, but compared with the Nazis, they seemed a tad less onerous. While everyone took refuge in a five-layered raspberry cream cake now being served, he alone refused to be distracted by the rich dessert.

"On the subject of purging," he said, "does our peace loving Fuehrer plan a second coming of the blood letting? Does he plan to eliminate those so-called weeds in our midst in the same manner he butchered more than two thousand citizens back in June? Some were his closest friends. People who'd helped him to power. People he concluded were traitors for reasons so obscure it escapes the rational mind. I hear amiable Adolf even had his own nephew arrested. I ask you, Kurt, will wives again be gunned down along with their husbands? Will Herr Hitler again show compassion for a chosen few by issuing daggers for the do-it-yourself option? Let me tell you Kurt, let me tell all of you, that brand of benevolence scares the hell out of me!"

Karl-Heinz finally ran out of steam. No one picked up the slack. A tomblike hush settled over the room. Servants melted away. There was no clatter of dishes in the pantry. The dining room was so silent that the soft hiss of burning candlewicks could be heard. A red rose petal fell from a bouquet on the table, dropping onto the white tablecloth like a bead of blood.

After some agonizing moments, Karin whispered in Danish to her husband, "Torben, what was all that talk of daggers and suicide about?"

The senior Lundgrens smiled nervously at Dorrit and shrugged their shoulders indicating that they, too, hadn't quite understood everything that was said.

Fritz found Lisbet's hand under the table and, lacing his fingers with hers, squeezed gently.

250

Chapter Seventy-four

The dark cloud that had descended over the dining room eventually lifted. The men went into the library to smoke their cigars, while the women gathered in the drawing room with demitasse and mint wafers, everyone enjoying this quiet repose while waiting for the musicians in the salon to tune their instruments in preparation for the dancing. Politics now set aside, guests retreated into trivial conversations, and by and by the festive mood was restored. Dorrit forgave Karl-Heinz his outbursts, if only because she knew that Johann would have held the same opinions; the difference being that he would have sparred with Kurt in private.

Kurt could never admit it publicly, but of course the blood purge had shocked him as well. However, he'd convinced himself that the end would eventually justify the means; after all, everything had its price and he was sure that once stability had replaced the turmoil of the past, Herr Hitler would call-off the violence. His stronghold on the nation was a temporary measure. In the meantime, Kurt would make sure that Karl-Heinz's opinions did not seep past these walls. Karl-Heinz was Lillian's cousin, Kurt had no choice but to protect him or he, too, might come under suspicion. And if any of the servants talked, he had ways of discrediting them; being a high government official had its advantages.

Much later that evening, well into the early morning hours after the last of the guests had left or retired upstairs to their rooms, Lisbet and Fritz walked out on the terrace to escape the heat of the house. A fine mist hung suspended in the air, too light to settle on the grass as morning dew, too heavy to blow away on a nonexistent breeze. Dawn came early in summer and was already erasing the shadows of night from beneath the trees dotting the sloping lawns. Stars were fading from the sky as it changed from black to gray with

251

the first hint of a new day.

Before heading upstairs, Cassandra and Max came out on the terrace to announce they were finally calling it a night. Cassandra hugged Lisbet, saying, "I hope we'll always be the best of friends."

"Anyone who shares her gowns is a friend for life," Lisbet promised.

Embracing Fritz, Cassandra whispered, "I wish you and Lisbet a long life and all the happiness in the world!" No sooner had she uttered those words when, in spite of the warm evening, an icy chill ran up her spine. A bad omen, she realized, but one that might be thwarted if she spit over her left shoulder. But she couldn't spit here. Fritz would think her weird, Lisbet would laugh at her, and Max would tease her. Would it be too late to spit once she got upstairs?

"Happy, darling?" Fritz asked after closing the terrace doors behind Cassandra and Max to keep morning moths from following them into the house. He walked back to where Lisbet stood, studying the slowly awakening landscape by the steps leading down into the rose garden.

"Umm..." she murmured, plucking absently at the ivy clinging to the raised stone pillars bordering the terrace. Coming up behind her, Fritz put his arms around her waist and drew her back against him, the tulle of her full skirts rustling about his legs.

"After everything you heard at dinner tonight," he said against her soft yellow hair. "Aren't you crazy to marry a German?"

"Yes, I'm crazy..." she smiled toward the pale and vanishing moon before turning and snuggling into his embrace, "crazy about you."

Fritz cradled her head against his shoulder. "And you're willing to live in a police state ruled by a man I have every reason to believe is utterly mad. A man with barbaric tendencies and no human conscience whatsoever."

"Herr Hitler doesn't scare me."

"An individual who would have us both shot for voicing a contrary opinion doesn't scare you?"

"I don't frighten easily."

Fritz chuckled. "Unless old Buttercup breaks into a gallop."

"That's low!" Lisbet sputtered and raised her hand to level a blow at his shoulder; a thrust he warded off by grabbing her arm in midair and twisting it gently behind her back. She was at his mercy. He took full advantage of it, kissing her in a surge of passion.

"We've got to find some privacy," he whispered, his breath hot against her face.

"Privacy? Tonight?"

"Yes. Tonight. Or I will go mad. Mad as Adolf."

"Tonight is gone," Lisbet mumbled dreamily. "It's almost morning."

"Morning is a long way off, darling. No one will stir until noon. We have all the time in the world."

"And nowhere to go." Lisbet sighed, knowing the house was full of guests. She reminded Fritz that she was sharing her room with Julianne.

"May I suggest mine?" he said, devilishly smug.

"What about Helmut? He's sleeping on your day bed."

"If so, he's a fool. I informed him less than ten minutes ago that Julianne would be alone in your room tonight."

"Frederick Alexander von Renz!" Lisbet scolded with sham indignation. "You're a rogue and an opportunist!"

"Thank you, darling," he grinned.

"And I love you..."

"I know," he said against her lips.

Chapter Seventy-five

Lisbet and Fritz were married in a four-centuries-old cathedral in the heart of Copenhagen on a Sunday afternoon in mid September.

Having booked a block of rooms at Hotel D'angletaire on the King's Market, Fritz traveled to Denmark the Thursday before, suggesting others in his party arrive at their own leisure, the only requirement being that they meet Saturday in the hotel's lounge for the drive to a luncheon hosted by Lisbet's aunt and uncle at their waterfront home on Strandvejen. Several additional prenuptial events followed the lunch, and Fritz secured three Bentleys to chauffeur his entourage to the various parties. On Saturday morning, glancing out the window of his suite, he saw the cars were already parked at the curb; one was pulling away to meet his mother's train. Satisfied everything was going according to schedule, he turned back to the mirror to fasten his neck cloth.

He was about to leave and go downstairs for the rendezvous in the lounge, when he got a telephone call from Dorrit. At first he believed she was calling from the train station, having somehow missed the car he'd sent, but a moment later he was dismayed to learn that she was still in Berlin. Of course he was even more troubled when told that Sigrid, who'd been ill before he left, had not improved sufficiently to give Dorrit the necessary peace of mind to travel. Sadly, his mother would miss the wedding.

Distracted by this disappointing news, Fritz left his suite, quickly walking down the hall toward the elevator. Stepping out on the ground floor, he crossed the lobby, ignorant of the many admiring female glances cast in his direction. He was wearing well-fitting gray gabardine slacks and a loden blazer. A navy striped ascot was tied in the neck of his white shirt and heavy gold cuff links glinted at his wrists. Tall and lean, he was the picture of casual elegance, and the fact that he appeared preoccupied made him all the more attractive.

Robert and Linda Grantham had arrived from the States the previous evening and had gone directly to bed to adjust to the time difference. Fully rested, they were the first to arrive in the lounge and were sitting at the bar when Fritz walked in. He kissed Linda with great affection and embraced Robert in a backslapping male hug.

"It's wonderful to see you!" he said, now standing back, eying Linda. She was six months pregnant, wearing a red maternity dress and a large feathered hat, both flaunting her condition. Frankly, he was amazed at the long, grueling flight she had endured. "I can't believe you're here."

"I had no choice," she grinned. "Robert was planning to swipe a P51 and fly solo to your wedding. To keep him from getting kicked out of the air force, I decided to come along, which forced him to go legit and find seats on a cargo fight. Of course the long haul over the Atlantic did nothing for my ankles." Balancing her weight on the bar stool, she stuck out her feet and swiveled the swollen appendages to garner some sympathy. "They are as fat as my waistline."

Looking at her ankles, Fritz was mumbling his concern as Helmut, Edith and Ulrich walked into the lounge, followed by the Horstmanns. The early hour notwithstanding, Fritz figured the group might have an appetite for Danish beer. Turning to the bartender, he signaled for a round of Tuborgs.

"Where's your bride-to-be?" Linda nudged him as she studied the approaching group. She didn't see anyone resembling the description from Fritz's letters.

"She's not here. She and Julianne are staying in Gentofte at her parents' home. They'll link up with us at the lunch."

Cassandra and Max were late strolling into the lounge. They had just flown in from London where Max had been consulting with fellow archaeologists at Oxford in preparation for a dig near Rcykjavik scheduled for early next year. On Monday he, Cassandra, and Ernst, would leave Copenhagen for Iceland to do the preliminaries before returning to Tunisia to wrap up their work. Having arrived at the Hotel D'angletaire right on time, they were only delayed coming down to the lounge by a telephone call from Dorrit; similar to the one Fritz had received.

The two calls were placed after Dorrit had spent the better part of the morning pacing the floor in the library on Lindenstrasse, wringing her hands in silent anguish, tormenting herself over whether or not to alert anyone of Sigrid's illness. The child had suffered flu-like symptoms on Thursday the day Fritz left for Denmark, and it quickly developed into a sore throat, followed by vomiting and a bright red rash. Ben Tarnoff was summoned Friday afternoon and his diagnosis of scarlet fever hit Dorrit like a thunderbolt. She decided not to go to Copenhagen and instead spent a sleepless night, wondering how best to report the devastating illness to the child's parents and to Fritz. Saturday morning she checked on her little granddaughter repeatedly in the hope of a sudden miracle. But each time she walked into the sickroom, Nurse Heller shook her head, saying there was no change; in fact, her expression became graver as the morning hours went by. Finally, Dorrit had no choice but to place the calls.

Still dressed in her robe and slippers, she sat down at Johann's desk, holding her head between her hands, preparing herself for the difficult assignment. By the time she reached for the telephone and had the long-distance operator on the line, she had formulated a terrible lie. Instead of reporting the true nature of Sigrid's illness, she would claim that the child suffered from a touch of the common cold. This deception was necessary, she rationalized, because she couldn't possibly upset Fritz with disastrous news the day before his marriage. And if she told the truth to Cassandra and Max, they would rush home to Berlin, which would cast a pall over the wedding and not benefit Sigrid in the least. The child was too ill to recognize anyone.

Peddling the falsehood to Fritz turned out to be easier than Dorrit expected because she caught him just as he was leaving his room, which gave him little time to rattle off a lot of questions. As it happened, she reached Cassandra and Max as they, too, were preparing to go downstairs. And although her hand on the receiver shook with her fabrications, her voice remained steady during both calls.

"I've already informed Fritz," she said to Cassandra. "He will extend my regrets to Lisbet and her family. Of course I'll call the Lundgrens myself after the wedding when they have more time to talk."

Surprised with Dorrit's decision not to travel, Cassandra urged her to reconsider before handing the telephone to Max.

"Don't be so quick to cancel," he pressed her. "Sigrid is bound to feel better tomorrow. If you leave first thing in the morning, you can still make the wedding. The ceremony is not until five in the afternoon."

"I know, Max. Actually, Sigrid's cold is not the only thing keeping me home. I just discovered that I've let my passport expire. As you know, government offices are closed on Saturdays and the lines at Anhalter Bahnhof for getting a temporary stamp are notoriously long. Especially on a weekend. I simply can't travel."

After ringing off, Dorrit dropped the receiver into its cradle as if it had burned her hand, same as the lies had burned her tongue. Only the part about her expired passport was true. Darling Sigrid was critically ill, something she had purposefully withheld from the parents. *Gott im Himmel*, would they ever forgive her? She put her head down on Johann's desk. *What would you have had me do?* she asked him, frightened beyond belief, knowing that Sigrid might die. Tears blinding her, she recited every Yiddish prayer Herman Zache had taught her, begging desperately for her little granddaughter's life. *Please...God! She is so small...please leave her with us. Don't take her...*

"Why do you suppose Sigrid's cold is keeping Dorrit home?" Cassandra asked as Max put the telephone down.

"Sigrid is not the entire reason," he said, leaning into the mirror over the dresser to run a comb through his hair. "My mother's passport has expired."

"That's not a problem. She can get a temporary validation stamp at any train depot."

"It appears she can't be bothered. Sometimes it's hard to figure her out."

"Can't be bothered? She was looking so much forward to this wedding." At a loss with Dorrit's strange behavior, Cassandra shook her head as she put on the bolero jacket matching her mauve dress. Twisting her hair into a bun, she fastened it with a silver comb before placing a black satin beret on her head. "It makes no sense," she said, pulling the hat's decorative net down across her forehead. "Sigrid is frequently ill. Both Nurse Heller and Mademoiselle Morisot are on hand. Surely they can care for her. And Dr. Tarnoff is right down the street."

"You know what I think?" Max said as they left their suite and headed for the elevator. "I think my mother has gotten cold feet and is looking for an excuse not to come. She didn't come to our wedding in Athens either."

"Yes, but that was a much longer trip and she was in mourning."

"I believe she's still in mourning. It may sound odd, but except for the trips between Berlin and Bernau, she has not traveled since my

257

father died. I don't think she can leave him."

"Leave him? What do you mean?"

"My father is buried in Bernau and the house in Berlin is a shrine to him. His clothes are still hanging in the closets. She can't bear to part with anything of his. Likewise, she can't bear to leave."

"I can understand her keeping his clothes. But not traveling?" Cassandra frowned. "That's strange."

"Not as strange as her conversations." Max looked pensive as he stepped into the elevator behind Cassandra.

"Conversations?"

"Fritz has told me that he often finds her in the library late at night, looking at her wedding picture and having a lively discussion with Johann."

"Oh..." Now Cassandra understood. Years ago on Aiyina, when she'd felt alone and miserable, a small photograph of her parents had given her comfort.

The elevator reached the ground floor. They stepped out and crossed the beautiful wood paneled lobby that smelled pleasantly of lemon polish and expensive pipe tobacco. Well-dressed people were sitting in clusters of leather club chairs, drinking coffee and reading the noon papers.

"Let's call Dorrit tomorrow evening," Cassandra said, as she and Max entered the lounge and approached the familiar group gathered at the bar. "We'll call right after the wedding and describe everything in detail. I think she'd like that."

Max nodded. "Come to think of it, it might be our last chance. Once we leave for Reykjavik Monday morning it'll be difficult to telephone. Iceland lives up to its name. I've been told utility lines regularly play dead from the stress of the wind."

Chapter Seventy-six

Dorrit spent her days and nights by Sigrid's bed, alternating with Nurse Heller, both anxiously watching the small fever-flushed face sink further into the pillows. The child's cheeks grew hollow, purple circles spread beneath her eyes; she was not aware of her surroundings or of anyone in the room. Still, Dorrit held her hand and stroked her forehead while Nurse Heller bathed her with a damp cool cloth.

The fever refused to subside.

Ben came by each morning to examine the small patient. Dorrit watched his expression, taking a small measure of comfort in the fact that as time passed he began to look less worried. Gertrude also visited the tense household and, knowing full well that Dorrit had been up most of the night, ordered her to bed.

Staggering obediently into her own rooms, Dorrit lay down on the bed, but her sleep was troubled. Crushed with fear for Sigrid, she was also anxious about Fritz in New York where he and Lisbet were honeymooning. Scarlet fever was highly contagious and he had been exposed before he left. Each day Dorrit expected bad news. She jumped when the telephone rang, and when someone knocked on the front door she prayed it wasn't a telegram. Of course, as the days passed and she heard nothing from America, she began to relax. Fritz must have escaped the contagion and, as Ben explained, children were the most susceptible, which was why everyone kept a watchful eye on Peter, and why he was not allowed to go to school for the duration. He remained healthy, thank God, showing no signs of suffering anything more serious than acute boredom at being housebound in a quarantined environment. Mademoiselle Morisot did her level best to keep him occupied with games and French lessons.

259

"I think she'll make it," Ben said one morning in early October after examining Sigrid. "We're into the third week. The rash is peeling away and I see no other complications setting in. I believe we can afford to be optimistic at this point."

"Oh, Ben..." Sobbing with relief, Dorrit clung to him.

A few days later when Sigrid began to tolerate solid food, elation broke out among the women tending her - women who had carefully counted each and every spoonful of chicken broth that slipped down her throat, now celebrated her tolerance for Gertrude's homemade applesauce.

On an afternoon in mid October, Sigrid finally opened her eyes and saw her grandmother for the first time in weeks. Turning her small head on the pillow, she spotted Dorrit dozing on the davenport in the sickroom.

"*Oma?*" the voice was weak, but persistent. "I'm...I'm hungry..."

Dorrit leapt to her feet with energy repudiating her years. It had rained steadily all day with gusty winds rattling the windows. But the moment Sigrid spoke, the darkened room brightened as if the drapes had been thrown open to a sunny day. Dorrit rushed over to the bed, fell on her knees and hugged the thin child to her chest while tears of joy ran unashamedly down her cheeks.

It was over! It was over at last! God had spared a frail little girl from a disease that routinely took far more robust victims.

"Save your tears, *Oma*..." Sigrid whispered in a voice raw and unsure from lack of use. "Save them for tomorrow...you m...might need...them."

Dorrit laughed and cried all the more with the poignant reminder of her own timeworn advice now so suitably offered.

"Nurse Heller!" She yelled at the top of her lungs and banged on the wall, rousing the woman from her room next door; it was a rude summons, one that was totally out character, but this was not the time to stand on ceremony.

"Run to the kitchen!" Dorrit ordered, as the flustered nurse rushed in, adjusting the stiff collar on her uniform and smoothing her hair. "Sigrid needs food. Tell Frau Schmidt to get something ready at once!"

"Wh...what?" Momentarily confused by this sudden call to duty from the depths of a well-deserved nap, Nurse Heller's professional demeanor was further ruffled by the baroness' loud voice and wet face. "What shall I tell her to prepare?" she asked, blinking the sheen of sleep from her eyes.

"Something nourishing." Dorrit pulled a handkerchief from her pocket and blew her nose. "Oatmeal. Soup. It doesn't matter. Don't just stand there. Hurry!"

Collecting her dignity, Nurse Heller made a good imitation of running from the room.

By mid November Sigrid had regained her former strength, frail as it were. Lisbet and Fritz returned from their honeymoon and moved into a spacious apartment at 137 Uhland Strasse near the Kurfurstendamm. The housing shortage across Germany had eased, a fact that Herr Hitler regularly reminded his listeners of during his weekly radio broadcasts.

By Christmas when Cassandra and Max came home to Berlin for their holiday visit, the house on Lindenstrasse was festively decorated and a cheerful ambiance greeted them. They never guessed that their little girl had hovered so close to death only two months before. Needless to say, Dorrit didn't belabor the subject.

Despite her advanced age, Frau Schmidt outdid herself on Christmas Eve, serving two roasted geese stuffed with plums, apples and oranges, along with a wide array of side dishes. The meal was topped off with her acclaimed cinnamon-glazed rice pudding, a favorite with everyone.

Dorrit's heart swelled with pleasure as she and her family, now including Fritz's wonderful wife, gathered around the holiday table.

They were seven this year.

A lucky number.

Surely that bode well for the future...

www.ingramcontent.com/pod-product-compliance
Lightning Source LLC
Chambersburg PA
CBHW030121180626
46812CB00002B/509